Assassination

at the
State House

by

RON ELLIOTT

McClanahan
Publishing House

Cover design and book layout by James Asher Graphics

Cover photograph courtesy of The Kentucky Historical Society
Cover photograph computer alteration by James Asher Graphics
Back cover photograph by John Snell

Manufactured in the United States of America

All book order correspondence should be addressed to:
McClanahan Publishing House, Inc.
P. O. Box 100
Kuttawa, KY 42055
(502) 388-9388
1-800-544-6959

Dedication

To my father,

Herman Elliott
1912 - 1977

If you're in touch with your Uncle Berry,
find out what he knows.

Preface

Any student of Kentucky history has read a line of text something like, "As Governor-elect William Goebel approached the State House on the morning of January 30, 1900, he was felled by a bullet fired by an unknown assassin from the office of the Secretary of State." To quote Paul Harvey, "now you're going to hear the rest of the story." I herewith offer the facts of the matter, such as I could determine, in a manner which is hopefully entertaining as well as informative.

Every event of any historical significance described in these pages actually took place and every major character was an actual person. The material presented here was gathered from period newspaper accounts, historical records, the few available books, and, in large part, the actual trial transcripts. All places, dates, and times mentioned in the narrative are offered as historically accurate.

No liberties were taken with the facts, and as few as possible with the people. In some cases, several conversations which occurred at various places were combined. Josh Sousley, James Young, Sam Readnour, Alvie Vaughn, Melvin Ballenger, T. J. Ashby and George Whittaker were invented to voice some of the typical comments.

Conversation between and among the various characters is largely fabricated, but is constructed from the actual sequence of events and is presented in the vernacular of the time and place depicted. For example, there was, to my knowledge, no meeting at Berry Howard's residence to organize a trip to Frankfort. Caleb Powers did, however, travel to that section of Kentucky in January of 1900, and did meet with various parties, including Frank Cecil, for that purpose. Additionally, Berry Howard did attempt to induce various men to go along on the trip. So, while that particular event is fictitious, it is representative of the events that did, in fact, occur. In many cases, conversations recounted in one of the trials have been adopted to fit at an appropriate spot in the narrative.

All dialogue between the attorneys, witnesses and judges in the courtroom scenes are direct quotes of the trial transcripts. In a few cases, I altered/added punctuation to clarify meanings. The gestures of the various characters (with the exception of Mr. Youtsey's "fit," which is documented) and side comments by the major characters are of my invention. The description of Mr. Weaver, the strolling barber, as a "volunteer perjurer" is as published in Irvin S. Cobbs' *Stickfuls* (New York, 1923).

A few words of explanation may be helpful to the reader. As Kentucky entered the twentieth century, there was no such thing as a state police force. So, in times of turmoil, the governor had little choice but to call out the militia, which was sometimes called the state guard. That civilian-soldier organization was the equivalent of the modern National Guard. Also, given the economy of 1900, the $100,000 reward fund approved by the General Assembly had as much appeal as a couple of million dollars would in today's market.

The project which culminated in this book began as an investigation of family history, but soon evolved into a wider view of American history. That view is, of course, influenced by the culture and technology existent during the period. Politics and jury trials were the prime sources of entertainment in the early part of this century, and any event which combined these two elements, as the Goebel affair did, was big time news. Today, surrounded by televised ballgames, movies and VCR's, it is difficult to imagine the environment in which these events occurred. The research that produced this work recreated that environment for me. Soon after I began the project, I found myself on a train speeding toward Frankfort on a snowy night in January of 1900. I've done my best to recreate that atmosphere to share with the reader. I hope you enjoy the trip.

I've learned the truth of "no man is an island." I gratefully acknowledge the contributions of my wife, Debbie; my brother, Allan; the staff at the Kentucky State Archives, especially James Prichard; the staff of the Kentucky Historical Society, especially Ron Bryant; Joan Stafford; Jessica Browning; and special mention to Trish Faubion and John Snell.

Clichéd—but fact—without the help and support of these folks, this book would not exist.

Chapter 1

Washington Post, August 4, 1899.

Tuesday, November 7, 1899
Election Day

"Well boys, you got it all decided yet?" Ike Livingston was just making a little joke with the men gathered around the potbellied stove in Bradshaw's store, just up the Right Fork of the Straight Creek branch of the Cumberland River.

"Ike, you know damn well that it was all decided last year," Robert Bradshaw answered for the group.

Ike worked his way near the stove for warmth. Huddled around the stove were Leonard Brock and his young son, Wendell, "old man" T. J. Ashby and Berry Howard. In the rear of the store, Josh Sousley lay on a stack of feed sacks. The men had long since learned that four feet from the stove was the distance required for proper warmth—any further was too cold, any nearer was too warm. Hence, these men were arranged in a four-foot radius circle. Bob Bradshaw was sorting the mail behind the grid that separated the post office from the store proper.

"Reckon you're right, Bob," Ike said as he kicked the base of the wood-burning stove to clear the winter mud from his boots. With each kick, a glob of mud dropped to the floor, and a shower of sparks shot from the red-hot sides of the stove. Ike's joke was that each of the men present knew that— although the polls were just now closing and the ballot counting not even begun yet—Kentucky's gubernatorial election had, for all intents, been decided back in the spring of '98 when the State Legislature overrode Governor Bradley's veto and allowed the infamous "election reform bill" to become the law that would dictate the outcome of this election. Berry Howard knew it especially well.

Berry was a former member of the Legislature from Bell and surrounding counties and had been elected to the post several times. Being re-elected from a district in which all voters were Republicans—at least nobody ever publicly admitted to being a Democrat—qualified Berry Howard not only as a major figure in local party political circles, but as one of the more influential spokesmen, without regard to party, in the eastern part of the state.

There was almost always a political discussion going on in the store, but Ike had made an extra special point of stopping in today. He figured that—it being election day—the debate would be extraordinarily lively, and that Berry would probably be present. Talking politics was the main form of entertainment for these men, and these days the discussion centered on the current campaign and the nominees: W. S. "Hogjaw" Taylor and his Democratic rival, William Goebel. Berry had served in the legislature with Goebel and Ike wanted to understand the political environment better than he presently did. Berry Howard was the man to ask.

"Berry, you know the man," Ike began. "How the hell did he manage to get that election reform law passed?"

"Don't nobody 'know' Bill Goebel," Berry said. "I'm acquainted with him, and I suspicion that's the most anybody can say. He's probably the most intelligent man I ever met, and easily the most determined. And there's your answer; he just ain't a man to be put off of what he's got in mind."

"But that Goebel Election Law's a scandal," Leonard protested. "It allows the Legislature to appoint a board of three state election commissioners who appoint, in turn, the local commissioners. Then, betwixt the bunch of 'em, they determine who can vote and settle any disputes. That's about the same as leavin' a fox in charge of the hen house—with that law in place, whichever party has control of the Legislature has a lock on any election."

"You see the plan pretty well," Berry said. "Except, in this case, it ain't the party in control; it's 'Boss Bill' himself."

"So, you're sayin' that Goebel hisself hand-picked the election board what'll certify the votes? Hogjaw ain't got a snowball's chance in hell." Bob was serious.

Berry Howard was a big man. At six-feet-two, with two-hundred-sixty pounds distributed on his frame, he was considerably larger than the average man in the mountains. His wide nose tapered upwards to just fit between a pair of bushy eyebrows. The thin hair on top of his head exposed a great amount of forehead that wrinkled when he was excited, as he was now. Given his stature—physical and political—when Berry Howard talked, people listened. He was in an expansive mood at the moment. "Don't be so sure about that, Bob. They's plenty of Democrats in John Y. Brown's faction that hates Goebel as bad as we do. Taylor's gonna get a lot of votes. All us Republicans, of course, and lots of the Democrats would sooner vote for Taylor than take a chance on Goebel gettin' elected. Even though the election board will probably throw out a bunch of the votes, Taylor may yet come in with the most. Besides, the honest citizens in this state might just make it hot enough that they'll be forced to do right by us."

"The Republicans pledged to repeal that election law, didn't they?" Bob asked. "That alone should get us a lot of votes."

"It should," Berry agreed, "but don't forget that there's plenty of people who'll vote for any Democrat, no matter what."

"Tell about the yeller dog, Berry," Brock said. "Young Wendell here ain't heard the story."

Berry smiled. "Well, the Lord knows there's little enough in this campaign to smile about. It's the only story we got this time that's worth tellin' again, I guess." He turned to address the boy. "After Goebel got the nomination, many of the Democrats knew they couldn't support him, so they decided to run ex-Governor John Y. Brown as a third candidate. Some of the old-line Democrats went out to stump for Brown.

"Ted Hallam, who's as fine a speaker as old Kentucky ever produced, was speaking for Brown at Bowling Green when somebody jumped up out of the crowd and allowed that he wanted to ask Ted a question.

"Ted informed the man that it wasn't a debate, but he'd answer the man's question if he'd then let 'em get on with the speakin'.

"The questioner asked, 'Didn't you, not four weeks ago at the convention in Louisville, say that if the Democratic party, in convention assembled, nominated a yeller dog, you'd support him?'

"Ted admitted that what the man said was a fact. So, he asked Ted how, then, he could not support William Goebel? Son, I hear that the roof pert nigh come off that place with the laughter.

"Ted just waited 'til they quieted down afore he spoke. Then he said, 'I did say that if the Democratic party, in convention assembled, nominated a yeller dog, I'd support him, but, lower than that, you shall not drag me.'"

Bob Bradshaw left his post behind the counter to join the cluster around the stove. He pulled his stool between Ike and Leonard into what he considered the prime location for Berry's attention. Ike and Leonard both shot him looks of disgust as he horned his way into the conversation.

"If the Democrats hate him and the Republicans hate him, how does he keep gettin' elected?" Bob asked.

"Like I said, he's a smart one," Berry replied. "For one thing, he was the first Kentucky politician to realize that gettin' elected nowadays don't strictly depend on stump speakin' ability and party faith like it always has before. He's bright enough to see that since most of the voters is farmers, presentin' some program that appeals to them and callin' in your political favors is enough to get you elected. Then, too, he figures that with the economy as bad as it's been, there ought to be somebody to take the blame. He's seen fit to blame the Republicans and the railroads. He don't really care about people—just cares about their votes."

"But still, he ain't taking no chances, is he?" Ike asked. "That's the real reason behind that damned Goebel election reform law, ain't it?"

"You're right as rain," Berry said. "Since we elected a Republican governor in Bradley last time, they aim to make sure that don't happen again. The only purpose of that particular piece of legislation is to ensure his election as Governor. In plain truth, I really believe that the old son of a bitch would sell his first born child—if'n he had one—for a vote."

"No woman would have him," Bob said. "The only chance that man'd have at a child would be to find one under a rock just like his own Pappy musta found him." A round of laughter followed that comment.

T. J. Ashby shot a stream of tobacco juice at the brass cuspidor resting at the base of the stove. The amber stream missed and hit the stove, which responded with a violent hiss of steam. "Hell boys, we shoulda seed what was gonna happen when Goebel paired up with William Stone durin' their convention. Goebel don't care no more for them Rebels than I do—his Pappy was a Union soldier, same as me—but any fool could see that somethin' weren't right about that."

"T. J., you ain't gonna tell us again about how you and Gen'l Grant whupped the Confederates all by yourselves are you?" asked Leonard, knowing he'd get a rise out of the old man.

"By God, I'll tell you this, you damned whippersnapper," T. J. shot back, "I knew damned well that Goebel'd renege on his promise to Stone. Stone's got so many votes just because he lost a leg defendin' their cursed cause that he's got the idea that anybody will keep their word with him. He should of known that Goebel'd drop him like a hot 'tater once he got what he wanted—typical Johnny Reb thinking."

"Hold on there, T. J.," Ike said. "The war's over."

"The hell it is," the old man said with the fire of youth once more in his eyes. "We just left off using bullets, that's all."

Ike thought that there was probably more truth in that than the old man realized. In many ways, the political divisions that had split the Democratic party were the same issues that had resulted in the Civil War 40 years earlier. The blood-letting had settled some disputes, but many old ones still smoldered, and new difficulties boiled. The passions left unresolved by the fighting had allowed many men to exchange military garb for political trappings. So, in a political sense, the war did go right on after 1865, only using words rather than bullets.

That fact was part of Ike's problem. Having been born some ten years after the end of the war, he simply couldn't relate to some of the ideas that were carry-overs from previous days. Today was the first time in quite a while that he'd caught Berry in a talkative mood, and he meant to make the most of the opportunity. To get the conversation back on track, Ike said, "We'll fight the war again some other time, T. J." Then, turning his attention back to Berry, he continued, "As I understand the deal that they struck at the Democrats' convention, Stone and Goebel both claimed to support the farmers and ganged up on Wat Hardin. That right, Berry?"

Berry tilted his ladder-back chair on its back legs and let the back of the chair touch the wall. He hooked the heels of his boots over the bottom rung and assumed his best legislative tone. "That's right, Ike. He figured that he and Stone could unite to defeat Hardin, and it worked, too. Perfect example of the sayin' that the Democrats take greater pleasure in beatin' each other than in beatin' us Republicans. I was in Louisville back in June when it happened. I didn't go near that Music Hall, though. There was enough racket pourin' out of the place that you didn't have to get very close to have a good idea of the turmoil goin' on. Ever'body thought there was gonna be shootin' all the while. Stone understood that once they'd disposed of Hardin, Goebel'd support him. When Goebel refused his end of the deal, you'd thought the roof was comin' off that place. The story made the rounds that whoever was left standin' when the smoke cleared would get the nomination. There really weren't never no doubt, though."

"What do you mean?" Bob asked.

Berry shifted his bulk slightly to get more comfortable. He crossed his left leg over his right as he warmed to his subject.

"Ever'body in the state knew that Goebel'd do whatever was necessary to get that nomination. Didn't make no difference to him how many people he had to back-stab or lie to.

"Bill Goebel ain't the back-slappin', baby-kissin' kind of politician we're used to. Can't speak in the old-time fashion worth shucks, either. I don't mean to say that he ain't an effective speaker, just that he ain't likely to inspire no howlin' at the moon with his oratory. He's a back room deal maker, and he used ever' trick he knew to get that nomination. It cost him plenty of favors and a lot of support, but he was determined that he'd be the candidate for Governor. He would have said or done anything in the world to get it. It split their party worse than it already was and made Goebel a flock of new enemies, but, by hell, he got his way—as usual. I couldn't tell you no plainer how the man is, boys. He don't give a tinker's damn for nothin' or nobody 'cept Bill Goebel."

"So you say there ain't much danger of a Goebel rally bein' confused for a tent revival meeting, huh?" Leonard asked.

Berry gave Leonard a sour look, then softened as he caught the intended humor. "Only to the extent that they would have to sing a few hymns to settle the place down." He paused, as if to consider his next comment, then went on.

"Now you boys know that I ain't one to go out of my way to be fair with a Democrat, and I hate Bill Goebel as much as any man alive. But, by God, I got to say that I do believe he started out with the good of the people of Kentucky at heart. He soon found out, as all politicians do sooner or later, that you can't do no good for nobody 'til you got the power.

When he made that discovery, that's when the trouble started.

"He was workin' so hard to get hisself in power that he forgot the reason he was doin' it was to do good for the people. Oh, of course he still says that he stands for this and that—bein' again' the Louisville & Nashville Railroad, for example—for the benefit of the people, but all the son of a bitch really thinks about is how to get hisself elected. If he thinks bein' for somethin' will get him the most votes, he's for it. If he thinks most folks are again' it, then he's again' it. Always put me in mind of a willow saplin'. Just the least little bit of a breeze will cause it to lean way over in whatever direction the wind happens to be headin'. He ain't wishy-washy in his convictions—he's a fighter—but, he ain't gonna waste any energy fightin' for somethin' unless he see votes in it."

"But he must have political supporters," Ike commented.

"Oh, yeah, he's got supporters," Berry replied. "There's plenty who think that Goebel'll give 'em some state job or owe 'em a favor if they help him get elected. I wish 'em well on him keepin' his promises."

The front door of the store flew open, admitting a blast of frigid air and one of the Hoskins boys, who stood in the doorway eyeing the group around the stove.

"Push that door to, son," Bob shouted. "Was you raised in a barn on a hillside where the doors close by themselves?"

The boy closed the door. Bob stood and moved toward the counter. "What can I do for you, Nate?" he asked.

Nate's eyes darted back and forth between the group of men, who were ignoring him, and Bob, who was waiting expectantly. The hum of conversation started up again from the back, and Bob did not want to miss any of the discussion. Finally, he decided to take the initiative. "Poke of coffee?" he suggested to the boy.

The boy's eyes switched back to the storekeeper and widened a bit. Wordlessly, he nodded.

Bob weighed the coffee and handed Nate the paper bag. "I guess your Ma wants it on her bill." It was more of a statement than a question. After a moment's hesitation, Nate nodded again, then left.

Bradshaw searched the bank of credit books lining the wall behind the cash register. Finding the one labeled "Hoskins," he pulled it from the rack and started back toward the stove.

"That boy's a talker, ain't he?" T. J. joked.

"More kin to his Ma than his Pa, I'd say," Ike responded.

"What I've been wonderin', Berry," Leonard said as he edged his chair in to get closer than Bradshaw, "is how Goebel managed to get away with killin' that feller up in Covington?"

Berry let the chair fall forward. His weight gave the front legs so much momentum that they struck the poplar puncheon floor with a resounding thud. All in the same motion, Berry rocked forward to address his audience at closer range and punctured the air with his right index finger for added emphasis.

"A hell of a good question, son. Like I said before, Goebel's a smart man. He got out of that mess the same way he got in it—brains, money and political influence. Even though Goebel and John Sanford were both Democrats, they'd had their political differences. Goebel bought a newspaper—he's a successful lawyer, you know—just so's he'd have the last word. I gather that Sanford took exception to some of the things he printed.

"The way I heard it, Goebel crossed the street to get to him when he saw Sanford outside. They exchanged a few words, and bang-bang, they both shot. Sanford missed and Goebel hit."

"Sounds like an old-fashioned duel to me," T. J. remarked.

"The newspapers called it 'a duel without honor' didn't they?" Leonard asked.

"Some did," Berry said. "Some of them just called it murder."

"But he come clear of it, didn't he? How'd he manage that?" Bradshaw insisted.

"Back room politics," Berry said. "He took care to have the whole affair take place in his home county in broad daylight. Then he used his political influence to make sure that he'd never come to trial. Like I said, he's a smart 'un, but it's tricks like that that ensure that nobody wants to be associated with him.

"And I'll just tell how bad it is, too. Even that Louisville Democrat rag, the *Courier-Journal*, came right out after the convention and said that it was 'compelled' to support the Goebel ticket. Didn't want to, see, but had to."

Josh Sousley stirred beneath the dirty black slouch hat that covered his face. He had been motionless since Ike had entered and had added nothing to the discussion up to this point. Leonard, who was closest, thought he was asleep and was content to let well enough alone. Josh Sousley was one of the most unsavory characters in a land of tough customers, and everyone knew that his type was best left alone. Suddenly, Josh lifted himself up on an elbow and pushed his hat back exposing a shock of greasy black hair. "If somebody was to shoot that son of a bitch, we'd all be a damn sight better off," he growled.

A silence fell over the group. A gust of wind just beyond the weather-boarding behind Ike caused him to shiver. The sound of a tree branch scraping on the roof of the store added a touch more chill to the atmosphere inside. All eyes turned to Sousley. Ike thought that Josh was joking, but that thought was short lived. All present knew better than that, and the dull red glint in Sousley's eyes removed any doubt. Berry shot a desperate look at Bob Bradshaw, asking for a way to break the tension.

"Say, T. J., tell us about that time you met General Grant." They'd all heard the story many times, but Bob knew that T. J. enjoyed the telling, and that it would bring some relief.

"Well, it was back in the summer of '64 at the Wilderness," T. J. began the familiar tale. "It'd been hotter than hell all day. About dusk, the Rebs quit shootin' at us, and we had a chance to grab a bite to eat. One of my mess mates happened to let his slab of bacon slip his grasp. The bacon hit on a rock and was fried—done to a turn—by the time he could pick it up offen that rock.

"Anyway, when night fell it was dark as the inside of a cow's stomach, and smelt twice as bad. And turned off so cold that we had to take the brass monkey inside. I crawled up inside a bomb crater that somebody had put a roof over, and was just about asleep when somebody else crawled in there with me. Mighta been a Reb for all I knew.

"Just as I was trying to decide whether to say 'Howdy' or shoot, a hand sticks something in my face and somebody says, 'How about a smoke? Got a Lucifer?' It was a see-gar—damned fine one, too. 'I got me a light here someplace,' says I, and I pulled them Lucifers out of my knapsack and struck one. Well, what do you think I seed when that light fell on his face? It were Gen'l Grant. Yes sir, U. S. Grant, hisownself. 'Howdy do, Gen'l,' says I. I lit his see-gar, then I lit mine. 'Thankee kindly, Private,' says he as he crawls out. 'I'll let you know if I need further help, but you might want to stop by my headquarters now and again just in case.'

"Boys, I'll swan you coulda knocked me over with a feather. I was so proud of that moment that I carried the stub of that see-gar the rest of the war. I'd still have it yet, but some yellow-bellied son of a blood sucker stole it out of my packet."

Even though they'd all heard the story before, everyone laughed. Ike thought it was interesting that T. J. never told it the same way twice in a row, and with each telling it got hotter, colder and darker than before. Also, General Grant became more grateful. Ike figured that in another four or five years, Grant's gratitude would result in an officer's commission or maybe a cabinet appointment.

"You been around some and seen some things, ain't you?" Leonard teased.

"Some," T. J. allowed.

"You recollect when Lincoln was shot?" asked Leonard.

"Recollect it very well."

"How 'bout the fall of Rome?" Ike threw in.

The old man cocked his head to the left, lifted his chin, and squinted as if in deep thought. When he spoke, his eyes betrayed the slightest hint of a twinkle. "Now that you mention it, seems like I do recollect hearin' somethin' drap."

Chapter 2

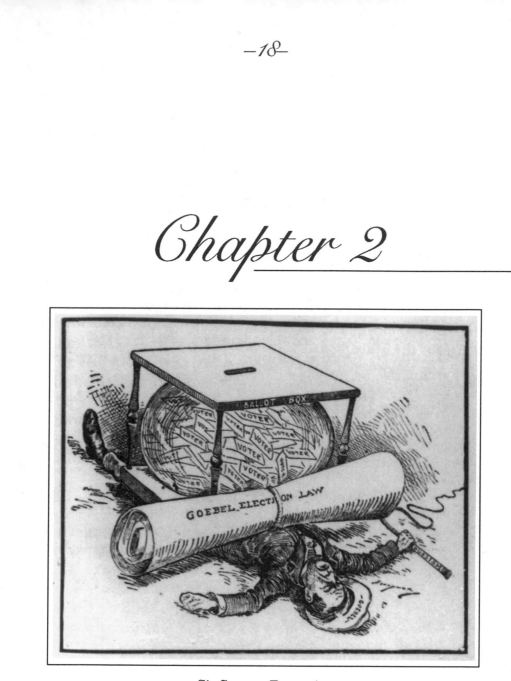

Sic Semper Tyrannis
Washington Post, November 21, 1899.

Sunday, December 24, 1899

"The only mistake that son of a bitch made," Ike said aloud, "was in failing to anticipate that the men he appointed as commissioners might just possibly be honest."

His wife, Ellen, was on the way in from the kitchen with a steaming mug of coffee in each hand. She knew that Ike was reading the *Courier-Journal* he'd purchased in town yesterday. That meant that he'd be studying up on the political news, and it was all good. Less than two weeks ago, the state election board had reviewed the returns and disallowed all votes it considered illegal. To the great surprise of most observers, the board had brought in the official count showing Taylor with 193,714 votes, Goebel with 191,331, and Brown with 12,140. Hence, "Hogjaw" Taylor was the winner by a difference of 2,382 votes. While that margin represented less than one percent of the total votes cast, the verbiage of the Goebel election reform law dictated that all rulings of the election board were "final and conclusive." So, on December 12, 1899, William S. Taylor had been duly inaugurated as the 31st Governor of the Commonwealth of Kentucky—only the second Republican in the state's 107 year history to be so honored by the people. With so much good news abounding, Ike's outburst was unexpected.

"Lands sakes, Ike Livingston, you watch your mouth. On Christmas eve and a Sunday to boot." She handed him a coffee mug. "What does that paper say that's got you so upset?"

Normally, Ike liked Sunday mornings. Keeping current in the conversations down at Bradshaw's store and the courthouse required reading the newspapers to do his homework. To do justice to a newspaper, he had to have a nice fire going in the fireplace, a good breakfast in his stomach, and the time to sift out the partisanship from the facts in a story. Especially if he were reading a Democratic newspaper such as the *Courier-Journal*, which was usually all he could get. All these elements usually came together only on Sunday, and he didn't like to be disturbed when they did. Ike shot Ellen a quick sidelong glance, his eyes betraying only a mild irritation. In his opinion, a man just didn't discuss politics with a woman, not even his wife, and not even if she did happen to be a fully accredited and educated school teacher. Ike thought that everybody knew that politics was nothing for women to worry about. Besides, she always made an effort to see both sides of the question, and he was in no mood to put up with that kind of foolishness. All other things aside, if men encouraged women to talk politics, first thing you know, they'd be wanting the vote.

"Ellis and Pryor resigned from the election board Friday," he replied. "They were Goebel Democrats, tried and true, but they were also honest men, so they reported the will of the people. Now, as a reward for their honesty, that son of a bitch has, no doubt, persecuted them to the extent that they had to resign, leaving only Poyntz on the board." He managed to get a sip of coffee between sentences.

"There you go again," she said. "Santa will leave you only a lump of coal if you don't mind your mouth."

"I'd be happy enough if Santa just left us a Republican Governor," he retorted.

"What's the problem?" she asked. "God's in his heaven, Taylor's in the State House, and all's right with the world, isn't it?" She sat in her favorite rocker and blew on her coffee to cool it.

Ike resigned himself to the fact that he was going to have a discussion with her, like it or not. He inhaled deeply, sucking in the pleasant scent of the cedar Christmas tree standing in the corner of the room. "Yes, but it won't be for long. As Berry said, Goebel ain't a man to let anything stand in the way of what he wants, and what he wants is to be Governor.

"The first thing he's gonna do is replace those election commissioners. And you can bet that he'll find some this time that ain't got as many scruples as Ellis and Pryor."

"Let him replace them. Who's on the election board isn't going to make any difference at this point—all the horses have crossed the finish line, so to speak. After all, the very thing that's so contemptible about his own election law is that there's no recourse from the board's decision." She rocked placidly.

"Like I just told you, he ain't a man to give up easy. There's no question in my mind that he'll think of some way to keep the pot boiling," he spat. He raised the coffee mug to his lip and then jerked it away quickly. "Speaking of boiling, this coffee has been about the fire."

"Now, Ike, don't get yourself all in an uproar. The coffee and the political situation will both cool off if you'll just wait a bit. Whatever else there is to say about William Goebel, he's a reasonable man. He let Taylor go in office, didn't he?"

"Let him, hell. Hung himself with his own rope is what he did. His cronies are in there, thick as flies, urgin' him to do something."

"I suppose you're right. He's already demonstrated that he's in control of the Legislature and that the law only applies as William Goebel sees fit for it to. So, even if there isn't any current legal path left open, he'll likely find some way to create a new one." This was said more as if she was thinking aloud than speaking to Ike.

That woman's got a good mind, he thought. Maybe the world wouldn't stop spinning if women did get the vote. The consensus among the men was that women would just vote for the best looking man, but that might not be so bad, he thought. Given what had been going on lately, even he would have to admit that women would be hard pressed to do worse than the current mess.

He began to study his wife as if he hadn't seen her for a time. Strange how a man just began to overlook things. It was only four short years ago that they'd run off to get married over at Middlesboro, and already he'd begun to take her looks and her intelligence for granted. She was a fairly handsome woman, tall and thin like all her family. She had a nose that was slightly too large for the delicate features of her face, but she had a way of arranging her auburn hair so that one did not notice. She wore lace collars to accent her long neck and overall, her appearance was quite striking.

Ike Livingston had no choice concerning their relative levels of education—he had not even finished grade school—so if anyone asked, he had to admit that she was the more educated. Although he knew that his wife's wealth of knowledge and problem solving ability far exceeded his, he was not about to admit to that, either in public, or even to himself. If it had to be, he'd just get out of her way when it came to a math problem or writing a letter, but when it came to politics. . . .

A shout from the gate at the foot of the path broke his reflective mood.

"Hullo—anybody home?"

Ellen recognized the voice of her younger brother. She hurried across the room and opened the front door. "Good morning, Willie. And Merry Christmas, too. Come on up."

Will Elliott was a slight young man. At nineteen, he was the youngest of Ellen's nine surviving siblings. He was of average height and weight, but the distribution of his weight made him appear somewhat thin. The way he brushed his hair into a peak on the right side always made Ellen think that his head looked lopsided. She knew better, though. Will was a very level-headed young man, and Ellen thought he was a fine looking boy even if he did appear somewhat frail. He had recently gone through the growth spurt typical of boys his age, leaving the pants legs of his Sunday-go-to-meeting suit a little too short. That, coupled with the uphill slant of the path, caused an exposure of a great expanse of white socks as he moved up to the porch.

Ellen held the door open as Will entered the front room and crossed to the fireplace. After warming his hands, he turned to face his sister and brother-in-law. "It's just about cold enough for us to have some snow for Christmas," he remarked.

"Just about," Ellen allowed, resuming her seat in the rocker. Ike reluctantly laid the newspaper aside, the urge to keep reading losing out to the necessity of being polite. While Will warmed at the fireplace, Ellen spoke. "Oh, Willie, I'm glad you stopped by. Did you get an invitation to the Slusher's New Year's party?"

"Sure did," Will said. Then as an afterthought, he added, "But don't you be trying to fix me up with some gal."

Will was painfully aware from long experience that teasing him about girls was a favorite pastime for his brother-in-law and sister. The gleam he thought he saw in Ike's eye caused him to think this question was a set-up.

"No, no, nothing like that," she laughed. "Ike and I've been having this running argument that you can settle. You know the Slushers are calling it the 'end of century' party? Well, I've been trying to convince Ike that the century doesn't end until next December. You're the math whiz—what about it?"

Will turned to Ike, looking for assurance that his sister wasn't pulling his leg. The expectant look on Ike's face told him that this was a legitimate question. Will had given that very question some thought and happened to be prepared, but decided to proceed with a bit of caution. In any given situation, he thought it best that the men stick together so he wanted to back Ike whenever he could. This did not appear to be one of those times.

"Okay, Ike," he began. "The very first year was year 1, right?"

"Right."

"So, at the end of year 1, one year had passed, right?"

"Right."

"All right then. On December 31 of year 2, two years had passed; at December 31 of year 3, three years and so on down until December 31, year 99. How many years had elapsed?"

"Ninety-nine," Ike replied.

"Correct. So, on December 31, year 100, one hundred years had elapsed, and that was the end of the first century. Now, to extend that thinking on out, the second century ended on December 31, year 200; the third century on December 31, year 300; and finally, the 17th century ended on December 31, 1800. You with me, Ike?"

"Yeah, I guess so," Ike mumbled somewhat reluctantly.

"O.K. then you have to agree that the 19th century will end on December 31, 1900, a whole year from now."

"Just exactly what I've been trying to tell him for a month now," Ellen said.

Ike thumped his coffee mug down on the table hard enough to cause the popcorn strings on the Christmas tree to sway. "Aw, who asked you, anyway? Makes no difference to me, I'm gonna celebrate it with ever'body else next week."

Will smiled. "Well, I suppose that folks celebrated in 1799 and I guess they will in 1999, too. We might as well go ahead and be wrong right along with 'em." Will had warmed to the point that he had to turn to expose another side to the fire. As he rotated toward Ike, he saw a knowing grin spread over his brother-in-law's face.

"Did either of you know-it-alls realize that 1900 will not be a leap year?" he asked.

"Of course it will," Ellen replied. "Everybody knows that if the year is a multiple of four, then it's a leap year."

"Well, I've got news for you," Ike said triumphantly.

"What you say is true, provided it's not a century year."

"What do you mean?" Will asked.

"I mean the year ends in double zero, like 1800 or 1900."

Will thought that the fact that Ike referred to any year which ended in double zero as a "century year" settled the previous argument, but he said nothing.

"In the case of a century year," Ike went on, "it has to be multiple of 400 to be a leap year. So, neither 1800 nor 1900 is a leap year, even though they're divisible by four, but 2000 will be a leap year."

"You've been reading those books down at the judge's office again, haven't you?" Ellen accused playfully.

Will rotated his other side to the fire. As he turned, he shot an uneasy glance at his sister. Although he liked her and respected her opinion, even more than Ike's sometimes, he knew that Ike would not want him to bring up the reason he was there until she left the room.

In her rocking chair with her needlepoint on her lap, Ellen rocked away contentedly, but she had caught Will's glance and was aware of what the lull in the conversation meant. She had long since adjusted to the fact that men would discuss politics with women only on a one-on-one basis, so she knew that Will and Ike wouldn't talk until she left the room. But, she had decided that since she had the upper hand on her husband at the moment, she'd just press on the opportunity to stir Ike up a bit more anyway.

"What brings you by this morning, Willie?" she asked with a quick wink in his direction.

Although they were at opposite ends of the age scale—at 30, Ellen was the oldest of their parents' children—Will and his sister were a great deal alike. He readily saw what she was doing and was willing to play along. He didn't often pass up an opportunity to pay Ike back for his teasing.

"Oh, I thought I'd check in and see what Ike's voting plans for the new year are. How 'bout it, Ike? Going to vote the straight Democratic ticket?"

Ike snorted. "I think it's about time I told you a little story. I was sittin' here on the porch one evenin' when a wagon come over the hill with an old man and a hound dog sittin' up on the board. Just as he come even with the house here, the mule stepped in a pothole. The mule let out a scream, and the whole she-bang went down in a heap on the side of the road.

"I figured that the mule's leg was probably broke, so I got my pistol and went down to see what I could do. When I got down to the road, I seen right off that the mule's leg was sure enough broke, so I naturally had to put the beast out of its misery.

"About that time, I heard a whine from the other side of the road. I looked over in the ditch on that side, and there was the poor ole hound dog. I seen that he was in a world of hurt, so, bad as I hated to, I shot him in the head.

"Then I saw that the old man who was drivin' was pinned underneath the wagon. I looked down at him and said, 'How you doin' old timer?' He looked up at me and quick as a wink, he says, 'I ain't never felt better a single day in my whole life.'

"Now the moral of that story, son, is if you go around asking stupid questions, you're probably gonna get stupid answers."

"I'll get you some coffee, Willie," Ellen said as she took her cue to head for the kitchen.

"What's up, Will?" Ike asked as soon an Ellen was out of the room.

"Not much," Will replied. "Berry feels sure that Goebel is going to contest the election in the Legislature."

"But there ain't a legal basis for him to do so," Ike said.

"Berry said that made no difference. He didn't tell me anything specific about the plans, but I think he's in on some scheme the Taylor administration is cooking up. At any rate, Berry is holding a meeting at his house Tuesday week, and he asked me to make sure that you're invited."

"Wouldn't miss it for the world," Ike said.

Chapter 3

Washington Post, January 16, 1900.

Tuesday January 2, 1900

"Y ou ready to go, Ike?" Will yelled up toward the house. The door burst open and Ike shot from the porch like something evil was hot on his tail and gaining on him by the second. At six feet, one-inch, Ike was taller than most men, and his 165 pounds seemed just right on his frame. His brown hair had just the least bit too much curl, but the square jaw balanced the whole into a picture of masculinity. Bouncing down the path destroyed the effect, though, and Will thought that Ike really shouldn't hurry—he looked slightly comical. By the time he reached the gate, Ike was panting for breath.

"You bet I'm ready, I'm just not as young as I once was," Ike managed to gasp.

"There's really no hurry," Will said as they began to walk.

"I know, but the weather has been so rainy and cold the last few days that I've got a slight case of cabin fever. Besides, I'm anxious to find out what Berry has in mind. Him being on the inside with the administration and all, it should be interesting," Ike said, unconsciously quickening the pace slightly.

They walked along in silence for a bit. It was one of those bright, sunny winter days that made one think that spring was just around the corner—even if it was only early January. Ike was happy to be out of the house and lost in his thoughts about what might be afoot on the political front. When they'd walked ten minutes, Will spoke what was on his mind. "Ike, would you mind explaining something to me?"

Ike liked Will and considered him bright. Will had done quite well in school and had shown an aptitude for math and working with numbers. Ike and Ellen had discussed recently that now that Will's "schooling" was over, it was time for his "education" to begin. Ike was flattered that Will would turn to him.

"Be happy to help if I can. What's on your mind?"

Will began hesitantly. "Well, I understand that Kentucky is a Democratic state, but I never really understood why. Everybody I know is a Republican."

"You've got to look over the ridges of these hollers, son. There's other places in this state besides Bell County. But you're certainly not alone in your confusion. I'm not sure that I understand all there is to it myself. It goes back at least to the war. As you know, Kentucky was a border state and never left the Union. So, at that time—mid-sixties—we were considered a Republican state.

"While the war was going on, Kentucky had to suffer with what you might call an 'occupation' of Yankee troops. Well, needless to say, some things happened that didn't make everybody happy. Perhaps that's what started a little Democratic leaning—away from President Lincoln's party, see?"

"That seems clear enough," Will said.

"It's hard for men as young as you and I to understand, but it's a fact that the English language is not adequate to describe how bad the people who comprised the Confederacy hated Abraham Lincoln and his Republican party."

"I guess that's where the term 'the solid South' comes from?"

"Sure is. No self-respectin' Confederate veteran is ever gonna vote Republican."

Will's face reflected confusion. "But, like you say, Kentucky wasn't a Confederate state. So what's the impact on us?"

"Well, Kentucky furnished more soldiers for the Union than for the Confederacy, but more of the Confederate veterans seem to run for office. Of course, they're all Democrats. Then, too, the way that reconstruction went following the war made many Kentuckians feel closer to the southern states. It's been said that Kentucky waited until after the war to secede."

"That's funny."

"Not to the serious politicians, it ain't."

"I thought you were a serious politician."

Ike smiled. "Me? Nah, I just like to talk politics for the entertainment value. After all, there ain't that much else to do around here."

They were approaching the forks of Straight Creek. As they took the first bridge to head up the Right Fork toward Berry Howard's house, Ike asked if Will wanted to stop in Bradshaw's store.

"Too late," Will said. "Bob's done closed up."

"Then let's just sit and rest a spell out here on the bench," Ike said.

The late afternoon sunshine felt glorious as they lounged on the bench and soaked up its warmth. Ike stretched his long legs out toward the road and leaned back in a relaxed pose. He felt good to be out of the house and he was enjoying the walk and the conversation. He sat contentedly until Will was ready to continue the discussion.

"If I understand you right, then Kentucky's chock full of Democrats, each of whom is an ex-Confederate. Ain't there any Union loyal Democrats?" Will asked.

"Sure there is," Ike answered, "lots of 'em. And that's a part of the reason their party's so split up. The old-line faction depends on fancy oratory and family ties, while Goebel and his backers represent a new breed of cat. The two factions usually find some way to smooth over their differences around election time well enough to beat us, but, with Bill Goebel in the game, there's so much hatred that they didn't manage to do that the last two times."

They sat in silence for a few minutes, enjoying the last fading rays of sunshine that managed to stream over the peaks on the ridge to the west. At this time of year, the sunshine darting through the swaying bare tree limbs created a fabulous dancing light pattern. "I 'spect we best get on," Ike said as he unfolded himself up from the bench.

"One more thing, Ike," Will said, moving into position alongside. "The way you make it sound, Kentucky's a pure Democrat state now. How come we're all Republicans?"

"Why hell, son. Anybody with the brains God gave a goose wouldn't be a Democrat!"

Will had heard that kind of comment all his life and was a little disappointed. He thought that his brother-in-law was treating him like an adult for once. Ike saw the look on Will's face and realized that it was a time to be serious.

"Well, we've been Republican ever since I can remember. That's one reason for it—might not be a good one, but it is one. Eastern Kentucky and Eastern Tennessee were hotbeds of Unionism during the war. That meant supporting the Republican party, and we just never stopped.

"Then, for another thing, the central and western Kentuckians—who are mostly Democrats—are pretty much farmers, while about all there is for us up here in the mountains is minin' coal. One of the biggest issues the politicians have got to argue about these days is railroad regulation. The Democrats—farmers—like to blame the bad economic times we've had lately on the railroads and are always trying to put stricter rules on them. But for us, it's a fact, son, that we'd starve if weren't for the Louisville & Nashville Railroad. So, it just kinda works out that bein' partial to the railroad makes us anti-Democrat."

"I can see that the L & N brings in most of the goods we get and employs a few folks, but that don't seem all that important. Why would we starve?" Will was deep in thought.

"Because nothin' wouldn't happen if they didn't haul the coal away. I'll show you what a difference the L & N's made. What would you say is the population of Middlesboro?"

Will figured Middlesboro to be the biggest town in Bell County. "Oh, I'd say 10,000."

"That's about right," Ike agreed. "In the winter of 1889, I was 'coon huntin' in what's downtown Middlesboro today. The L & N come in there that fall, and by the summer of '90, there was probably upwards of 6,000 people livin' there. That's what kind of difference the railroad made, and if they was to take those tracks out, Middlesboro would dry up and blow away pretty quick."

Will got a smile out of the image of someone pulling out the Louisville and Nashville tracks. "Railroads don't move the tracks around much do they?" he asked.

"No, they don't," Ike said. It was his turn to see the humor in the discussion. "If they did, they'd done took 'em out during the depression of the '90s, I reckon."

"I can understand that the railroads don't particularly want any regulation, but do they really care that much about who gets elected?"

Ike snorted. "Well, I've heard estimates that the L & N spent upwards of half a million dollars on Taylor's campaign."

Will tried to digest that figure and all the information Ike was providing for him. He had to admit, it made sense.

"Didn't you ever think that a Democrat was the best man for the job?" Will wondered.

"I'll tell you the truth, son." Ike made a show of looking right and left to ensure that no one would overhear his next comment. Then in a conspiratorial tone, "I did vote for a Democrat one time. And it's the God's truth that the corn never got more'n knee high that summer, and what they was of it come out as yeller as an acorn squash."

The water gushing into the Right Fork told them that they had reached the mouth of Stoney Fork. From here, only a short walk brought them to the Howard's house. Although there were plenty of men gathered on the porch who saw Ike and Will at the gate, Ike followed the mountain custom and let out a whoop to announce their arrival.

"Evenin', Ike. Who's that you got with ya?" Ike recognized Berry Howard's large bulk through the gathering dusk.

"I thought I'd best help keep an eye on Ike," Will laughed as they climbed the steps onto the porch.

"How you boys doin'?" Berry roared. He extended his hand and exchanged greetings all around. "There's some folks inside you'll want to meet. Gettin' cold out here anyway. Let's go in the house."

Berry went in first and promptly disappeared into the milling crowd. The roaring fire felt good on Will's face as they entered the front room. He had been so involved in the talk with Ike that he hadn't realized that the temperature had dropped quite a bit when the sun ducked behind the hills. The room was filled with all manner of men. Will recognized the Gross boys, T. J. Ashby, Bob Bradshaw, Josh Sousley and many other residents of the Right Fork community. As they entered the room, an attendant posted by the door offered a printed handbill to each person. At the front of the room, on the left of the fireplace stood Berry deep in conversation with a tall, handsome man and a stockier man with a handlebar mustache. Will did not know either man but thought that the taller one looked familiar.

"Okay, ever'body lissen up here," Berry shouted over the hum of conversation. Berry's deep voice was as commanding as his presence, and an expectant hush fell over the room. "I want to introduce these gentlemen," he continued. "Many of you know Frank Cecil, our deputy sheriff, and one of our Republican friends."

The stocky man stepped forward and smiled. He was of average height but more than typical weight, making him appear just a bit chubby. He had sandy-reddish hair and a ruddy complexion to match. Will knew Cecil as a deputy but didn't know that he was climbing in these political circles.

"And this," Berry said, placing his hand on the shoulder

of the taller man, "is our newly elected Secretary of State, Caleb Powers." A gasp went through the room. Although he was a native of adjoining Knox County, everyone present knew that it took a special event to attract such a major political figure to such a remote area. Tucked away in the geographical triangle formed by the borders of Kentucky, Tennessee, and Virginia, Bell County is far from the center of political power.

Berry and Cecil found chairs as Powers began to speak. "We appreciate all of you men showing up here this evening," he began. Will hung on every word. He'd been to political rallies before, but here he was in the very same room with the man who was the third highest ranking official in the entire state. Will knew that Powers even advised the Governor. "I know that you're all curious as to what's going on and what our plans are, as well you should be, and I'm not here to waste your time. So, let's get right to it. As you all know, we were legally elected, certified and inaugurated. Nevertheless, this very day, William Goebel has filed a notice of contest for the Governor's seat, and other Democrats have followed suit. So, even as we speak, many of the offices legally occupied by Republicans are being contested. The handbill that each of you has details the charges that Mr. Goebel has leveled against us. I suggest that you read it when you have a chance. I'm sure you'll each see for yourself what they're attempting."

A murmur went through the crowd. Will heard someone behind him say, "I'll personally shoot the son of a bitch afore he steals the election away from us."

Powers held up his hand for quiet. "Soon, the Legislature will select committees to decide the contests. We want those committee members to know that we plan to resist such awful encroachment of our most sacred rights. So, we're asking loyal Republicans from all over the state to come to the Capitol to protest this travesty of justice before the Legislature.

"The reason I'm here, then, is to ask all Bell County men who love liberty and are willing to stand up to protect their rights to be ready to go to Frankfort on the 24th of this month. At that time, the Legislature will be hearing the contest evidence, and we want them to hear us, too.

"Let there be no mistake, we want men of good character—good citizens—who will stay sober and present a favorable image of the Eastern Kentucky voter to the General

Assembly, to convince them that we want the duly elected state government to retain the offices."

The room exploded with applause. Powers turned to shake hands with Berry, and the look on his face said that he was pleased with the reception. "I told you that these Straight Creek boys would be behind us," Berry yelled above the din.

Powers waved his hands in the air asking for quiet. "Two more things, men," he yelled as the noise subsided. "I'm sure you all can see that there are those elements that'd like to see us not get to Frankfort. On that basis, let's keep our plans as quiet as we can—not involve anybody who doesn't need to know about what we're doing. And, finally, those of you who belong to the local militia company will want to take your uniforms along just in case the Governor calls out the military. With those cautions, I wish you good night and good luck."

Will turned to face Josh Sousley and Chas Whitt. "You goin'?" Chas asked Sousley.

"Damn right," Josh replied. "And I'll bring Goebel's head back on a pole. How 'bout you, Will?"

Will hesitated. Although he was pretty sure that such rough talk was just talk, he really didn't want to make any commitment before he had a chance to think the situation over carefully and seek some calm advice. "I'm not sure I can get away from the house," he mumbled. He needed to talk to Ike.

He looked around the room and finally spotted Ike in conversation with Berry, Cecil, and Powers. He made his way through the thinning crowd. As he approached the group, he heard Berry speaking. ". . . but the L & N don't own all the tracks. We might have to have some money."

"There's nothing for you to worry about. We'll take care of it when we get to Frankfort," Cecil said.

Will decided that this conversation was of no concern to him, so he moved over and sat in a chair near the fire to wait for Ike. As he dropped into the chair, he discovered that he was very tired. Rather than risk falling asleep, he started to examine the handbill he had been given. It listed a total of eight sections charging that the election was invalid because the Republicans had used thin, transparent ballots, called out the militia to be in charge of the polling places, and entered into various conspiracies to intimidate voters and defeat specific contestants. Will's eyes became heavy as he waded through the legal verbiage.

He awoke with a start. "Wake up, son," Ike was saying. "It's time to head on back home."

Will did not know how long he had slept, but he was refreshed and the night air felt good. The full moon illuminated the path along the silver ribbon that was the right fork of Straight Creek. Will moved into place by Ike's side as he pulled his heavy wool coat closer against the cold wind.

"Ike, are you going to Frankfort?" Will found the whole idea a matter of grave concern.

"Did I ever tell you about the time that wagon wrecked in front of my house?" Ike chuckled.

"You know you did. What's that got to do with going to Frankfort with this rough bunch?"

"The moral's the same, son. Don't ask stupid questions. Nothing could keep me from going."

"Did you get any details?" Will asked.

"Sure did. The L & N's gonna have a train at the Pineville depot on the night of the 24th. We'll leave about 10 p.m. and be in Frankfort early the next morning. Then we'll tell the Legislature just how the cow ate the cabbage."

"What was Mr. Powers saying about keeping our plans quiet?"

Ike turned serious. "He's afeared that someone might blow the tracks to keep us from putting on our protest. We've arranged for the L & N to run a freight right in front of our passenger train, just in case."

"That kind of talk scares me some," Will admitted. "I'm not too sure I want to go."

"Then don't. Nobody's twistin' your arm."

They walked in silence for a moment, each lost in his thoughts. "That ain't exactly the kind of reply I was hopin' for," Will said.

"What did you want to hear?" Ike was serious.

"Well, this whole thing scares me," Will said. "I'm as good a Republican as anybody, but I heard some rough talk there tonight."

"It's time for some rough talk, son. And, if need be, it's

time to back it up with action. It ain't just the Governor's chair that's at issue here. It's whether we'll stand by and let that son of a bitch steal away the rights that we've fought wars to gain and keep. That's why I'm determined to go. You're right that there might be trouble, but as far as I'm concerned, if there's gonna be another civil war over this, I'm willin' to fight."

Will turned the matter over in his mind as they walked in silence for a bit. Finally, the matter resolved, he turned to Ike. "So am I," he said quietly.

Chapter 4

Gov. William Goebel.

Wednesday, January 24, 1900

A light snow was sifting down on what seemed to Will must be every man in Bell County congregated at the Pineville L & N depot. He was beginning to think that maybe his parents and sisters were right—that it would be wiser to just stay home. While he realized that these were, in fact, the very same men who he had thought to be a rough crowd at Berry's house, that group was downright tame compared to the bunch assembled here. There were some fifty men on the platform, and each was equipped with at least one weapon. Long rifles, squirrel guns, carbines, shotguns, and pistols were all in evidence, along with a multitude of different kinds of knives. The talk about being ready to do battle if necessary certainly appeared to be more than just idle chatter at this point. Many of the men carried earthenware jugs of corn whiskey, and the shouting and cussing left little doubt that they knew what to do with the contents.

He was beginning to seriously consider going back to the warm comfort of home, and might very well have done so except for the excitement of it all, when he felt a hand on his shoulder.

"Hell of a crew, ain't it?" Ike observed.

Will began to realize the limits of his experience. He had never been out of Bell County and had only ridden the train once before. And that was only to Middlesboro. Yet here he was waiting in the middle of the night with a group of ruffians to board a train that seemed to stretch for miles beyond the cones of weak light projecting from the station. In actuality, there were fourteen passenger cars lined up, ready to go. In several of the cars he could see men standing and sitting. A banner made from a bed sheet hung from the windows of one car. It proclaimed: **Republican Patriots from Middlesboro, Kentucky. Plain or fancy shooting performed on request. Very short notice required.**

A hell of a crew, indeed, he thought. Then realizing that he hadn't answered Ike, he said, "Sure is. Who's in charge of this travelin' circus?"

"I think Frank Cecil's around here someplace," Ike replied glancing around the platform. "Somebody from

Middlesboro should already be aboard."

"Is this all that's going?" Will had the idea that they had been discussing a large protest meeting.

"Not by a long shot," Ike replied. "We'll be picking up more men at ever' stop along the way. Matter of fact, Berry said there'd be a double dip at the next stop."

"Barbourville?"

"Yep. The Knox contingent will be there, of course. And Berry said that the Governor had a man named Culton who's gettin' up a group from other counties. They'll join up there, too."

"Where's Berry? I thought he'd be here with bells on."

"Left Monday on some errand to Louisville," Ike replied. "But he said there's nothin' for us to worry over."

"Well, I'm worried all the same," Will said. "Do you know anything about this fellow Culton, anyway?"

"He works in Frankfort is all I know. Looks like this show is about to go on the road. You ready?"

"Yeah, I'm ready, but I ain't too anxious to get in there with this bunch," Will admitted.

"Don't have to. Me and you'll ride up here in the first car."

An L & N conductor came walking along the platform swinging a lantern. "All aboard," he shouted. "Anybody wants to go to Frankfort get on and find a seat."

Ike took Will's arm and started toward the front of the train. The conductor put out a palm to halt them. "Where you boys think you're goin'?" he demanded in a hoarse voice. Reaching inside his vest pocket, Ike extracted a folded document and handed it to the conductor. He unfolded the paper and held it up to the light. As he scanned the page, a look of recognition crossed his face. "Yes sir," he said to Ike. "Any friend of Berry Howard's is most certainly a friend of the Louisville and Nashville Railroad and can ride right up here in the front car." He lowered his arm in a sweeping gesture motioning them forward.

"Say, mister," Ike asked the conductor. "I saw another train roll through here not ten minutes ago. Was that one loaded with people going to protest, too?"

"Naw," the man peered down the tracks, waving the lantern, "that was a freight the company's runnin' in front of this here train just in case somebody might blow the tracks to try to keep us from gettin' there. You best get aboard now."

"Do you still have any questions about the seriousness of what we're doin' here?" Ike asked as they moved toward the front of the train.

Will heaved a sigh of relief as they entered the plush car. The interior presented a picture of stark contrast to the one the ruffians outside had created in his mind. The seats were upholstered in cream-colored leather that contrasted perfectly with the deep red carpet. The crystal light fixtures dangling from the ceiling projected a diffused light over the scene. The sole occupant was a distinguished looking gentleman wearing a gray pin-stripe suit and smoking an elaborately carved pipe. The aroma of the pipe tobacco created a pleasant atmosphere throughout the car. He looked up from the newspaper he was reading as Ike and Will entered and smiled pleasantly. He stood and offered his hand to Ike. "Hello, men. I'm D. G. Colson from Middlesboro."

As the man extended his right hand to him, Will noticed that Colson's left arm was in a sling.

Ike introduced himself and Will.

"Are you in charge of the Pineville group?" Colson asked.

"No," Ike replied, "I'm a friend of Berry Howard. Will and I are part of the Straight Creek crowd."

"Right Fork?"

"Right," Ike answered. "How'd you know?"

"Any friend of Mr. Howard's would have to be from the Right Fork."

Ike was deep in thought for a moment. "Did you say your name was Colson?"

"Yes."

"I've heard Berry speak of you. You're his lawyer from over at Middlesboro, ain't you?"

"That's correct, Mr. Livingston. Mr. Howard and I have been friends and colleagues for many years."

"Berry said he'd meet us at Frankfort," Ike offered.

"Very good," Colson said, returning to his newspaper with an air that made Will feel that they'd been dismissed.

"I like this set up pretty well," Will said to Ike. "I wasn't much looking forward to riding all the way to Frankfort with that gang back there." Settling back into a plush seat, he flashed a boyish grin and asked, "How long'll it take to get there?"

Ike had only made the trip once before himself, and that was with Berry. Still, he would let his young brother-in-law think he was an old hand. "Depends on how many times we stop and how long we wait at each stop," he said.

I could have figured that out for myself, Will thought but decided against saying anything. He and Ike had just settled into seats facing each other when the train started with a jolt. Will jerked toward Ike, and then recoiled into the back of his seat, banging his head roughly. Ike chuckled as he watched Will grimace and massage the new sore lump on the back of his neck. Soon the train settled into its steady clackety-clack, swaying motion over the rails.

Will leaned out into the aisle to sneak a glance at Colson. Seeing that the Middlesboro man was asleep, Will spoke softly to Ike. "Ain't that Colson fellow the one that was involved in that big shoot-out in Frankfort a week or so ago?"

"That's the man," Ike said. "I'm glad you had sense enough not to say anything to him about it."

"I ain't gonna say too much to a man the grand jury brung three counts of murder against," Will said earnestly.

"Don't forget about the two indictments for carrying concealed weapons," Ike added with a chuckle.

"What was that all about, anyway?" Will asked.

"Oh, Colson and another man had been spittin' at each other like a couple of cats for over a year now. They were both army officers in the War with Spain and had some fallin' out. I guess they just happened to meet in the Capital Hotel and the sparks flew."

"I heard it was more bullets than sparks."

"Well, given all the passions that's runnin' these days, I guess when they happened to meet, they happened to be armed, too. Matter of fact, Colson emptied two pistols before the shooting was done."

"He got his man, didn't he?"

"Got him, and two others besides," Ike laughed. "Are you sure you want to go to Frankfort?"

"Too late to turn back now," Will spoke hesitantly.

All along the way, Ike and Will could hear the sounds pouring from the cars of the train. None of the voices were intelligible, but from the general timbre, the riders were certainly in high feather. Ike attempted to ensure a desultory conversation lest Will discover that he was not exactly the world traveler that he had let on. About midnight the train pulled into the depot at Barbourville. The bustle on the platform put up such a racket that the need for conversation was temporarily relieved.

The scene was a repetition of the one at Pineville. Here, there were more like 175 men. Each appeared to be armed to the teeth and the whiskey jugs were very much in evidence. Will was looking back over his shoulder to watch the men pile into the passenger cars when he heard the door to their car open. A stocky man with a handlebar mustache strode in.

"Howdy, men. Bill Culton's the name." Ike stood and introduced himself and Will as friends of Berry's.

"Do you know Mr. Colson?" Ike asked.

"Sure do," Culton said. The two men shook hands heartily.

"Bill, what in the world are you doin' here?" Colson said.

"I'm workin' for Governor Taylor now," Culton answered. "He's real interested in gettin' a lot of us folks to Frankfort just to make sure that the Legislature knows that we're watchin' them."

Will saw the L & N conductor walk by outside waving the lantern. He could see the man's mouth moving but couldn't hear the words. Will took his presence as an indication that the train was about ready to move out. Everyone in the car had just regained their seats when the train lurched violently forward again. Will was prepared for the jolt this time and managed it quite well. "Happy to see you're becomin' a travelin' man, son," Ike smiled. The familiar clackety-clack sound soon dominated the scene once again.

"Where's Berry at?" Culton asked.

"Went to Louisville earlier in the week," Ike replied. "Said he'd be on hand to meet us in Frankfort."

"I hope he does, but it don't matter none," Culton said. "Ever'thing's done took care of."

"I've been wondering about that," Will said. "How long are we going to be in Frankfort? Where are we going to sleep and eat?"

Ike could see that the boy was upset. "Don't fret about it, Will. Berry said that if we have any problems, we should see a Mr. Pence at the Board of Trade Hotel and he'd take care of us." That knowledge was as much comfort to Ike as he knew it'd be to Will. "And if all else fails, he said we could call on Caleb Powers."

"Caleb's a fine man," Culton said. "I guarantee that we can depend on him for anything we might need." Culton pulled a silver pocket watch from his trousers and clicked it open. "Way past midnight. Big doin's tomorrow; we'd best get some sleep."

It appeared to Will that Culton was asleep before he finished talking and Ike wasn't far behind. Will looked over his shoulder to see Colson snoring away. Left alone with his thoughts, he leaned back and tried to relax. He soon found that he was much too excited to sleep, despite the soothing rhythm being transmitted by the train wheels. He tried watching the countryside out the window, but there was not even a light in what few farm houses they passed. So many unknowns were turning in his mind. Finally, he gave up the effort to sleep and wandered out to the landing between cars.

A couple of men were standing out there smoking cigars. As Will did not know either man, he assumed they were part of the Knox County contingent. As Will approached, he overheard what one of the men was saying.

"I hope we get to stop at the Capital Hotel. I've heered tell that it's as fine as any palace the European Royalty have."

"I've been there," the other man said. "It is a nice place." Noticing Will coming out of the car, he turned. "Howdy."

Will nodded a smile.

"You from Bell?" the man who had spoken asked.

"Yes, name's Will Elliott."

"Happy to know you, Will," he replied. "I'm Zack Steele. This here's Ike Hoskins." Will shook hands with both men.

"Too cold to stand out here," Zack said. "Let's go back inside. Come on along, Will." They pitched their glowing cigars into the rushing darkness and started into the car behind them.

Although he was hesitant to enter, Will was sure that he'd still be unable to sleep. Steele's smile was reassuring, so he accompanied the men back into their passenger car. This car was not nearly as plush as the other one, and its atmosphere was more like he'd originally expected. Men were lounged over the seats in every conceivable position, and tobacco smoke hung in the air like a velvet curtain. Now, in the light, he could see the faces of his companions, and he took an instant liking to Zack Steele. He was a tall, thin man with a tuft of honey blond hair sticking from beneath a felt hat cocked back on his head. His triangular face was lined from the effects of a constant smile, and his good nature was evident. Will walked with Zack into the middle of an argument.

"No, damn it, I'm telling you the L & N's providing this transportation free of charge. They're more interested in seein' that Goebel don't become Governor than any of us ever even thought about. I know for a fact that they spent a pot full of money to get Taylor elected," one of the men was saying.

The other contestant spotted Will and Zack. "Here's the man what'll know. Zack, is the Republican party payin' for this ride for us?"

Zack flashed his disarming smile. "The official position of the Louisville and Nashville Railroad is that they have no interest in politics and don't support any candidate. They did appeal to all Kentuckians to 'reject the antagonistic Goebel' however."

"So, they don't support any particular candidate, they're just against one," Will laughed.

"Aw, come on, Zack, what's the story on the train?" the man persisted.

"What the hell's the difference it makes to you, Frank Burch?" Zack said. "You're getting a free ride and the prospect of a few free meals, ain't you?"

"And a night away from the house to boot," someone shouted.

"And the chance to shoot some Democrats!" from the back of the car.

"We'll kill enough of the Democrats to create a Republican majority in the Legislature. Then, by God, it won't make no difference what Bill Goebel does," shouted Josh Sousley.

"That's if the son of a bitch is still alive to do anythin'," came from somewhere. Shouts of approval followed.

Burch leaned forward and offered Sousley a drink from his jug. Sousley hooked his finger through the jug's handle and turned his wrist over so that his arm supported its weight. He drank deeply and then wiped his mouth on the sleeve of his coat. "You know," he slurred to Burch, "I've heered tell that Goebel wears a breastplate of armor under his shirt."

Burch took the jug and drank. "Don't matter if he does." He pulled his rifle up across his knees and patted the stock. "Armor won't do him no good unless he wears it around his damned head."

Zach Steele saw the look of shock on Will's face. "Come along, Will," he said, taking Will's arm. "Your Bell County friends will be thinking you fell off the train if you don't get back." Although Will knew that Ike and the others would still be asleep, he let himself be led back out onto the landing. Once outside, the smile faded from Zack's face. "Don't let the talk upset you, son," he said. "These boys are just away from home for a spell and having a little fun." With a handshake and a smile, Zack Steele turned and walked back into the car.

Will re-entered the front car just as the train pulled into the Corbin station. Here the familiar scene was enacted once again. The platform was crowded with drunken men brandishing guns of all descriptions. They piled into the cars as Will made his way back to his seat facing the sleeping Ike. As soon as he settled in place, he found that he was exhausted and was almost asleep when a man entered the car.

The new man swept the car with a glance. Seeing the sleeping men, he spoke quietly to Will. "Evenin'. I'm Bob Noakes," he said.

"Happy to know you," Will said sleepily. "I'm from Bell County. You from Knox?"

"Yeah, I'm the captain of militia here in Corbin," was the last sound Will heard before he fell asleep.

Ike shook him awake as a cold, gray light of early morning streamed in the window. Looking out, Will saw a countryside nothing like Bell County. The hills were low and rolling, and it seemed as if he could see forever. There was not the feeling of being hemmed in by the trees and ridges that the Bell County landscape usually presented. There were trees sprinkled around, but nothing like as thick as his mountain home. "Where are we?" he said.

"Almost to Frankfort," Ike answered.

Will might have guessed that had he been more awake. The scenery out the window matched all he'd heard about central Kentucky. The train was slipping diagonally down a sheer cliff toward a river that was much wider and muddier than Bell County's Cumberland. He knew that'd be the Kentucky River. When the train reached the bottom land, the limestone palisades closed in, leaving the tracks little choice other than to parallel the water's course. As suddenly as if someone had flipped a switch, the weak gray light changed to darkness as the car plunged into a short tunnel chiseled through a limestone hillside.

Emerging from the tunnel, the train slid slowly past the sleeping depot and ground to a halt directly in front of the State Capitol building. As soon as the wheels stopped turning, a flurry of sound and activity shattered the stillness of the early morning air.

"Ever'body out!" someone shouted. "This here is the place to do what we come here to do. Ever'body out."

Ike, Will, D. G. Colson, Noakes, Culton and some other men exited the front car. Will assumed that the others had boarded the train at stops while he slept. Berry Howard came sweeping up the street, mist and fog swirling around his ample bulk as he walked. "Good morning, gents. Welcome to Frankfort." He seemed to be in high spirits.

The passenger cars disgorged the crowd of men. Guns seemed to point in all possible directions. Someone Will did not know climbed up on the fence railing and addressed the group.

"All right men, you all know that we're here to let the law-makers know that we're not gonna let them steal the election. Now nobody wants any trouble, and we want all of you to act like decent citizens. General Collier's office is in that red brick building yonder, and you can check your guns there, if you've a mind to. We want you to move through this gate here and assemble in the yard. As you go in, these men will give each of you one of these badges." He held up a white silk ribbon seven or eight inches long. Will thought he could see some kind of a picture on the ribbon. "There's folks comin' from all over the state, and these badges will help keep us all straight. Now move on in to the grounds, and we'll get you some breakfast directly."

Somewhat to Will's surprise, many of the men started moving toward the building the speaker had indicated. He wondered why they bothered to bring those guns along if they were just going to stack their arms. Someone handed him one of the badges. In the faint light, he could see that the ribbon was adorned with W. S. Taylor's picture. He pinned the badge to his vest.

Will stood aside while Berry talked in hushed tones with the others. He was awed by the gleaming white of the Capitol building made from limestone that he'd heard called "Kentucky Marble." It was crowned with a towering rotunda that had glass on all sides. The light escaping from within slanted upwards and seemed to support a wreath of fog that surrounded the tower like a halo. This central building, the Capitol—or State House, as it was usually called—was flanked on the right by a taller building fashioned from the same white limestone. Will knew that this building housed the executive offices of the government. To the left of the State House stood the red brick building called the Agricultural Building, which housed the State Adjutant General's office. The entire city block containing the three buildings was enclosed by a six-foot tall wrought iron picket fence. Two gates in the fence in front of the State House allowed entrance onto a wide brick sidewalk. Directly in front of the center pair of the six white columns, the walkway split, creating an elliptical grassy space that contained a water fountain. Will was puzzled by the lack of water before it dawned on him that it had been drained for the winter. Ain't nothin' the like of this in Bell County, he thought to himself. Any one of these buildings was the largest he'd ever seen; taken together, they were a sight. In a few moments Ike returned to his side. "Let's me and you go on over to the Board of Trade Hotel," he said. "Ain't nothin' gonna happen here for a while yet."

"Where is it?" Will asked. He could see nothing but fog beyond the State House.

"Just across the street here," Ike said. He led Will around in front of the locomotive to the side opposite the government buildings. A short walk brought them to the hotel.

In the lobby, a sleepy clerk tried to look alert as they approached the desk. "Good morning," Ike said. "Are you Mr. Pence?"

"Nah, I just be the night clerk. What can I do for ye?"

"Well, right now, we'd like some breakfast."

"Dining room's right through thar," he said pointing down a dimly lit hallway. "You'ns with that mountain crowd?"

It was more of a statement than a question as he eyed their badges.

"Yeah, I reckon we are," Ike answered.

"Then they're 'spectin' you. Eat hearty."

Will's eyes widened as the men entered the dining room. He'd heard about such things, but he had never eaten a meal anywhere but in a kitchen in someone's home. The sight of tables with white cloths, carpeted floors and waiters with white aprons was something from a dream. They found a table and were seated. In a few moments, Berry, Mr. Colson, and William Culton joined them.

Waiters swarmed around the table with platters of eggs, bacon, sausage, hot biscuits, and urns of coffee. Will sat in wide-eyed wonder as they dug into the meal. Through a mouthful of eggs, Ike asked Berry, "What's the plan for this morning?"

"The Legislature will be meetin' about 10:30," he said. "We'll meet over across the street and let 'em know that we're here and that we aim to stop the steal."

Will had grown accustomed enough to his surroundings to be enjoying the food. He had not even thought to wonder who was going to pay for the meal. He had a butter-laden biscuit half way to his mouth when the most beautiful sight he had ever seen appeared before his eyes.

She was wearing a pink bustle dress trimmed in white ribbons. The lace at the hem touched the floor, while the matching lace at the collar was topped with a pink and white ribbon choker. Her tiny waist was circled with a pastel leather sash. Her strawberry blond hair was piled high on her head in a bee-hive type affair that spiraled gracefully to an apex that seemed to point in the same direction as the parasol over her right shoulder. She had her left hand on a gentleman's arm but Will only noticed that she glided rather than rocked as she moved. Definitely ain't nothing in Bell County to match that, he thought. Melted butter dripped on his shirt front.

"Close your mouth, son, afore a fly gets in there," Ike said. That brought a round of laughter. Will closed his mouth but kept his eye on the girl as she found a table on the far side of the room. He snatched up a napkin and daubed away at his shirt.

"Now just what do you reckon your Ma'd think of you droolin' away like that?" Ike said. "That gal's really somethin', ain't she, Will?"

"Any of you know who she is?" Will was embarrassed, but he'd decided that, teasing or not, he'd find out.

When they had finished their breakfast, they moved back across the street to the State House grounds. The day had faired up; a faint sunlight had burned off the fog and visibility was good. The train on which they had arrived was backed up even with the L & N depot up the street, and the grounds were crowded with the mountaineers. It really didn't seem like the same bunch that had been on the train; few guns were in evidence, although Will suspected that most of them had handguns hidden away. The group seemed transformed once again, from the wild bunch of last night into a much tamer gathering. Will guessed there were maybe 1,000 to 1,200 men there—the number he had figured the train carried—and each and every one of them was sporting the white badge.

The man who earlier had asked the crowd to check their guns approached as they entered the gate of the Capitol grounds.

"Mornin', John," Berry said. "You ready to get this show on the road?"

"Ready. This should work out fine."

Berry turned to Ike. "I don't think you and Will have met John Powers," he said. As John shook hands, Berry added, "John's Caleb's brother, and captain of the Knox militia. He's a hell of a good man to have on our side."

They moved up the broad walk, past the fountain that stood before the august building. The rest of the group stopped as Captain Powers mounted the low steps of the Capitol building. The crowd quieted as he spoke. "Now, men," he began, "let's get down to business. The State Legislature is meetin' right on the other side of these doors here, and they're hearing the election contest right this minute." He gestured over his shoulder with a thumb. "We want them to know that we're here, and we want them to know what for. To start things off, here's our ex-Secretary of State, your friend and mine, Charles Finley."

Finley climbed the steps to thunderous applause. He

eyed the crowd with the presence of an accomplished speaker as the noise subsided.

"Fellow citizens, your presence here shows how vitally the people of Kentucky are interested in what is going on in this city. If you are not vitally interested you would not have made the long journey hither from the mountains. . . ."

Will caught himself wondering about the girl he had seen in the dining room. Who was she? Was that her husband? How would he find out? He awoke from the daydream with a start—he had not "made the long journey hither" to moon over some girl that he didn't know and would probably never see again.

". . . You are not here as revolutionists. You are still loyal to the form of government and to the good laws of the state. You are not here as criminals or conspirators, nor to do aught that is unlawful. You have simply come here. . . ."

She sure didn't look like any of the Bell County girls, Will found himself thinking. There were some pretty girls in the mountains, but. . . . His thinking was interrupted by applause. Finley had finished speaking.

Captain Powers had returned to the steps and was introducing someone else when he stopped in mid-sentence, his attention drawn to something behind the crowd. As if by command, each man fell silent and turned to see the source of the change in climate. Will felt slight pressure against various points of his body as the men surrounding him pushed gently in several directions. He quickly saw that, without conscious thought, the crowd was falling into two sections just as if an invisible knife were being drawn through the group. A pathway opened up through the group, leading from the gate right up to the Capitol doorway. Two men were approaching from the street. One was a well dressed fat man; the other was the focus of attention. He was a man of medium height and weight, wearing a salt and pepper suit topped with a black hat. Strands of black hair slid from beneath the hat down a neck that had folds of skin drooping over his white linen shirt collar. Will thought that the jet black eyes projected an evil beam that would burn through any obstacle it might meet. The morning light gave the skin a yellowish tint that conveyed no hint of a warm-blooded being. Will involuntarily shuddered.

"Who's that?" someone asked.

"Goebel." The name was a hiss.

"The son of a bitch looks like a lizard," Will heard himself whisper. He was embarrassed that he had spoken his thoughts aloud, but no one noticed—all eyes were riveted on Goebel.

He moved forward slowly, starting into the open corridor between the two groups of mountaineers. Will's eyes were locked on William Goebel's, which betrayed a look of slightly bemused distaste. It was clear that the man considered himself superior to everybody and everything around him. Just as he was about to enter the opening in the group, the fat man who was accompanying Goebel took his arm and, ignoring the waiting path through the crowd up to the front door, moved along the perimeter of the group and into a side door of the building. Will was sure that he saw a smile on Goebel's face when he disappeared inside.

Chapter 5

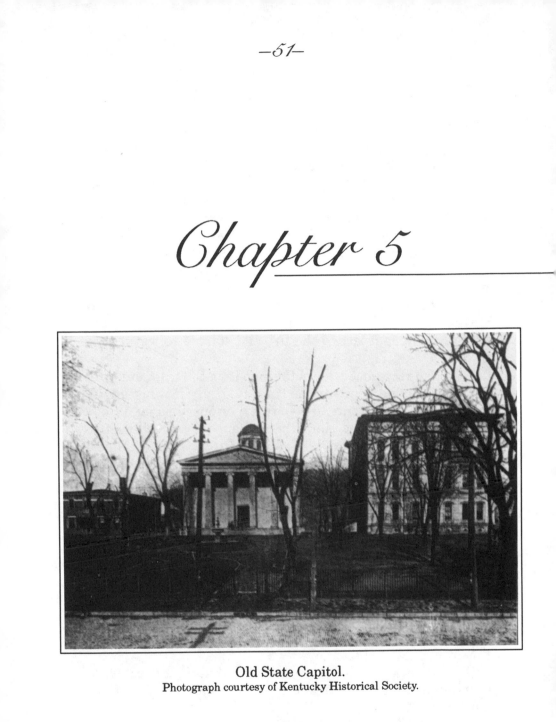

Old State Capitol.
Photograph courtesy of Kentucky Historical Society.

Thursday, January 25, 1900

T he group of protesters had elected Judge Jere Morton as chairman of the meeting and charged him and a committee with the chore of drafting a resolution to present to the Legislature. With the break in the action, Will and Ike had wandered out into the Capitol grounds, which were littered with the debris of the men camping there. They were discussing the significance of a Democrat having been elected chairman as they walked up to share a campfire.

"Hello men," Ike said. "Mind sharing some of that heat?"

"Seems to me it's plenty hot enough around here without no fire, but help yourself," one of the men replied. Will and Ike approached the fire and started to warm their hands.

Will recognized one of the men from the train but could not recall the name. Was the train ride only just last night? It seemed ages ago already—he'd experienced so many new and exotic sensations since then. Ike said something that made the man smile and Will realized that he was Zack Steele.

"Hello, Zack," Will said. "How're you country boys holding up to this cold weather?"

"Fair to middlin', Will," Zack said, flashing that smile that made it easy to see why everyone liked him.

"You all have any news about what's going on inside?" Ike asked, glancing toward the State House.

"Did you hear about how the members of the committee hearing the contests were chosen?" Zack asked.

"I'd heard they were simply going to draw names from both houses," Ike replied. "Is that what they did?"

"Yeah, it is," Zack answered, "but there's some talk that the drawing was rigged."

"What's the talk? It seems to me that if they just wrote everyone's name on a slip and threw them all in a box, it'd be hard to rig that."

"Well," Zack began, "they drew eight names from the House and three from the Senate for the Governor's contest and the same for the Lieutenant Governor's. Now, we all know that there's a slight Democratic majority in the Legislature, but only three of the twenty-two names drawn were

Republicans. Now, I put it to you, does that sound right to you?"

"No, it don't," Ike said. "I'd allow that, by rights, we should have had four or five on each committee."

"A man would think so, wouldn't he?" Zack mused.

Will had pulled a pencil from his vest pocket and was working furiously on a piece of paper while they talked. He was sort of mumbling to himself as he scribbled on the paper.

"What's he doing?" Zack asked, pointing at Will.

"Cipherin'. He always talks to himself like that when he's workin' with figures."

"The way I heard it," Steele went on, "is that they rolled the slips with the Republicans' names real tight and the ones with the Democrats' names real loose. That way, when they shook the box, the Republicans' names went to the bottom and the Democrats' names came to the top. That made it easy to tell which was which."

"Didn't anybody supervise the process?" Ike asked.

"One of the Republicans made a motion to the effect that somebody ought to oversee the thing and got ruled out of order for his trouble."

"The way I heard it," someone else spoke up, "was that the president simply called a Democrat's name no matter whose name was on the slip the clerk had drawed."

"That'd make it a heap simpler."

"I'll keep that in mind for the next time we draw names for Christmas gifts," Zack said. "I'll make damn sure that I don't get cousin Elmer's name again this year."

"I guess it might have happened the way it did by chance," Ike said thoughtfully.

"Yeah," Will spoke up, replacing the pencil in his vest pocket. "And, they might have to cancel the Fourth of July parade due to heavy snow, too." He waved the paper in the air.

"What's all that cipherin' you're doin' there?" Ike quizzed.

"I'm no statistician, but according to the way I figure it," he said, "drawing ten Democrats and one Republican for the Governor's contest would happen by random chance about once in ever' 1,000 times."

Ike let out a long, low whistle. "I don't care much for those odds."

"And that ain't even the worst of it," Zack said.

"How could it get any worse?" Ike countered.

"Well, several of the Democrats whose names were drawn—well, their names were called anyway—to serve on the committee to hear the Governor's contest are the same ones who urged Goebel to contest the election in the first place. And, just to top that, I hear tell that a couple of 'em have got money bet that Goebel'll end up as the occupant of the Governor's office."

"I'd like those odds," Will said. "Sounds like a pretty safe bet to me."

"Well, the ones that bet will sure as hell lose their money if I have my way," Zack interjected.

"If any of what we're saying here is true," Ike said, "the only chance there is of this whole thing comin' out fair is for us to get somebody's attention right here and now."

Will looked up toward the State House and saw Berry coming down the steps in the company of several men. That group approached where they were squatting around the fire. Noting the miserable look on Will's face, Berry asked, "You havin' a good time, Will?"

"This is the most fun I've had since that time old man Kelsey's cows got out," Will said, pulling his coat closer about his body.

"Ike, I need you to come with me to a meetin' up in Caleb Powers' office," Berry said. Turning to Will, he continued, "Tell you what, nothin' excitin' is gonna happen around here for a while. Why don't you go out and see the town? We'll meet up over at Kagin's Restaurant about 5 o'clock this evenin'."

"Sounds good to me," Will said. At least it'd be warmer moving around, he thought. Ike and Berry started to move off toward the State House. Will turned toward the gate when he heard Ike yell.

"Wait up a minute, Will. Do you have any money?" he asked.

Money had not even crossed Will's mind, not that he could have brought any if it had. "No," he confessed.

Ike held out three wrinkled one dollar bills. Will hesitated. "Take it, son, and go have some fun."

Will smiled sheepishly as he accepted the money and turned to walk away. "Don't spend it all in the same place," he heard over his shoulder.

Will walked out the gate of the Capitol grounds, across the street and railroad tracks and turned left toward the Board of Trade Hotel. Colson had said that the Capital Hotel was up that way somewhere. Even if they weren't going to stop there, he saw no reason why he couldn't see the place for himself. When he reached the corner, he looked to his right to see a big building that would have to be the place. He turned up that way.

On the way up the street, he had the thought that he had come a long way in the past 24 hours. For a boy who had never been out of the county before, he was getting rather independent. Then it occurred to him that he hadn't even thought to ask where Kagin's was. That thought put a dent in his newfound confidence. Oh, well, he'd find the place somehow.

The building he was walking by was a huge stone edifice that greatly resembled the State House. It, like the Capitol, was constructed of large limestone blocks. But, letting his hands drag along the side of the building, he noted that these blocks were of a much rougher texture than the government building. Rounding the corner of the building, he saw that the hotel also sported six tall, white columns and was topped by a domed rotunda.

Before the porch, a group of legislators huddled in overcoats were having a heated discussion. Moving around the group, Will stumbled on an uneven brick in the pavement and brushed against one of the men. As they bumped, Will felt the hard outline of a pistol in the man's pocket. "Sorry," Will mumbled and hurried on into the building. Everybody in this town must be armed, he thought as he entered the front door.

A wave of warm, welcome relief rolled over him as he entered the building. The splendor of the lobby of the Capital Hotel was just the latest in the series of things of which Will had never seen the like. The walnut and oak furniture was polished to such a gloss that the light from the crystal fixtures overhead was reflected from the surfaces in a blinding flash. This was the first he'd seen of electric lights, and the thought that it sure beat coal-oil lamps went through his mind. He ran his hand along the wall to discover that the wallpaper was textured with red velvet flowering figures the color of which was an exact match for the color of the plush carpet underfoot. He took off his coat in response to the changes in temperature and sensation and leaned against a white fluted column to catch his breath.

"I'm telling you what's the truth," Will heard a voice say from the other side of the column. "Bradley called out the militia in Louisville for the simple reason of keeping legal Democratic voters away from the polls. That's how Taylor won Jefferson County, pure and simple."

"And those ballots that Finley sent to the mountain counties," another voice added, "were the lowest Republican trick yet. They were clearly designed to confuse the voter. The Democratic ticket box was the smallest one on it and the Republican one the biggest. And the paper was tissue thin. Even when it was folded, anybody that looked could see how you voted. The railroad and mine bosses hung around the polls, and if a man's vote didn't suit them, then he was out of a job. Intimidation, that's how Taylor got the votes to win those counties."

Will started around the column to protest that last comment when his better judgment stopped him. He thought that, first of all, it'd probably be a good idea to get the white ribbon badge off his vest. No need to advertise in this situation. He removed the pin, folded the ribbon and placed it in his pocket. Secondly, it occurred to him that, as he wasn't old enough to vote, he hadn't been around the polls in Bell County, not to mention Jefferson County. Hence, regardless of what his instincts told him, he did not know any of the facts of the election, the use of militia, or the ballots. Finally, it occurred to him that these men were surely Democrats, and he'd never knowingly said a word to a Democrat before. He was slightly embarrassed to find himself thinking that it was a surprise that Democrats spoke English just like he did.

"Here, now what's all this?" one of the men said when he saw Will come partially from behind the column. He grasped Will's arm with his left hand as he moved his right hand inside his jacket. Will was both frightened and embarrassed. "I'm very sorry," Will said. "I was just resting here against this post and before I realized it, I was eavesdropping." His face was beet red.

The man gripping Will smiled. "I guess that's understandable, young man," he said. He looked Will over thoroughly and slowly withdrew his hand from beneath his coat. "We're just all a little jumpy at present," he said. "My name's James Young." He released his grip on Will's arm and extended his hand.

"Will Elliott," Will said, shaking the proffered hand.

"My friend here is Sam Readnour," Young said indicating the taller man. "We're not talking about anything worth making an effort to overhear, anyway."

"Thank you," Will said with a sigh of relief. "You gentlemen were presenting a point of view that I haven't heard much of."

"How's that?" Readnour asked, tilting his head quizzically.

"Well, I'm from Bell. . . ."

"Enough said," Mr. Young interrupted. "Not to worry, young man. Despite the fervor of the present moment, I've always thought that every man is entitled to his own opinion and his right to voice it. Truth to tell, as I'm a lawyer, I'd be out of work unless I was accustomed to dealing with both sides of a question. Besides, Sam here is not a Goebel Democrat."

"That's right," Readnour said, "I back Governor Brown."

As embarrassed as he was, Will was keenly interested in these men's opinions. The wisdom of Ike's remark about seeing beyond those Bell County hollers was sinking in. He was just beginning to stretch the limits of the environment in which he'd been reared. "Please go on with what you were saying. If you gentlemen don't mind, I'd like to hear what you think."

"Well, you might find this interesting," Mr. Readnour said, looking Will up and down. "The local folk are calling that crowd that came in on the train this morning the 'mountain army.' Are you a party to that?"

"I came on the train, but I'm no soldier."

"No, it doesn't appear that you are."

"The talk around town—among the Democrats, anyway—is that your mountain army came here for the simple purpose of intimidating the contest committees," Young said. "What have you to say about that?"

"I wouldn't pick the word 'intimidate,' but we do want them to know that we're here watching," Will replied. "As far as I'm concerned, I just aim to see that whatever's done gets done fair."

"Can't argue with that," Readnour smiled. "That's exactly why we call our party the 'Honest Election' Democrats."

"I've got a question for you," Mr. Young said. "If all you mountaineers came here just to watch, why'd everybody have to come armed to the teeth?"

Will had to confess that he had no good answer for that. "Boys will be boys," he said at length.

"Say," Will said, emboldened by their treatment of him. "Do either of you happen to know Senator Goebel?"

Both men looked slightly shocked. "Personally, no," Mr. Young said. "Why do you ask?"

"I just can't believe that he's as bad as folks let on," Will said. "Just thought one of you might know how I could get to talk to him."

"I wouldn't count on talking to Senator Goebel," Mr. Young said with a shake of his head. "He ain't exactly what you'd call personable, and he tries to limit his contact with voters to public speaking engagements. But, for whatever it's worth to you, I do happen to know that he lives upstairs right here in the hotel, Parlor A."

In the Secretary of State's private office in the southwest corner of the first floor of the executive office building, Caleb Powers was presiding over a strategy conference. In attendance were John Powers, Charles Finley, Wharton Golden, John Davis, Ike Livingston and Berry Howard.

"John, do you think this gathering is doing any good?" Caleb asked his brother, gesturing out the window with his head.

"Hard to tell until we get to talk to somebody in the Legislature. Anybody got any ideas on how we can poll them?"

Berry had. "As a former member of the House, I can get inside, and I can speak with some folks to find out what they're thinking."

"Good idea," Caleb said. "Charlie, what's the plan for these folks we've got outside here?"

"As soon as this crowd presents its resolution to the Legislature, they'll have accomplished about all they're going to," Finley said. "I say we send them home this evening."

"I'm in favor of that," Davis said. "You live in my boarding house, Caleb. You know we've got 'em sleeping in the halls and eating off the floor."

"Yes, I know it's crowded, John, but I think we ought to keep a few of them on hand. If the whole bunch leaves, the Legislature might think we've given up." To his brother, Powers went on, "John, fix up a train to take most of this bunch home later today."

Turning to Golden, Caleb said, "Wharton, you're here as an emissary of Governor Taylor. What's on his mind?"

"He thinks that the contest committees will be making their decisions late next week," Golden said. "He wants us to get another group to come in to protest Tuesday or Wednesday."

"Hold on, Wharton," Caleb said. "I don't know what happened the last time. I understood that groups were to come from all over, but all I see out there is the ones I brought." He gestured out the window behind him.

Golden glanced past Caleb's shoulder at the men milling around the grounds. "Governor Taylor changed his mind after you left for the mountains, Caleb," he said. "There was no way to get ahold of you to let you know he'd called off the dogs. Anyway, he's asked that we get up another bunch from the western part of the state."

Caleb opened a desk drawer and consulted his appointment book. "I can't go until Tuesday," he said with a sigh of resignation.

"That'll be the 30th?" Golden asked looking at the calendar.

"That'll be the 30th. Okay, you, John and I will go to Louisville next Tuesday." Caleb closed his appointment book with a snap. He was about to dismiss the group when a soft knock came on the door.

"Come in," Caleb called.

The door to the reception area opened to reveal a well dressed man of small stature. His dark hair curled over his ears in a manner that accentuated his chubby cheeks, making him appear much heavier than he actually was. A look of mild disgust crossed Powers' face.

"What do you want, Youtsey?"

"Just delivering this stuff from the auditor," he replied, depositing a stack of papers on the desk. Youtsey glanced at each of the men in the office. "You all plotting more election protection strategy?"

"You just tend to your business in the auditor's office," Caleb spat. "Let us worry about the election."

"My job's on the line here, too," Youtsey said. "If we get thrown out of the offices, I don't know how I'd make a living." After a moment's thought, he added, "You know, if I could only get my hands on $300, I could settle this election business right quick."

"What do you mean?" Finley asked.

"Never mind, Charlie," Powers said. Then to Youtsey, "Anything else, Henry?"

Youtsey appeared in no hurry to answer. He peered over Powers' shoulder out the window facing the railroad tracks out front. The window afforded an excellent view of the brick sidewalk that enveloped the fountain before the adjoining State House. Holding his left hand out in front of his chest and his right hand under his chin, he pulled an imaginary trigger. "This'd be a hell of a good place to knock off a few from," he said.

With that, Caleb leapt up from his desk. "That's it, men. We've all got work to do; let's get to it."

As the men stood to exit the office, Golden turned to Ike and, in an off-hand manner, said, "We'd all be a lot better off if somebody did knock off Goebel."

Caleb shot from behind the desk and grabbed Golden by the arm. "I'm sure you're joking, Wharton," he said, "but we cannot afford that kind of talk, not even in jest. Something like that would be the worst thing that could possibly happen for the party."

Wharton Golden assumed a sheepish posture. "I'm only saying the same thing that's being said outside."

"I know that," Caleb said. "I can't control what's said out there, but we don't need that kind of loose-mouth talk in here." The Secretary of State was clearly upset.

Outside the office, Caleb stopped a tiny man who was passing by in the hallway. "Mac," he said, "I need to see you about Youtsey." Turning to Ike and Berry, he asked, "Do you boys know Mackenzie Todd, Governor Taylor's private secretary?"

Todd shook hands with both. Turning back to Powers, he said, "I saw Youtsey in your office the other day with a rifle. When I asked him what he was doing, he said that if trouble came, he was going to be prepared."

"He's crazy, Mac. Can you speak to the Governor about it?"

Ike leaned closer to Berry and whispered, "What say you and me clear out of here?"

"Best idea I've heard in a while."

They took leave of Powers and Todd and exited the building through the door facing the Capitol. As they walked the short distance between the buildings, a group of the Bell County men approached them. "Hold up a minute there, Berry," one of them yelled.

Berry and Ike stopped while the men walked up. "Berry," Jim Gross spoke for the group, "can you get us a look at this Goebel fellow we've heard so much about? We were all eatin' breakfast when I understand he put in an appearance this mornin'. We just want to see what the man stirrin' up all this fuss looks like."

"You bet I can show you, Jim," Berry said. "You boys just come along with Ike and me."

Berry led the way into the side door of the State House. The group strung out behind Berry as he moved around to the front of the stone double spiral staircase and followed in single file as he climbed to the Legislative meeting rooms on the second floor. The doors to the Senate chamber were closed as Berry moved to a post beside the left-most double door. He motioned Jim Gross into position on his right side so that Jim could peer through the glass window in the door. Berry pointed to Senator Goebel, who was seated at his desk in the Senate chamber reading a newspaper. Goebel was turned in his seat so that he presented a profile to the men at the door. "That's the man," Berry said quietly.

Jim said nothing; he merely moved aside so that the next man in line could take his spot. One by one, the men strung out on the descending curve of the staircase stepped into position and Berry pointed out the object of their trek to Frankfort. Watching from Berry's left side, Ike thought that either Goebel's presence or just a sense of reverence for the building commanded each man to silence. Each, in turn, pivoted and exited down the other side of the staircase without a word.

Bill Culton was the last man in the line.

"Surely you don't need me to point Goebel out to you," Berry smiled.

"No, I already know that he looks like a damned old ferret."

"I'm glad you showed up here, Bill. Caleb Powers just asked us to try to find out how the House members are responding to the little demonstration we're putting on outside. Do you mind helping Ike and me ask a few questions?"

"No, I don't mind, but how are we going to get at 'em to ask?"

Ike thought Culton slurred his speech just a little. Perhaps he'd been sharing a jug with some of the boys outside.

"I know the doorkeeper," Berry said. "His name's Bill Lyons; he'll let me in."

They moved around the railing of the stairwell to the opposite side of the building and stopped in front of the doors to the House chambers. The doorkeeper was in position at the door.

"Hello, Bill," Berry greeted.

"Mr. Howard, how are you?" Lyons nodded.

"Tolerable. We'd like to go in and see what's goin' on in the House." Berry reached to push the door open.

Lyons moved quickly to step between Berry and the door. Given Lyons' small size compared to Berry's, it was an act of considerable courage. "Hold on there, what business do you have in there?"

"As a former member, I have a right to go in if I want to."

"Well, I suppose you do," Lyons said. Then indicating Culton and Ike, he continued, "but these men here ain't got no business at all in there."

Culton assumed a menacing posture and moved his right hand to his left side beneath his coat. He started to say something to Lyons just as Charles Finley approached.

"Hello, men. What's going on?" Finley said in a friendly voice.

"These men are trying to get in the House chamber," Lyons said. "They ain't got any business in there, and I aim to keep 'em out."

Finley placed an arm around Culton's shoulder and smiled. "Let's go on downstairs, and we'll talk about this thing a little." Motioning to Berry, he guided Culton around the stairwell to the opening in the railing on the other side of the building. Lyons heaved a sigh of relief as the group disappeared down the stairs.

⚜

I wonder how long I've been standing here, Will thought as he pulled his watch from his pocket. He was surprised to see that it was almost 4:30; the time had passed quickly in the bustle of the Capital Hotel lobby. He had observed that the desk clerk seemed to have an answer for any question, so he moved across the room toward the counter.

"Pardon me, could you tell me how to get to Kagin's?" Will inquired.

"Opposite the State House." The clerk didn't even look up from the papers he was sorting. Not as friendly as the folks in Bell, Will thought as he moved out the front door and down the massive stone steps. As soon as he was out of the building, he was assaulted by a wave of noise from behind the building. Moving in that direction, he saw a flurry of activity around the L & N depot. It appeared as if all the men that had arrived that morning were assembled at the station. The shouting, shooting and yelping told Will that they were ready to relieve their boredom. With all the shouts and stray bullets flying around, he decided it'd be a good idea to just move right on by. Walking quickly, he soon saw the sign announcing Kagin's Restaurant. As he entered the door, an insistent clanging of the engine's bell announced the train's departure.

"Well, the wayward traveler has returned." Ike waved Will over to the table where he and Berry were seated. "You didn't do anything I wouldn't do this afternoon, did you?"

"I'm not too sure what you wouldn't do, but probably not," Will laughed. "Where's everybody out there going?" he asked, gesturing toward the depot.

"They presented our resolution to the Legislature, so they're going home," Berry said.

The train was picking up speed as it puffed by outside the restaurant. The tracks were so close that the tremendous noise caused the windows to vibrate and the tables to walk across the floor. Will waited for the noise to fade before he attempted to speak. "We're stayin' here?" He looked at Ike.

"Did I ever tell you about the time that wagon wrecked in front of my house?" Ike laughed.

Chapter 6

Scene of the Goebel Shooting
Adapted from the *Cincinnati Enquirer*

Monday, January 29, 1900

Today is the day I'm going to talk to Senator Goebel, Will thought as he exited the Board of Trade Hotel. He'd been hanging around the Capital Hotel since his conversation with the two men up there last week. By now he thought he had a pretty good idea of how things worked here in Frankfort. He turned the corner and on the way up toward the Capital Hotel, he went over possible approaches in his mind. "Good morning, Senator, my name's Will Elliott." No, he doesn't care what my name is. I'll try, "Pardon me, Senator, I just wanted. . . ." No, he doesn't care what I want, either. "Hello, Senator Goebel, would you mind explaining to me. . . ." Yeah, that's good. The right opening would be necessary to get his attention. Then they could talk. Will felt sure that he could reason with the man once he got the Senator's attention.

He was so wrapped up in such thoughts that he had turned the corner, was up the steps, and entering the lobby of the Capital Hotel before he realized where he was. Once inside, he headed up the central staircase toward Parlor A, where the Senator lived. In the past few days, he'd observed Senator Goebel's routine every day, and it did not vary. So, Will knew that in about ten minutes, Goebel and his retinue would be moving into the hall and down the steps.

Will had assumed his post in the hall just outside Goebel's suite when the door flew open. Out marched a large man followed by Senator Goebel and then another big man. Will took one step toward the Senator and started into the opening he had practiced. "Pardon me, ..." The man in front jumped between Will and Goebel so quickly that it startled Will.

"What the hell do you want, boy?" the man said gruffly.

"I just . . . ." Before Will could get any more words out, the man had shoved him against the wall and pinned him there with a thick forearm across his chest. Will could only watch wide-eyed as Senator Goebel and the rest of his entourage moved on down the hall. Goebel passed the point where the man had Will stuck up on the wall just as if nothing at all unusual were happening around him. When the group was out of sight, the big man released Will and hurried down the hall in the departed Senator's wake.

It had all happened so quickly that Will was a little stunned. He was having difficulty breathing, and a swath of pain marked the path of the man's arm across his chest. He tried to relax as he pushed himself away from the wall with a backward thrust of his elbows. The push turned out to be more abrupt than he had planned. As a result, he propelled himself away from the wall and directly into the path of someone walking down the hallway.

Will hit the plush carpet on his knees in a shower of perfume, lace and paper wrapped packages. He scrambled quickly to his feet to find himself staring into the eyes of a beautiful woman. In fact, it was the same woman he had seen at the Board of Trade the day he'd arrived, the very one he been hoping to glimpse again somewhere in his roving about the town.

Will immediately felt his face flush. All the rehearsing of what he'd say to her when he had the chance was a waste now that he needed it; he could simply think of nothing to say. In a poor attempt to cover his embarrassment, he made a show of helping her pick up the packages.

"Oh, I'm so sorry," she said. "With these packages piled so high, I didn't even see you."

They both knew that Will's shove away from the wall was the cause of the collision. He wondered if she thought he'd done it purposely. She wondered if he'd ever speak.

Finally, he found his voice. "No, no, it's not your fault at all." They both happened to straighten at the same time, and he found himself staring into those liquid green eyes that he'd first seen in the dining room. He was at a loss for words once again.

She hesitated, then seeing that he was not going to go on speaking, blushed slightly and said, "My name is Mary Whittaker."

Will had barely spoken to any women other than his sisters before, and certainly none that mesmerized him such as this lady did. "Happy to know you, Mary," he managed to stammer.

Again she hesitated, giving him the chance to go on. When the long seconds made it apparent that he would not, she said, "And your name?"

"Oh, I'm so sorry. I'm Will Elliott." He had picked up

the last of the packages and was now holding them awkwardly, not knowing whether to hand them to her or to offer to carry them. Finally, he decided to be bold. "Please let me help you with these."

She flashed a smile that, as far as Will was concerned, totally eliminated the need for the fire that was blazing away in the hearth at the end of the hallway. Before she could answer, Will heard a voice behind him, "Hello, Mary. Everything okay?"

Will turned to see the man he had seen her with that first day at the Board of Trade. She made the introductions: "Will Elliott, this is my brother, George Whittaker."

A wave of relief flooded over Will as they shook hands. Her brother! What good news that was. Will thought that, as usual, the various possibilities he'd considered about who her escort might be were all wrong.

"Will and I just had a slight run-in," she told George. She shot Will a knowing glance. He smiled at the pun and was warmed by the fact that they were sharing an inside joke. She took the packages Will was holding as she spoke to George. "Why don't you take Will in and entertain him for a bit while I deposit these packages in my room. I'll join you two in the dining room in a few minutes." With that, she was off down the hallway.

"I guess she decided that for us," Will said, watching her disappear down the hallway.

"Looks like she did. After you, sir." George pointed the way into the dining room. As they walked in, he went on, "She does have her ways of arranging things. You know how women are."

Will simply smiled. He was as keenly aware as he'd ever been that he didn't know how women were.

As they were being seated and ordering coffee, Will had his first opportunity to size up George. He was tall and large-boned. His short blond hair pointed in 25 different directions, rather like a porcupine's quills, Will thought. His oval face was kind, and the mouth seemed creased at the corners from the effects of a constant smile.

"I take it that you're not from Frankfort." Will voiced his deduction from the fact that they were staying in the hotel.

"No, I'm from Perry County," George said.

Will was somewhat taken aback. Perry County is near

Bell in the Eastern Kentucky mountains and just as isolated. He was surprised that there were people from his section here other than those who had traveled on the train. This knowledge put him more at ease—it had crossed his mind that these people might be Democrats. Will wasn't sure, but he assumed that there probably were some beautiful women of the Democratic persuasion. But, if they were from Perry County, they were just as Republican as he, so there was no need for him to worry.

"That's interesting," he said. "I'm from Bell County—Straight Creek, Right Fork."

"Right Fork? What's that?" George was puzzled.

Will was about to answer when Mary swept into view. She had changed clothes and looked just as she did when he had first seen her. The green velvet gown was trimmed with lighter green ribbons, woven in and out of the fabric at the neck, waist and hem. The colors accentuated her eyes perfectly. Her strawberry blonde hair was piled on her head in what Will thought must be a coiffure. He'd read that word, but had never spoken it—the subject never seemed to come up in the conversation in Bradshaw's store—but he was pretty sure that he was looking at one. As if that wasn't enough, she smelled of something Will had never encountered, and he liked it. He jumped up to assist her with a chair.

"Do answer that," she said. "I can't imagine what's the right fork unless you two are discussing the etiquette of silverware usage at a formal dinner party."

Will was not at all sure what she meant. She said it with a smile, so he went along by smiling also and decided that the right move was to answer the question straightforwardly.

"The Straight Creek branch of the Cumberland River splits in two just above Pineville. The two forks run more or less parallel about a quarter-mile apart in most places, but it might as well be a thousand miles. The folks on one fork don't have nothing to do with those on the other fork for some reason. So, when you tell anyone that you're from Straight Creek, you might as well go on and tell which fork, so they won't have to ask."

Will could see that both Mary and George relaxed with that explanation. He supposed that they were also relieved to find that he was from Eastern Kentucky. Not a word had passed about politics; nonetheless, all parties now knew where they stood on that score.

"So, what are you doing here?" George asked. "You're a long way from Straight Creek."

"I came on the train last week to protest the election contest before the Legislature."

George laughed. "I saw the newspaper headline announcing that 'an armed mob had invaded Frankfort.' So you're a part of the invasion force, huh?"

Will found that he was no longer so sensitive to that issue. "I guess so."

"The paper also said that you had to show a gun rather than a ticket to get on that train. Is that true?" Geroge was smiling.

"Well," Will sopke slowly, "it is true that we didn't have to have a ticket, but I'd allow that the part about showing a gun was made up by some damn fool reporter sitting in an office someplace."

"I thought all that bunch went back to the hills," Mary said.

"Most of 'em did," Will replied. "There's still a few housed in the Executive Office Building and here and there, though."

"Where are you staying?" George asked.

"I'm over at the Board of Trade with my brother-in-law."

Mary glanced up alertly at that. "Your wife's brother?"

Will knew that he was about as callow as anybody but the significance of that question hit even him. He blushed as he looked her in the eye. "My sister's husband."

Mary took her turn to blush.

The turn of the conversation was not lost on George, either. Pushing his chair back, he rose and said, "Well, I'll leave you two young folks to get acquainted." He peeled a dollar from a roll and let it drop to the table, and as he turned away, he said to Mary, "As long as you don't leave this room, there'll be no need to tell Pa you found a friend." Will and Mary both blushed as he walked away.

"He's teasing," she said. "It's a lovely day—for January, anyway." She lowered her chin then shifted her eyes upward to look at him. "Would you like to go for a walk?"

"You bet," Will said, jumping up from the table. He'd

become aware that he was uncomfortably warm, and the idea of cool air was appealing.

The weather was, in fact, quite lovely. It was another of those winter days that the abundant sunshine made it impossible to believe the thermometer reading. The young couple strolled out the door of the Capital Hotel and then across the narrow street that brought them to the bridge spanning the Kentucky River.

"Let's cross," she said. "There's a path by the water on the other side."

They paused on the bridge to watch a barge move up the river. The sparkling water refracted the sun's rays like thousands of prisms. The river banks and the bridge supports glittered with the effects of tiny rainbows.

Will had been trying desperately to think of something clever to say since they left the hotel. So far, he'd mentioned the weather three times. Time to try something different.

"So what are you and George doing in Frankfort?" he asked.

"Oh, George came to see Governor Taylor about something," she said. "I'm not sure what it is. Politics is too complicated for me to understand, you know." The flutter of her eyelids told Will that she was treating him the same way he'd seen his sister treat Ike on several occasions. Although it was a familiar situation, the sensation of being the recipient was new to him. He liked it.

"You don't say," he said in mock understanding. "Tell you what, the next time I talk to your brother, I'll find out what it is and then I'll explain it to you."

"Well, that will give me something to look forward to, won't it?" she said with a flick of her head toward him.

Will felt a warm glow start over him that stopped suddenly as he began to wonder whether she meant she'd look forward to seeing him or to finally understanding politics. He decided that he really didn't know much about women. At this juncture, that fact made no difference; he was having the time of his life.

They had reached a point where the path wound around a bend in the river. Going further would take them out of sight of town.

"We'd better start back," she said. "It's getting a little colder, anyway."

Will wanted to go on—maybe forever—but he made no protest. They turned and started back toward the bridge.

As they approached the slope in the path that would bring them back up to the bridge and hence into the town, Mary slowed the pace slightly. It was a moment before he realized that she was falling behind, and he was about three feet ahead before he stopped and turned. She took another step closer to him, stopped and slipped her hand into his. Will started to worry that his pounding heart would damage his rib cage. He had not the slightest idea of what to say or do.

From the look on Will's face, she thought he might bolt.

"Wait," she said, "I just wanted a minute to tell you how much I've enjoyed your company this afternoon." She patted his hand and then let it drop. He felt a warm sensation where she had touched.

"I've really enjoyed it, too," he said. Then, summoning all his courage, "How about we do it again tomorrow?"

"One more thing for me to look forward to," she smiled.

The late afternoon sun was a red-orange disc sitting on the ridge west of town when Will bounded down the steps of the Capital Hotel after delivering Mary to her brother. The temperature had fallen, but he was sure that her absence was the cause of the cold feeling within him.

Only as he approached the Board of Trade Hotel did it occur to him to hope that Ike had not seen him with that girl. If they'd been seen, Ike would tease him forever, and tell the home folks about it, too. Well, let them talk. As a matter of fact, when he went walking with her tomorrow, he'd do his best to give them something to talk about.

In the hallway, he heard voices coming from their room. He recognized Berry's voice, and while it was not quite angry, Berry and Ike were clearly having a heated discussion. When he opened the door, the voices became much clearer.

"It don't make much difference that most of 'em went home," Berry was saying. "There's still plenty of criticism of us coming here, and the fact that only a few stayed is lost on the press."

"But we've done nothing agin' the law; and overall, I'd say been pretty well behaved," Ike countered.

"I've got two things to tell you, then the issue is closed. One, Caleb Powers told me this morning—Caleb Powers who's been the very soul of reason all along—that he'd 'a thousand times rather we fight and be free than submit and be slaves'.'" Berry flipped a copy of the *Cincinnati Enquirer* to Ike. "And, two, that headline says that civil war is imminent in Kentucky. Now, case closed. You and Will are gonna get the hell out of here first thing in the morning."

Will's heart sank. He had arranged to see Mary tomorrow. It occurred to him now that he'd just assumed that they'd be here—he'd given no thought to the idea that they might go back home sometime. He started to protest, but Ike beat him to it.

"But, Berry, the contest committees will be voting soon, and you know that there's supposed to be another group of Republicans coming in this week. Caleb's going to Louisville tomorrow to see about it. I think we ought to stay."

"Damn it, Ike. There's likely to be trouble here. You can see as well as I that a firecracker going off would start a war to rival the one with Spain. If that happens, I aim to see that you and Will are not part of it. There's a train leaving here at 7:30 in the morning. It ain't the most direct route back to Pineville, but you two are gonna be on it, and that's that." The big man pulled a roll of money from his pocket and passed over some bills to Ike. "This'll take care of your hotel bill and train fare. In the morning, pay Mr. Pence downstairs and be at the depot by 7:30." Berry swung his huge bulk around and shot out the door, leaving Will with his mouth open.

With one more glance over his shoulder at the Capital Hotel, Will reluctantly followed Ike up the steps and into the waiting L & N passenger car. The ticket vendor had explained that this particular train was going to Louisville before heading back to the mountains via the Lebanon spur. As Berry had said, it wasn't the most direct route, but they were leaving Frankfort.

All he had been able to manage was a short note telling Mary that they were leaving town. He had had no idea about what to say concerning when, or if, he'd see her again. He had asked her to keep him in her mind. That was the best he could think of. He was glad that the lobby of the Capital Hotel was nearly empty when he'd delivered the note to the

desk clerk. He'd been nearly in tears. Now, as he stared out
the coach window trying for some prospective on the episode,
his thoughts were as unpatterned as the black swirling snow
flake border surrounding his reflected image.

"That's mighty strange, ain't it Will?"

Ike's attention was also directed out the window,
toward the State House grounds. "What's that?" Will asked.

"Ever' day we've been here, there's been a crowd of
folks around the State House. There ain't a soul up there this
morning. Mighty strange."

As the train began to pick up speed, Will noted that
the light snow was beginning to stick to the ground. In
combination with the falling temperature, that would probably
cause an accumulation. He noted that this was a considerable
change in the weather from when he and Mary had paused
on the bridge in the midst of the rainbows such a short time
ago. The memory of that image coupled with the bleak
weather did nothing for the gloom in his heart. Rolling along
through the central Kentucky countryside, he at least had
the consolation of seeing some beautiful scenery that he had
not seen before. Kentucky was beautiful, but it just wasn't
the kind of beauty he was longing for.

Ike was soon asleep, and Will was glad that he could
suffer in silence. He was sure that Ike had noticed the change
in his attitude, but he had not asked anything. Thank heaven
for small favors, Will thought. He didn't relish the idea of
explaining his foul mood to anyone, much less Ike Livingston.

The bustle and emotion of the last few days must have
caught up with Ike. He slept soundly through the stops and
starts at the various stations, and only stirred slightly when
they went through the confusion of the Louisville train yards.
Will had thought Frankfort was a big city, but he now saw
that it was a village compared to the "Falls City." It seemed
to take forever before they passed all the houses and were
once again in open country rolling along parallel to the banks
of the mighty Ohio River.

The sun was directly overhead when the tracks turned
southeast away from the river and seemed to cause the train
to begin a mad dash for the mountains. After about an hour,
the train came to a screeching halt, throwing everything and
everybody forward. Ike tumbled out of his seat on top of Will,
who was already in the aisle.

"What the hell happened?" Ike muttered, half awake.

"Train stopped," Will said, happy to have a chance to pay Ike back for some of his wise comments.

"Gonna be a slight delay, folks," a conductor called. Walking up the aisle, stepping over bags and bodies, he said, "We're in Lincoln County, just outside of Stanford. You can get off if you want, but don't wander too far. We're liable to get going again 'most any time."

"What's the problem?" Ike asked the conductor.

"Dammed old cow on the tracks," he replied. "She ain't nothin' but hamburger now." He laughed at his own joke and moved on.

Ike and Will climbed down from the coach to the gravel along the track. A couple of hundred yards ahead of where the train had stopped was a depot—Stanford, according to the sign on the end of the building.

"I think I'll just wander on down here to the depot and see what's going on," Ike said. "Want to go?"

Will sat down on the coach steps. "Nah, I'll hang around here." Nothing had happened to improve his mood, and he preferred to be alone.

Will's gloom deepened as Ike walked away down the tracks. Well, he decided, there's nothing to be done about it right now. What was his mother's saying about making the best of the situation? To help break the mood, he examined his surroundings. The land sloped gently away to the south. There were mountains in the distance, not nearly as high as he was accustomed to seeing, but just as beautiful. He found himself thinking that if he ever left Bell County, this Lincoln County might not be a bad place to live. He began to envision what the country might be like beyond those low hills he could see in the distance.

He was not sure how long he'd been daydreaming when the sound of running footsteps on the railroad gravel broke the spell. He looked to his left to see Ike approaching at a dead run. The fact that something was wrong was written all over his face. Ike stopped, panting, and gasped out, "Goebel's been shot!"

Chapter 7

Justice, superseding—"Back to your cave."
Chicago Chronicle, February, 1900.

Tuesday, January 30, 1900

Ike and Will had had no discussion about what they were going to do. They were in total agreement that they'd get back to Frankfort as quickly as possible. They had a spot of luck, too. They were able to catch the regular L & N passenger run through Stanford at 2:15 p.m., and they pulled into the Frankfort depot at 5:30 p.m.

They stepped off the train into a battlefield scene. In all directions, openly armed men appeared in the fading light. Some lounged against the fence surrounding the State House grounds, some dashed up and down the streets, and many crowded around the steps of the Capital Hotel. Will convinced Ike that they should go there first.

"What's going on?" Will asked a man at the back edge of the crowd.

The man turned and eyed Will suspiciously. "We're waiting for word on Senator Goebel," he said at length.

"He's inside, is he?" Will said.

"Yeah, they carried him over here so the doctors could do their work."

"He's still alive then?"

"Word came out a little while ago that he said himself that he'd live. Those damned Republican assassins can't stop a man on the side of right—not even with a bullet."

Will found Ike right behind him. "I'm going inside," he said.

"You're crazy if you think you can get through this mob. If you don't get shot afore you get to the porch, somebody'll sure as hell put a knife between your ribs." He could see that Ike was saying only what he thought.

As strong as his desire to get inside to try to find Mary was, he had to admit that Ike was right. The crowd really was a mob, and it would be foolish to try to get through it. "Well, then, what do you think we should do?"

"Let's get on down to the Board of Trade and see if we can find Berry," Ike said. "He'll tell us what's going on and what we can do to help."

More people had crowded in after them so that when they turned, they discovered that they were no longer at the rear of the crowd. Weaving their way through groups of standing people, they overheard several snatches of conversation.

"It's the worst crime in history. We ought to hang every one of those mountaineer Republican cut-throat assassins . . . ."

"I tell you, I was right there. The shots came from one of the houses on Lewis Street, east of the Capitol, and I'm sure the first shot was from a rifle and the rest of 'em . . . ."

"I'd bet money that some of the Sanford kinfolk finally found a way to pay Goebel back for the Covington killing . . . ."

"There ain't no doubt, the shots come from the third floor of the office building. I seed somebody up there . . . ."

Finally, they made their way out of the crowd and turned the corner of Broadway just up from the Capitol Grounds. "Would you look at that!" Will exclaimed, pointing at the grounds.

Ike squinted in the failing light. The State House and the executive office building were lit as if the government's business were going right on, and uniformed soldiers surrounded the entire city block. The black outlines of wheeled cannons and Gatling guns showed starkly against the white crust of the snow-covered ground.

"Hells bells," Ike said. "Where'd they come from?"

"They showed up within fifteen minutes of the shooting," a man lounging against a lamp post answered as they passed by. "Some say it's mighty suspicious that Taylor could get 'em out there as quick as he did unless it was prearranged."

"Why are they there?" Will asked.

"Hell, son, Taylor's afeared for his life. And his job, too, probably. He called out the militia to protect the life and property of the administration."

"Do you mean to say that he's still in there?" Ike asked.

"Ain't so much as peeked out of the building all afternoon. And, I'd have to allow, he don't show no signs of comin' out soon, either."

They moved on down the street toward the hotel.

"You know, Will, the wonder of the thing is that only one man's been shot. This place is ripe for an all-out war."

"It is a wonder," Will agreed. "I was afeared there'd be a shoot-out inside the State House. I know ever' one of the

Legislators was armed. Did you hear where Goebel was when he was shot?"

"I heard somebody say he was headed into the State House. They said the shots came from the office building—first or second floor—and that he fell halfway between the columns and the fountain."

"No longer than we've been here, I've already found out that there's plenty of rumors going around, and there's no consensus about where the shots came from."

"I'll go along with that," Ike said. "I even heard somebody say that Goebel wasn't shot at all—that it's just an elaborate hoax. Can you imagine that he hired people to fire shots and then carry him off to make it look like the Republicans did him harm?"

Will didn't have a chance to answer. They were at the door of the Board of Trade, and Berry Howard nearly bowled them over as he ran out the door. The Winchester rifle he was carrying nearly hit Will in the ribs. "Ike, Will, what the hell are you two doin' back here?" Berry Howard was not a happy man.

"We were stalled on the road when we heard the news," Ike replied. "We thought we'd get back here and see if you needed us for anything."

"I'd just as lief you two had gone on to Bell," he said. "But, as long as you're here, come on along with me."

They headed across the street and into the State House grounds. A uniformed soldier challenged them at the gate, his bayonet pointed in a menacing fashion. Berry extracted a piece of paper from his vest pocket and handed it to the soldier. He unfolded the paper and examined it in the poor light. He refolded the paper, handed it to Berry, and wordlessly stepped aside to let them pass. They moved into the grounds and over to the left of the Capitol to the red brick building. Will could see a figure with a rifle in each window.

"You boys just wait here for a minute. I'll be right back." Berry slipped inside the building.

"Will, ain't that Bill Culton in that window light up yonder?" Ike asked pointing up to his left.

"I'm not sure," Will replied, "but that's sure Zack Steele in the next window over. I'd know that hide in a tan yard."

They inspected the other windows. A man with a gun at the ready appeared at every turn. Will noticed that his feet were getting cold from the snow and began to wonder how the soldiers guarding the grounds must feel just as Berry reappeared.

"Okay," he announced, "I think ever'thing's calmed down for the night. What say we go get us some supper?" He seemed to be his old jovial self once again.

"Sounds good to me," Ike replied.

They moved back across the street and were approaching Kagin's Restaurant when a yell came from up the street. "Wait up there, Berry."

The man who had yelled was approaching quickly. He was a big man, about six feet tall and heavy, and he was dressed in a dark colored suit that did not fit him well. His dark hair and dark eyes made his face difficult to see in the dusk.

"Well, hello, Jim," Berry said as they shook hands heartily. "Let me introduce you to these folks. Ike Livingston, Will Elliott, this here is Jim Howard."

Jim shook hands with both men. Will noted that Jim had large hands and that his handshake displayed powerful limbs.

"Howard? Are you related to Berry?" Ike asked.

"No," Berry answered for him. "Jim's just one of our faction from Clay County. What do you think, Jim? Might we be related somehow?"

"Not that I know of," Jim said, "maybe way back."

"We're just going in to supper, care to join us?"

"I could eat."

As the group entered the restaurant, Ike tugged Will's sleeve, pulling him slightly behind the others.

"Watch what you say here, Will. I think that's the man who's involved in that White-Baker feud down in Clay County. I believe he's the one they call 'old bad Jim.'"

When they were seated Berry turned to Jim. "When did you get in town?"

"I just came in this morning."

Will and Ike were champing at the bit for news. "Well, Berry, fill us in on everything you know," Ike said.

"He's not like you, Ike," Will joked. "Berry can't tell everything he knows at one sitting."

"I'll smack you back to Straight Creek. I mean about the shooting. Come on, Berry, cut loose."

Their food was delivered, and Berry hesitated while the waiter moved around the table. No more than Will knew about restaurants, he had observed that waiters paid no attention to diners' conversations. He thought it strange that Berry was not about to say a single word until the waiter left. Not until the man finished and walked away did Berry begin to speak.

"I was upstairs in the State House talkin' to Will Lewis. I didn't hear nothin', but somebody came runnin' in and said that Goebel was shot."

"Will Lewis is your Representative from Bell, ain't he?" Jim asked.

"That he is, and Harlan and Leslie counties, too. Anyway, by the time we got downstairs and outside, they was carryin' him off. I started into the office building—I thought those nice thick stone walls looked fine for protection. Only got as far as the steps before I heard somebody talking about blowing the place up with dynamite. It come to me that there might be better places for a man to spend a little time. I high-tailed it over to the red brick building because I wanted to be near General Collier's office. Ever'body figured there'd be more trouble, you know."

"Looks like to me we can still figure on more," Ike said. "Was they guns in Collier's office?"

"You bet we had some hardware stashed in there. We thought that if trouble come, we might have to stand off an assault on the offices. It was a surprise to ever'body when the militia showed up."

"Apparently Governor Taylor thought there might be an assault too," Will said. "I overheard somebody saying that for the militia to get there, equipped and all, as quick as it did, there must have been a prearranged signal for them to move out."

"Not that I'm aware of," Berry said. "Anyway, by the time it started to look like there wasn't gonna be no more shootin', there was a dozen different stories making the rounds."

"We heard all of 'em," Ike said.

"I doubt that," Berry went on. "Some said that Chinn, Goebel's bodyguard shot him; some said that he wasn't shot at all; and my personal favorite is that he shot himself—just a mite more serious than intended."

Everybody laughed, but Will noticed that Jim Howard just kept on wolfing his food. Jim displayed no more than passing interest in any of the conversation, and Will became aware that Jim had had little to say so far.

"Then, there's the matter of where the shot that got him came from," Berry went on. "It was either from the south, or east, or west—we have to leave out north, or else shoot him through the closed doors of the State House—or from all three floors of the office building; or again, my personal favorite, the shooter was in the fountain."

Jim looked up for the first time, his fork halfway to his mouth. "Did anybody look in there?" He suddenly seemed interested.

"In all the confusion, I doubt it," Berry answered.

"A man could've shot him from inside that fountain, climbed out in all the fuss, and got clean away, you think?" Jim asked.

"Anything's possible, I allow."

"I hear they've done got the shooter in custody, anyhow," Jim said as he returned his full attention to the food.

"Well, they did arrest a man named Whittaker," Berry said.

"Whittaker?" Will fairly shouted, "What's his first name?"

"Howard, uh, Holland, no, it's uh, Harlan. Why are you so interested? You know the man?"

"Not if his name's Harlan," Will said. "Are you sure about the name?"

"Not for absolute certain," Berry said, "but I am sure of two other things. One, he's from Butler, Governor Taylor's home county; and two, he ain't guilty of nothing."

"I heard he was loaded for bear when they nabbed him," Jim said, once again more interested in conversation than food.

"If you'd call three pistols and a knife 'loaded,' he'd qualify," Berry said. "But, the fact is that all this Whittaker is guilty of is standin' in the wrong place at the right time."

"How's that?" Ike asked.

"He was simply standin' on the steps of the office building when the deed was done. By the time I got out there, a policeman thought this Whittaker fellow looked suspicious and tried to grab him. I guess that when the policeman held him, he went for his gun, like anybody would do. That, plus all the hardware he was carrying, is all they've got on him."

"But three pistols and a knife?"

"That simply puts him in the company of ever'body else that's been in Frankfort in the past month," Berry said. "Like I said, he was just simply in the wrong place."

Will was only semi-aware of the conversation. This might be Mary's brother, George, they were talking about. Berry said he didn't think so, but he wasn't sure. The man in question was, no doubt, lodged in the Franklin County jail, and if it was George, Mary'd just be at loose ends. He'd have to find out.

A tall, well-built man approached the table and said hello. Berry jumped up with a smile. "Hello there, 'Gate. Boys, this here's Wingate Thompson, the policeman we was just talkin' about."

Thompson shook hands all around. "Had some big-time excitement this morning, didn't we?" he remarked.

Berry started to say something, but Will jumped right in.

"You're the man that made the arrest?"

A smile of satisfaction spread over Thompson's face. He tilted back his chair and hooked his thumbs under his suspenders. "That's the fact."

"What's the man's name?" Will demanded.

"Whittaker."

"I know that," Will was exasperated. "What's his first name?"

"Harlan. At least that's what he said when we booked him over at the county jail."

Will relaxed a bit. It seemed as if Thompson knew what he was talking about—a rare commodity here today. The man in custody was, in fact, not George, so Will could move on to worrying about finding Mary.

"Are you boys going up to the Capital Hotel?" Thompson asked.

"What's going on up there?" Berry asked in answer.

"The word's out that the contest committees came to some decision this afternoon. Governor Taylor had asked them to suspend the hearings until things calmed down a bit, but they met anyway. I hear that there's going to be an announcement up there about 8 o'clock."

Will's pulse quickened at the thought of going to the Capital Hotel. He pulled his watch from its pocket and snapped the case open. It showed 7:45. "If we're going to be there by 8," he said jumping up, "we'd better get a move on."

Despite the fact that it was long past the time that the sidewalks were usually rolled up and stashed in the courthouse basement, the streets were still crowded. Gangs of men stood around on every corner discussing the events of the day. As the group approached the Capital Hotel, Will noted that the crowd there had dwindled somewhat, although there were several men on what he had already heard being called "the death watch."

Just as he entered the lobby, someone handed Will a printed handbill. There was a crowd milling around the lobby, concentrated primarily around someone speaking from the central staircase. He assumed that the expected announcement was in progress, but Will was more interested in getting to the hotel desk. Ike, Berry, and Jim Howard moved toward the speaker while Will veered off to the left toward the desk. Finally, he got close enough to get the clerk's attention.

"Could you tell me if the Whittakers are in?" Will shouted.

"Whittakers? You mean that lawyer and his good lookin' sister? They checked out about 15 minutes ago."

Will's mind raced. Had any trains left within the past 15 minutes? He'd been on the railroad street the entire time he'd been in town. Surely he would have noticed any trains. He dived into the crowd toward the staircase. Luckily, the announcement was over, and the crowd was thinning so he had little trouble finding his friends.

"Well, the fat's in the fire now," Berry was saying. "It's Taylor's move, and I can't think of a thing he can do."

"What happened?" Will asked.

"Read that handbill they gave you," Ike said.

Will pulled the paper from his pocket and his eye fell on the second paragraph:

"In view of these facts we do now adjudge, determine and declare that the said William Goebel was elected governor of this Commonwealth on the 7th day of November,

1899, and then and there received the highest
number of legal votes cast at said election, and
is now legally entitled to said office . . . .

"This is the committee's decision?" he asked.

"It's the committee's recommendation to the General
Assembly," Berry said. "The Legislature will have to meet in
joint session to vote on it. Then it'll become a fact."

"Speaking of votes," Ike said, "did anybody hear how
the committee voted on the contest?"

Berry glowered at Ike. "With ten Democrats and one
Republican on the committee, what do you think the vote was?"

Will leaned closer to Ike and said, "Did I ever tell you
about the time that wagon wrecked in front of my house?"

"Get away from me." Will could tell that Ike made
that comment only partly in jest.

"As a matter of fact, I just came to tell you that I'm
going over to the depot," Will said.

"What for?" Ike asked.

"To see a man about a dog," Will replied. "I'll see you
at the Board of Trade later." With that he was out the door.

He was happy to note that the streets were now nearly
deserted. Will thought that most people had probably decided
that all the excitement was over for the day and had gone
home. At any rate, he encountered practically no one on the
way to the depot. Once inside, he spotted Mary and George
at once. They were sitting on a wooden bench apart from the
other passengers. George had his head back against the wall
and his legs stretched before him. Although his eyes were
closed, Will thought he was awake. Mary sat beside him in
an alert posture. Her back and neck were perfectly straight
and her eyes darted around the room, not lingering long on
any person or object. Her gaze fell on Will when he was ten
feet away.

With a side glance at her brother, she leapt to her feet.
Will did not notice that she moved from where she was
standing, but suddenly found her arms around his neck. He
had never hugged a woman other than his sisters before, and
had certainly never been hugged by one, and was not sure
how to react. It didn't take him long to get his arms around
her waist, however. She clung tightly to him.

"I was afraid I'd never see you again," she whispered.

"We came right back when we heard about the shooting," he replied, pressing his cheek into the side of her neck.

She noticed that several of the men sitting around were staring at them and smiling. "We're making a spectacle of ourselves," she giggled, releasing her grip on his neck.

"I don't mind being a spectacle," he said, trying to hold on.

"Let's sit," she said, turning to move back toward her brother and the bench. Once seated, she noted that George had not opened his eyes.

"George decided that this was no place for us after the shooting," she said. "But we couldn't get a train until 8:45, so here we sit."

Will glanced at the clock above the ticket window. 8:40.

"I can't tell you how happy I am that I got here in time." Somehow, he found her hand in his.

Her reply was lost in the profusion of noise of an arriving train. The hiss of steam and screech of brakes drowned all possibility of conversation for a few moments. By the time the noise subsided, George was on his feet and picking up their baggage.

"Why, hello, Will. Where've you been all day?" George asked.

As they shook hands, a conductor stuck his head in the door.

"Train's goin' to Lexington and points east. All aboard."

George took Mary's arm and started out toward the platform. After a couple of steps, it occurred to him that she had good-byes to say without him. He released her arm, stepped onto the car, and extended his hand to Will. "Be sure and come see us in Perry County, Will. Mary, don't dawdle, the train won't wait."

"I think you can count on seeing me again," Will said. With a smile, George disappeared into the car. Mary turned to face Will.

"What do I say at this point?" he asked, taking her hand.

"How about 'I'll see you as soon as I can'?" she said taking his other hand in hers.

"May I call on you at home?"

"You'd better. Lothair, in Perry County."

The locomotive let out a hiss, and the cars jerked slightly forward. She looked deeply into his eyes, kissed him lightly on the lips and was gone.

With rapid ringing of the bell and a hiss of steam, the train lurched into motion. One by one, the cars clicked by until finally the caboose moved away from the station. The light streaming from the windows of the tiny red car encapsulated it as it moved with agonizing slowness through the tunnel and then disappeared around the bend. As he walked out of the depot, he became aware that his mouth was tingling. As his hollow footsteps resounded toward the Board of Trade Hotel, he found himself whistling tunelessly and scheming about how he'd get to Perry County.

"Evenin' Mr. Pence," Will said as he entered the lobby of the Board of Trade.

"Hello, Will. Welcome back. Your party's up in room 12."

"Thanks," Will shouted as he bounded up the stairs. Approaching number 12, he heard the voices inside. I wonder that these men don't ever get tired of politics, he thought as he opened the door.

"Why, hell yes, it'll work," Berry was saying. "If the Legislature don't meet, they can't adopt the committee's recommendation, and Taylor's the governor until they do, ain't he?"

"What's happened?" Will asked.

"Governor Taylor's adjourned the Legislature, trying to buy some time for things to settle down. They're to reconvene in London next week. I was just tellin' Berry that it won't work."

"I'll quote section 36 of Kentucky's Constitution for you. '. . . and its sessions shall be held at the seat of government, except in case of war, insurrection or pestilence, when it may, by proclamation of the governor, assemble, for the time being, elsewhere.' Unlike most of our legislators, I've read the thing," Berry declared.

"I don't know what 'insurrection' means," Ike said, "but William Goebel was surely a pest, and just looking outside, any fool can see there's a war on."

"That don't mean that a Democrat can see it," Berry said, unaware of the humor Ike and Will saw in the comment. "Anyway, what any fool can see ain't necessarily legal. It remains to be seen if the lawmakers will abide by Taylor's declaration."

"Why wouldn't they?" Will asked.

"Governor Taylor declared a state of insurrection," Berry said. "The General Assembly don't have to agree with that."

"The Republicans will, won't they?"

"That's just the point," Berry said. "Of course, they will. Some of 'em left for London on the train that just pulled out. If the Legislature manages to convene, only the Democrats will be in attendance, and Lord knows what they'll vote in."

Will felt a twinge in his stomach at the mention of the train headed east. His attention was diverted, however, when Ike said, "One thing's for damn sure: if that bunch meets tomorrow morning, William Goebel will be the governor of the Commonwealth of Kentucky tomorrow night."

"If he's alive," Jim Howard added.

Chapter 8

A Bluegrass Race
Washington Post, February 3, 1900.

Wednesday, January 31, 1900

Sunshine streaming through the window onto his face woke Will early. He rolled over on his pillow, surprised that he had been asleep. He thought he had tossed and turned all night, with Mary on his mind. He rubbed the sleep from his eyes to observe that Ike, Berry, and Jim were still sawing logs. He dressed as quietly as possible and tiptoed out of the room to the water closet down the hall. When he returned, everyone was up and ready for breakfast.

"What do you think's gonna happen today?" Ike asked on the way down to the dining room.

"Well, I guess the Legislature will try to meet, and Taylor will try to keep 'em from meeting," Berry replied.

"That ought to be interesting," Jim added.

When they had finished their breakfast, they strolled up the hall and by the front desk on the way outside. Tom Pence was at the desk.

"Mr. Howard, do you still want me to hold that package for you?" he called to Berry.

"Just keep it safe, Tom," Berry said. "I'll pick it up afore we go home."

"It's right here under the counter whenever you want it," Pence said as they moved outside.

Across the street, the capitol grounds looked like an army bivouac site. Columns of smoke spiraled skyward from multiple campfires blazing away in front of tents that showed up as a stark white against the background of the muddy ground spotted with patches of light snow. The muzzles of the cannons and Gatling guns ringing the buildings loomed black against the gray morning sky.

"Let's get over there and see what Powers has to say this morning," Berry said, starting across the street.

"I thought he was gone to Louisville," Ike remembered.

"He came back yesterday afternoon when news about the shootin' reached him. Got back here about 4 p.m." Berry said.

At the gate, an armed soldier challenged him. Again, Berry produced his pass, and the soldier stepped aside. Just inside the gate, John Powers approached them.

"Mornin' John," Berry said. "What's goin' on this

morning?"

"I was just on my way into Caleb's office to find out. Come on along." John started for the office building.

Although he'd never seen any such thing, the scene around the buildings matched the concept that T. J. Ashby's stories of an army camp just before a major battle had created in Will's mind. Three more times, they were challenged before they gained entry to the office building; it was clear that the militia was taking seriously its charge to protect the occupants. In the hall, just inside the door, they encountered Caleb Powers in conversation with Governor Taylor. Both men looked somewhat the worse for wear and had clearly had very little sleep. The thought crossed Will's mind that both of these men were virtual prisoners in this building.

"Good morning, Governor; good morning, Caleb," Berry spoke as cheerfully as he could manage.

"Good morning, gentlemen." Taylor almost managed a smile. "This is a terrible tragedy, isn't it?"

"Yes, sir, it is," Berry agreed, "but we'll have to see how it all turns out."

"No matter what happens to us, it's a tragedy. Affairs should never degenerate to the point that someone has to shoot a man over political convictions," Taylor said wearily.

"And, as deplorable as that is," Powers said, "it's only a part of the crime committed here. The eyes of the nation are upon us, and we've certainly done nothing to dispel the conception of Kentuckians as drunken, barefoot, gun-totin' ruffians."

"Yes, gentlemen, it's a black day for our state. Well, business goes on, just the same. So, if you'll excuse me." Governor Taylor turned and walked away.

"Come on in my office, men," Caleb said. Taylor moved slowly toward his office at the other end of the hallway, while the group filed into the Secretary of State's corner office.

"John, did you know that they're now saying that the shot that felled Goebel came from this room?" Powers asked his brother.

"No," John replied, "the last I heard, the only thing there was any agreement at all on was that it came from somewhere close to the ground. I heard it was so windy here yesterday that nobody could really place the sound."

"The doctors examined the wound and his clothing and

concluded that the bullet struck him moving right to left at a slight downward angle. The Democrats find that sufficient evidence to prove beyond any doubt that the shot was fired from here." He indicated the corner window behind his desk.

"Well, I'm damn glad that we weren't here, in that case," John said. "No way they can hang it on me or you. We were on the train, halfway to Louisville."

"I doubt that'll make much difference when they get rolling. I have a feeling that the Democrats are going to make an all-out effort to hang this thing on our party." Powers was thoughtful.

"But hell, Caleb," Berry said, "anybody with a lick of brains can see that Goebel gettin' hisself shot—while it's no more than he deserves—is the worst thing that could have happened for the Republican party."

"Well, we'll see what happens next. The Adjutant General, Dan Collier, is going to meet us over in the State House." Caleb extracted his pocket watch, glanced at it, and replaced it with a sigh. "It's about that time."

As the group moved out the side door of the office building heading toward the side door of the Capitol, Will noticed that a large group of Legislators was entering the front gates. The sentries were not interfering, but had their rifles at the ready.

Inside the State House, General Collier was posted at the base of the double spiral stairway. He stood with a defiant look on his face as the lobby filled with lawmakers. He was flanked on each side by two soldiers flourishing crossed bayonets. In a quiet voice, he began to speak, "Men, as you all know, the Commonwealth of Kentucky has suffered a terrible crime. In view of that, Governor Taylor has decreed that the Legislature is adjourned, to meet in London, Kentucky, on February 6. Each of you gentlemen will be allowed to go upstairs to collect your personal affects, but there will be no formal meeting here today."

South Trimble, the Democratic Speaker of the House stepped forward. "General Collier," he said, "I'm sure you are aware that the state constitution requires that the General Assembly meet in this place."

"I am aware of that, sir," Collier answered, "as I'm sure you are aware that the constitution provides exceptions."

"Yes, sir, I am aware. The present situation, however,

does not qualify as one of the cited exceptions."

"That's not a matter for you or me to pass on," Collier said quietly. "Governor Taylor has made the ruling."

Trimble turned to face the assembly. "Gentlemen, if they will not allow us our lawful right of assembly in the Legislative Halls, let us go meet in some large enough facility. I suggest the Frankfort Opera House."

General Collier shouted for quiet. "Men, let me remind you that the Governor has adjourned the Legislature. Any meeting before February 6 will be unlawful."

The words were wasted. Before he had finished speaking, the crowd was rushing out the front door of the State House and moving rapidly toward the Opera House. Ike, Berry, and Will slipped out the side door and hurried to keep up with the group.

As the assembly arrived at the Opera House, they were startled to find a line of armed militia, bayonets fixed, barring the entrance. The crowd milled around for a few minutes when someone shouted, "To the Courthouse. We'll meet in the Franklin County Courthouse."

The race was on, and a comical sight it was. Aged, corpulent, gray-headed legislators literally raced young militiamen for the courthouse. The soldiers won. By the time the lawmakers had arrived, bayonets once again barred the way. South Trimble mounted the Courthouse steps panting from the run. "Gentlemen," he yelled above the din of the crowd, "it appears that we've lost this round. Return to your places of abode but be prepared to meet as you may be called upon to do."

"Now wasn't that a lot of fun?" Ike asked.

"It'll save us a stop off at the health springs on the way home," Will giggled. Being the youngest present, he was enjoying the spectacle. Berry was looking at something down the street, his back to Will. Will was slightly startled when someone behind him whispered, "Meet at the Capital Hotel at 6 o'clock tonight."

Will turned quickly, but whoever had spoken was gone.

"Did you hear that?" he said to Ike.

"Hear what?"

"Somebody just told me to meet at the Capital Hotel tonight."

"Did you get her name and room number?"

Berry Howard had turned around in time to hear the last part of that exchange. "What're you talkin' about?" he asked.

"Somebody whispered in my ear to meet at the Capital Hotel tonight," Will said.

"I think he knows something we don't," Ike said with a wink.

Will felt a slight smug grin start over his face and quickly suppressed it before Ike noticed.

"That sounds like the Democrats are going to try to slip a meeting by on us," Berry said thoughtfully. "I guess that takes care of the excitement until tonight, then. I'm going over to the penitentiary to visit my nephew. You boys can just knock around town—I'll see you at the Board of Trade for supper."

When Will and Ike entered the dining room at the hotel, Berry was standing near the entrance entertaining the group seated at a table.

"So the mountain man was riding a mule while his wife walked along behind," he was saying. "One of the flatlanders allowed that it'd be nice if she could ride, too."

With a glance at Ike and Will to acknowledge their presence, Berry went on with his tale.

"The old boy studied on that and then allowed, 'I reckon it would, but the fact is, she just ain't got no mule.'"

Berry turned away from the table and motioned Ike and Will to the far side of the room. When they were seated, he said, "I talked to one of the doctors this afternoon. He says that Goebel's doing pretty good and may recover."

"You think he'll take office if he lives?" Will asked.

"I ain't sure what's gonna happen here," Berry said. "This is an interestin' situation. The first question to be answered pertains to Governor Taylor's proclamation."

Ike started to ask a question but paused while the waiter distributed plates of food around the table. When he was gone, "How's that?" Ike asked, sawing at his country ham.

"Is it constitutional for him to dismiss the Legislature? He says that we're in a state of insurrection while the Democrats say the only danger here is from the armed

Republicans. If Taylor's right, anything the Democrats do is illegal."

"What if the Democrats are right?" Will asked, spooning sugar into his coffee.

"Then we're in big trouble," Berry replied, wiping his mouth. "The Democrats'll meet, and since they won't have no Republican opposition, they'll vote in anything they see fit. Lord only knows what kind of legislation they'll pass."

Conversation lagged as the men attacked the food. When everyone had finished eating, Berry pushed his chair back from the table and patted his ample stomach as he stood. "Well, let's get on up to the Capital Hotel and see what they're up to."

The group sauntered out of the Board of Trade and started up the street. Will was worried. "But Berry, this is a clandestine Democrat meeting. We haven't exactly received an engraved invitation, you know."

"We ain't gonna bust in there like we own the place, son," Berry said. "Now listen up, both of you. There'll probably be a big crowd hangin' around on the death watch. We'll just stand around and look inconspicuous. Don't do nothin' to attract any attention to yourself."

"You should have brung a bandana to put over your face, Ike," Will joked. "You'd attract less attention that way."

"I'm gonna quit takin' you places if you don't learn to behave yourself," Ike quipped as they mounted the stone steps onto the porch of the Capital Hotel.

Berry was right. There was a large crowd in the lobby. There was no problem blending into the group. They had been in the room only a short time when a boy came through passing out handbills. Will held the paper up to the light and read:

". . . .declare that Hon. William Goebel was duly
elected Governor of Kentucky at the November
election. . . ."

"I guess that settles that," he said to Berry. All eyes in the room turned to a tall well-dressed man pushing his way through the crowd and onto the stairway.

"Who's that?" Ike asked.

"James Hazelrigg," Berry answered. "Chief Justice of

the Court of Appeals."

"What's he doin' here?"

"I imagine he's going up there to swear in the new governor."

Will was counting. "But, this ain't legal," he said. "There's names of 19 senators and 56 representatives on this handbill. That'd be a quorum, but there's no way they all met, and anyway, this isn't the 'legislative halls.'"

"It sure as hell ain't," Berry said. "They can't get away with this. There ain't no quorum present. Why this ain't even close to bein' legal."

"Goebel's been sworn in!" The word swept through the room like wildfire. And right on the heels of that news came a new rumor: "They gave the oath of office to a corpse."

Thursday's newspapers carried reports of Goebel's medical condition—critical according to some, stable according to others—the swearing-in ceremony, and much speculation about the legality of all the various actions. William Goebel's first act as governor was to issue an order firing General Collier and appointing J. B. Castleman as Adjutant General, dismissing the militia, and reconvening the General Assembly.

Berry Howard spent the day once again with his nephew at the penitentiary while Ike and Will simply "knocked about" the town.

Will awoke with Ike shaking his shoulder. "Wake up, son. It's Groundhog Day—and Friday, to boot."

Will rolled over on his cot so he could see out the window. "In that case, we're lucky it's overcast," he said, turning once again to face Ike. "I was afeared I'd have to keep you in all day."

"There ain't no chance of that. Berry says we're going back to Bell County on the 10 a.m. train. You best get dressed. He's gonna meet us at the station."

When they'd finished breakfast, they were walking out of the hotel on the way to the depot when Ike stopped suddenly.

"I pert nigh forgot," he said turning toward the front

desk. "Mr. Pence, do you have that package that belongs to Berry Howard?"

"Right here," Pence replied, lifting a small paper-wrapped box from under the counter. "Mr. Howard paid the bill and said you'd be along after this." He handed the box to Ike. "Stop with me again next time you're in Frankfort."

"We'll do that very thing." Ike and Pence shook hands.

On the way out the door of the hotel, Will pointed at the package Ike has carrying and asked, "What is that, anyhow?"

"Needle gun cartridges," Ike replied. "You know how hard it is to get these things for those old guns like Berry's got. He had somebody here in Frankfort order these for him."

The train came rumbling down the track just as they reached the depot. Berry was standing at the waiting room door and smiled as they approached.

"I see you got my cartridges," he said accepting the package from Ike. "Them Bell County fish and turkeys are in trouble now."

A hollow feeling crept into Will's stomach at the sight of the depot waiting room. He was happy at least that he did not have to spend any time waiting. The engine's bell was ringing by the time they could climb aboard the car.

The train pulled out of the Frankfort station, chugged through the tunnel, and glided along the wide, muddy Kentucky River. This ride was a little more like Will had expected on the trip down. Twelve or fifteen men had boarded the train along with Ike and him, and although Will was not aware of any kind of formal understanding, it did appear that Berry had assumed charge of the group. Most of the men were armed—even Berry had his Winchester close at hand—but the men were quiet, and it was clear to Will that the men were simply taking the guns home. The conversation in the car was subdued.

Before they were well settled in their seats, the train ground to a halt at the Lexington station. Will watched in amazement as some of the passengers left the train and boarded an electric street car.

"Makes you wonder how that thing gets around without no horse pullin' it, don't it?" Bob Noakes asked.

Will thought about trying to explain the principle of electric motors to him but then wasn't sure that he understood it himself.

"Are you going back to the mountains?" Will changed the subject.

"No, only to Crab Orchard," Noakes said. "My mother still lives there." The train was out of Lexington, moving southeast through the rolling hills of central Kentucky. Soon they descended a steep grade that told Will they were approaching the river again.

"Crab Orchard's in Lincoln County, isn't it?" Will asked.

"Sure is," Noakes answered, "heart of the Bluegrass Region."

"That's mighty nice country, around Crab Orchard there, Bob," Berry said. "I know a few of the folks around those parts."

Berry and Bob Noakes were off and running on a conversation about the people around Lincoln County, the relative merits of the Cumberland and Dix Rivers, and the difference between the inhabitants of the diverse parts of the state. Will had nearly forgotten that they could talk about anything other than politics.

It didn't last long. Will was enjoying the respite viewing the countryside when he heard Berry say, "I tell you boys, it's a mighty strange situation. We've got two state administrations, each with an army to back it up. Neither one will pay any attention to what the other says is the law."

"One thing's for sure, though," Noakes said, "there's no way there was any quorum of the legislature present at any one time for that vote. What they did is illegal as hell."

"I agree," Berry said, "but that still leaves the question of whether Governor Taylor's dismissal of the legislature was legal."

Berry carried on similar conversations with one and then another as the train made all the stops along the line: London, Corbin, Barbourville. Will discovered that he was quite tired of politics and paid little attention. He was more concerned about how he was going to get to Lothair, anyway. At last, the familiar shape of the Pineville depot hove into view. Ike, Will, and Berry were the last ones off the car. They stood in the late afternoon light as the train pulled out to continue its journey toward Middlesboro.

"Quite a little piece to walk out to Straight Creek," Will said. "We'd best get at it."

"Looks like T. J. Ashby's in his mill office yonder, yet," Ike said pointing toward the small building. "Let's stop in and make sure he's had his ration of grief for the day."

"I'd think you'd be anxious to get home to that good-lookin' wife of yours," Berry said.

Ike shot Will a look that led Will to believe that his presence had a bearing on Ike's reply. "I allow I'll see her soon enough," he said, "if she ain't run off with a flatland shoe peddler."

A shout from behind brought the group up short.

"Berry Howard. Wait up a bit, there."

They turned to see Henry Broughton, the Bell County sheriff, mounted on a mule approaching from the direction of town. Henry's brother, Anthony, was a few feet behind.

"Evenin' Berry, Ike, Will. Where you boys been?"

"You know damn well we've been to Frankfort," Berry replied.

Broughton shifted in the saddle and adjusted the pistol on his hip. "Didn't get in no trouble down there did you?" He eyed the rifle Berry was carrying. "I heard there was a little shooting."

Berry moved his rifle barrel to the crook of his left arm, his right hand resting lightly on the stock. "You know I don't shoot nothin' but gobblers," he said.

Broughton smiled. "Well it's good to see you back home. I'll see you again." He turned the mule's head and started back toward Pineville.

"There's been ill will betwixt the two of you since you refused to support Henry in the sheriff's election, ain't there?" Ike asked.

"You could say that," Berry said thoughtfully. "I thought Henry Broughton was a big enough man to overlook a little political difference. Maybe he ain't." Then, as an afterthought, he added, "I hope nothin' comes of it."

William Goebel
Photograph courtesy of Kentucky Historical Society

William Goebel in rear seat
Photograph courtesy of Kentucky Historical Society.

Caleb Powers

Caleb Powers, John Marshall, W. J. Deboe, W. S. Taylor, C. J. Pratt,
Sam D. Brown, G. W. Long, Vincent Boreing, W. H. Holt, H. S. Irwin,
McK. Todd, Attorney General Taylor and Republican Leaders
Taken at London, Ky., August 22, at the Campaign Opening.

Berry
Howard

Ike & Ellen Livingston

Will Elliott

Chapter 9

Cincinnati Enquirer, February 3, 1900, announcing Goebel's death

Sunday, February 4, 1900

"Well, the fat's in the fire now," Ike Livingston said as he laid the newspaper aside. He was so upset that it didn't even matter that Ellen provided the only ears available to hear his comments.

"What's happened?" She hardly looked up from her needlepoint.

"Goebel died about 6:45 last night." The lack of emotion in his voice caused her to drop her work and pay attention.

"Well, I'm sorry he died," she said, "but isn't that a good thing for the Republican party?"

"No. Matter of fact, it's the worst thing that could possibly happen. Last week, William Goebel was the most hated man in the state; tomorrow, he'll be the martyred leader of the Democratic reform movement. You mark my words, this'll set our party back for many years to come."

Ellen rocked thoughtfully for a few moments. "I'd allow you're probably right," she said, "but don't you think that with him out of the way, some sense of reason might creep back into the state's politics? After all, political rivals don't have to go around shooting each other."

The familiar look of mild irritation that meant she had thought of something that hadn't occurred to him crossed Ike's face. "It might be," he said. "There ain't much doubt that William Goebel was the main source of turmoil in politics. Such men as Gus Willson and even Beckham may be able to come up with some kind of peace treaty."

After a bit of thoughtful silence, Ellen said, "Ike, what do you think would have happened if Goebel hadn't got himself killed?"

"One of two things," Ike said thoughtfully. "He'd soon have been President of these United States, or he'd have totally wrecked the entire national Democratic party, just as he did in Kentucky. Either way, William Goebel would have become a household name."

Chapter 10

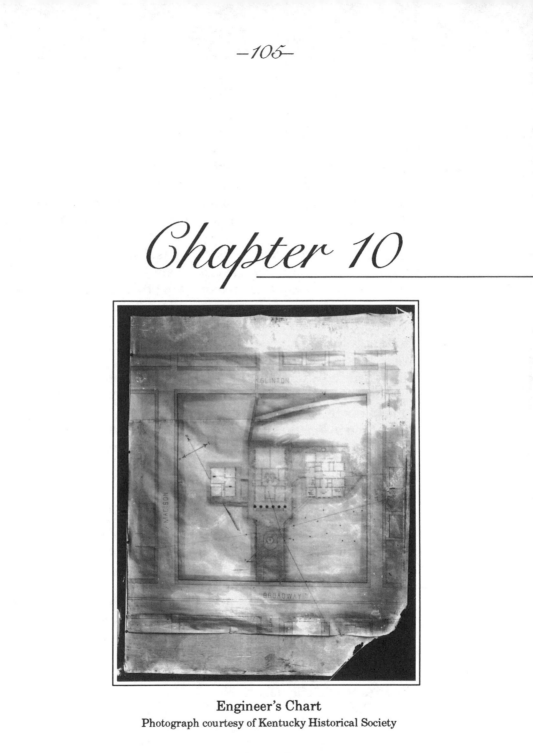

Engineer's Chart
Photograph courtesy of Kentucky Historical Society

Monday, February 19, 1900

"Ike, you up yet?" Will yelled up from the gate.

Ellen stuck her head out the door. "You'll wake the dead, Willie. 'Course we're awake, come on up."

Will climbed the hill to the house and entered as quickly as he could, keeping the cold air out. He crossed the room to the fireplace and extended his hands, palms out, to warm.

"Are you going to the courthouse with us?" he inquired.

"Yes, Ike finally condescended to let me go to town. I had to promise to stay away from the Judge's office though."

Will smiled. His hands being warm enough, he turned his back to the fire. "Ellen," he said hesitantly, "I've been wanting to talk to you."

"We're talking now, aren't we?"

Will heard Ike stomping the mud off his boots on the back porch and knew that he'd soon be inside.

"I mean about something personal."

She paused in her stowing of the breakfast dishes. "You mean you want to tell me something that's not to be discussed with Ma and Pa or Ike?"

"Yeah, I guess that's what I mean."

"It's a deal," she said. "Fire away."

"Well, I met this girl in Frankfort, you see, and I . . . ."

"So that's it. Ike said something strange was going on with you the last few days there." She was grinning broadly.

Will immediately got angry. "Now you promised," he shouted.

"I'm sorry," she said. They heard the back door open and Ike enter the house. "He'll be right in here. What did you want to ask me?"

"Well, not about the birds and bees if that's what you meant. I need your help to figure out a way to get to Lothair."

"Where's that?" she asked.

"Perry County," he said just as Ike walked in.

"I'll study on it," she said quietly.

"Buggy's hitched up," Ike announced. "You all ready?"

"We're ready, but you best warm up a bit first," Will replied.

Ellen got out of her chair and started for the bedroom

to get her coat. Ike waited until she was out of the room before he spoke.

"Did you hear that the so-called 'peace conference' failed?" he said. "I had thought that since Goebel went and got hisself killed, the biggest obstacle was removed."

Ike was referring to the meeting that Democratic and Republican leaders had held at the Galt House Hotel in Louisville on February 6, while the Republicans were assembled at London and the Democrats at Louisville.

"That thing had several provisions, but as I understand it," Will said, "the Republicans would concede that Goebel was rightfully elected in return for immunity from prosecution. I don't blame Governor Taylor one bit, I wouldn't sign the blessed thing, either."

"Well, they did promise to repeal the Goebel election law," Ike reminded him.

"That makes no difference," he said. "That damn thing is such a blight that it'll be repealed no matter what else happens."

"Oh, by the way, there's hot news from down at Bradshaw's. Did you hear that Goebel's got new last words?" Ike smiled.

"According to what I read in the newspaper, his last words were, 'Doctor, I forgive them; they were not the ones.' What do you mean by new last words?"

Ike laughed. "You're a week behind, son. As of now, just afore the poor martyred soul lapsed into a coma, he said, 'Tell my friends to be brave, fearless, and loyal to the great common people.' What a joke."

"What's so funny about that?" Will was puzzled.

"The whole thing," Ike replied. "In the first place, the son of a bitch didn't have no friends to worry about. In the second place, an intelligent man like Goebel would never use two words back to back that mean exactly the same thing, and finally, he didn't give a damn about the common people. That whole thing is just one more act of the farce they're playing out."

Ike fell silent as Ellen came back in the room dressed for the cold buggy ride to town. "Let's go," she announced.

Ike needed all the skill he had acquired in years of buggy driving to navigate the rutted dirt road. The constant freezing and thawing, combined with the wheeled traffic, caused the road to be in the proverbial washboard condition. At last reaching a stretch that did not require all his attention, Ike spoke.

"Will, did you hear that they've arrested another suspect in the Goebel killing?"

The first thought that went through Will's mind was of Harlan Whittaker, which led his mind off to Mary. "No, who's that?" he asked, clearing his thoughts.

"A man named Silas Jones from Beattyville, Lee County."

"What've they got on him?" Ellen asked.

Ike started to protest her joining the discussion but decided that he should have not brought it up if he hadn't wanted her input. "Nothing. He was one of the people that Culton man took on the train. He was in the waiting room to see Governor Taylor when the shots were fired."

"That ain't much to arrest a man on," Will said.

"They don't need much. It appears that the powers that be are gonna do anything and ever'thing they can to hang the shooting on as many Republicans as they can get their hands on. The way it's going, if you were a Republican and within ten miles of Frankfort, you're a suspect."

"That includes you and me, doesn't it?" Will was concerned.

"Me and you ain't big enough fish, Will."

The road began to roughen, requiring Ike's attention. The remainder of the ride passed peacefully enough. There was a chill in the air, not unusual for this time of year, but also a promise of spring. As the buggy moved onto the bridge spanning the Cumberland River, the uneven plank flooring caused the occupants to bounce up and down in place. Ellen leaned over the side of the buggy to view the muddy water swirling around the supports far below. She noticed that the water level was a little higher than normal.

"It's getting to be spring of the year," she said. "I'll bet the river's going to come a tide before the month's out."

"I wouldn't be surprised," Ike agreed. "Seems like the water runs some of these folks around here out of their homes almost ever' year." He looked to his left at some of the houses lining the river bank twenty feet below the level of the bridge.

Will snorted. "I've always said it wouldn't run me out but one time. I've never understood why these people will go right back in there as soon as the water goes down."

"They ain't got much choice, son," Ike said. "The property they own is what they've got and that's all." They had reached downtown Pineville. Ike stopped the buggy in front of Mason's store.

"Get your shopping done, woman," Ike said. "Will and me'll go kill some time over at Judge Smith's office. We'll be back to pick you up about noon."

Ellen started to make some reply, but she decided that if it made him happy to think she believed they'd come to town because she wanted to, she'd let well enough alone. "I'll try to be finished on time," she said dismounting the buggy.

Ike and Will could hear the voices inside Judge A. B. Smith's office as soon as they entered the upstairs hallway in the Bell County courthouse. "Go on in, Will. They're expecting us," Ike instructed as they reached the door.

Through the bumpy, translucent glass in the door, Will could see the forms of several men. Opening the door, he saw Berry Howard, Judge Brantly Smith, Judge W. B. Rollins, and Judge J. S. Bingham sitting around the large red oak table.

"I'd bet $10 you boys are talkin' politics," Ike laughed, closing the door.

"No bet," Judge Smith replied. "Come on in, Ike. Will, take off your coat and sit a spell."

"Now then, Bill," Smith said turning to Rollins, "what was you sayin' about the two Adjutants General?"

"I was sayin' that they're both Masons and been friends for years," Judge Rollins resumed. "They've agreed that just because Goebel's proclamation replaced Collier with Castleman doesn't destroy their bond of brotherhood. So, the two of 'em have pledged not to use the militia to fight this thing out."

"The two of them have got more sense than the whole damned General Assembly put together," Judge Bingham remarked.

"Well, sense enough to not start shootin' on the whims of the politicians, anyway," Berry added.

"Ike, ever'body here already stated his opinion. It's your turn—who's the rightful Governor?" Smith asked.

"Tough question, Judge," Ike said. "Taylor won't give up the office, and I don't fault him for that. The Democrats held their meetings and declared Goebel in, and then when he died, they gave the oath to Beckham. I think the idea the Republicans come up with at London is the best idea—let's hold another election this November, and this time, let's make it fair."

"There's a problem there, Ike," Berry said. "Even if all the Republican assemblymen were at London, which they ain't, there ain't enough of 'em to represent a quorum of the whole legislature."

Judge Rollins spoke up. "There ain't enough of 'em to pass the idea into law, but it don't take too many of us to see that the idea makes sense."

"Whether it makes sense or not, the Legislature'll have to vote it into law before it can happen," Bingham said.

"And the Democrats ain't gonna vote it in by themselves," Smith added. "The whole shootin' match is gonna have to get back together, and in Frankfort, I hope, before anything that's legal can happen."

"That's scheduled for this morning, you know," Smith said.

"That ought to provide some interesting discussion in the General Assembly," Berry commented.

"How do you mean?" Will asked.

Berry leaned back in his chair and assumed his familiar role as the local unofficial legislative emissary. "We've got two of ever'thing right now," he said. "We've got two governors. Taylor's barricaded in his office; Beckham's holding fort at the Capital Hotel. We've got two adjutants general; we've got two lieutenant governors—each one of them will try to preside in the Senate—and the same thing in the House with two speakers."

"I thought I read in the paper that Taylor sent the militia home," Rollins remarked.

"He let all but about 200 of 'em go," Berry replied. "I guess he thought that'd illustrate his good will."

"Well, men, how're we ever going to resolve this mess? I'd allow that the Democrats will soon be demanding possession of the offices. They might even try to take the office building by force." Judge Bingham was concerned.

Berry let his chair's front legs drop to the floor and leaned into the table as if he were imparting secret information.

"I think that all concerned parties are going to put it to the courts," he confided.

"Whew, I wouldn't want to hear that one," Judge Rollins said.

Now it was Bingham's turn to take the floor. "I doubt you'll get the chance, Bill. You know damned well that if the Democrats are going to file any suit, they'll do it in the Franklin County court to get Judge Cantrill. Likewise, the Republicans will go for the Jefferson County court, so we'll still have dichotomy."

Berry didn't understand that word, but—as was his nature—he saw a little humor in the situation. "If the Democrats file a suit enjoining the Republicans from filing any suit to enjoin the Democrats from filing suit, where'll they file that?"

A laugh went round the table, but Will was thinking seriously. "Even if both parties file suit, somebody will have to hear the case, won't they?" he asked.

The judges assumed a more serious posture.

"Yes, somebody will," Judge Smith answered for the group. "I allow that both parties will have to agree to abide by whatever decision the court renders, too."

"Subject to appeal, of course," Judge Rollins added.

Ike checked his pocket watch. "Will, it's nearly noon. We better go pick up that sister of yours." He stood up and pulled on his coat.

"Ike, if you're going back out to Straight Creek, I'd like to ride along," Berry said.

"We've got plenty of room. Come on."

As Ike, Will, and Berry left the room, Judge Smith turned to Rollins. "You know, Bill, the Commonwealth of Kentucky would give $1,000 to hear what Berry Howard knows about the shooting of William Goebel."

The departing trio had just entered the downstairs hallway in the courthouse and turned toward the door when a voice boomed out behind them. "Howard, hold up!"

They turned to see Henry Broughton emerging from the Sheriff's Department office. He approached down the hallway with his right hand resting on the butt of the revolver strapped to his hip.

"What can I do for you?" Berry's voice showed slight disgust.

"It ain't so much what you can do for me as what I'll do to you," the sheriff sneered.

"I ain't got time for riddles, Henry," Berry said. "In plain English, what are you sayin'?"

"Will and me'll wait for you outside," Ike interjected, moving toward the door.

"No, you both stay here," Berry gripped Ike's arm. "I want you to hear whatever this man's got to say."

Broughton shot a sour glance at Ike and Will, then turned his attention back to Howard. "Just thought you'd like to know. I got a telephone call from the Commonwealth's Attorney in Frankfort this morning. Seems like your old buddy Robert Franklin has somehow got the idea in his head that Governor Goebel's death was the result of a large Republican conspiracy."

"You mean Senator Goebel, don't you?" Berry said with a slight smile. "So what?"

"Title don't matter—he's been murdered, just the same. Seems as how it come to Mr. Franklin and Colonel Campbell that the bringing of all those armed men to Frankfort was part of the conspiracy that resulted in Goebel's death. Seems as how the Franklin County grand jury might just return indictments again' all them what organized that little sashay down the river." A smirk was evident on the sheriff's face.

"Let 'em indict away," Berry said. "I've done nothing to worry about. That august body would indict a jay bird if Rob Franklin told 'em that it'd fouled the sidewalk." He motioned to Ike and Will and turned to walk away.

"Like I said," Broughton called, "just thought I'd let you know. I'll see you again." His laughter burned in Berry's ears as they left the courthouse.

Outside on the sidewalk Ike asked, "Berry, who's that Colonel Campbell he was talking about?"

Berry smiled sarcastically. "The infamous Colonel Thomas Campbell used to be a lawyer in Cincinnati. Goebel's brothers have hired him to prosecute any upcoming legal actions."

"Why do you say 'used to be?'"

"His practice up there was so corrupt that it was a haven known to every criminal element in the country. A few years ago, using his typical legal tactics, he managed to get a fellow off that ever'body knew was guilty. Campbell's conduct enraged the local citizenry to the point that an armed mob determined to lynch the prisoner. When the police and militia tried to turn 'em back, the mob got out of hand and burned the courthouse. Colonel Campbell was charged as responsible for sixty-some deaths that occurred in the riots that lasted three days. Sometime after that, it come to the good Colonel that he'd be a whole lot happier as a resident of New York."

"Is he all that bad?" Will asked.

"I'd say he's got the same trouble Goebel had," Berry replied. "He gets so caught up in trying to convict or acquit, as the case may be, that he forgets people got rights. I don't envy Rob Franklin his chore of working with that man."

"I'd allow that the state of Kentucky has got more lawyers per square yard than any other place in the world. Don't you reckon one of them might do?" Ike asked.

Berry laughed. "You're right, son. It'd be hard to throw a stick without hittin' at least one lawyer in the eye. I suppose that the Goebel family probably has ties to Tom Campbell goin' way back. Anyway, the man is perfect for the kind of work they've got in mind."

"What's that?" Will inquired.

After a pause, Berry answered, "Intimidatin' witnesses before and after the fact is his legal specialty."

They walked a few paces in silence, each in his own thoughts. At length, Berry said, "Say, Ike, it's dinner time. What say me and you take Will here for his first visit over to Mrs. Pat's restaurant?" He grinned at Ike.

"Are you crazy?" he shouted. "Ellen's waiting for us over at Mason's store. She'd skin you and me both if she caught us taking her baby brother in there."

"It's just a restaurant. A man's got to eat, don't he?"

Ike chuckled at Berry. "You know as well as I do that not ever'thing a man can get in that place is on the menu."

They were in front of Mason's. "Yeah, and not ever'thing a man could get in there is somethin' he'd want, either." All three were smiling as Ellen came out the door to join them, loaded with packages.

"Let me help you with those," Will said, taking some of the bundles from her.

"Thanks, Willie. It's nice to see that chivalry is not totally dead," she shot a look at her husband.

They all piled into the buggy and headed out of town.

Before they had gone far, Ellen fished around in her packages and came up with a newspaper that she handed to her brother.

"Here's something you all will find interesting, but especially you, Willie."

Will took the paper and unfolded it. The headline story detailed the fact that a Frankfort policeman, Zack Thomasson, had happened to find a bullet hole in a hackberry tree near the western gate of the State House Grounds. The story had it that the bullet in the tree was the one that had killed Goebel.

"That is interesting," he said. "But why especially to me?"

"Turn on over a page or two," Ellen said. "There's a chart."

Will turned the pages of the paper. The Commonwealth had hired a civil engineer to make a chart of the grounds, showing the buildings and the tree. The chart had various lines converging at a point between the fountain and the Capitol steps.

"I thought you might like to put your math skills to work on that," she commented.

Ike pulled the horse to a halt in front of his house to let Ellen out. She reached for the packages, but Will stopped her. "I'll get those."

"Berry, you want me to run you on to the house?" Ike asked.

"No, thanks. I'd druther walk on a day like this."

"Pretty cold to be out strollin' around," Will observed while gathering up packages.

"You think this is cold?" Berry asked. "Let me tell you about the time I was down in Texas. I had me a pot of water boilin' on the stove and decided I didn't want it, so I took it outside to pour it out."

"Froze afore you could get it poured, did it?" Ike said with a smile.

"Sure as hell did," Berry grinned.

"That's pretty cold," Ike said, pleased that he had spoiled the punch line.

"So I carried the pot back in the house," Berry went on, "and the thing is, as I sat it down on the table, I noticed that it was still warm."

"Froze, but still warm?" Ike said skeptically.

"Froze solid," Berry said triumphantly. "It was so cold

that the water froze so quick it didn't even have time to cool off."

"Makes today seem like a heat wave, don't it, Ike," Will laughed.

"Get yourself on in the house with them packages," Ike mumbled.

Will carried the packages into the house while Ike tended the horse. Ellen was puttering about the kitchen when he came inside.

"I've given your problem some thought," she said, pouring coffee.

"What problem is that?"

"How we can get you to Lothair."

Will was surprised that that idea had not crossed his mind in the past thirty minutes. New world's record for longest time without thinking about Mary, he thought.

"And?"

"And it's going to be a problem," she said. "It appears to be about thirty miles from here, as the crow flies. That means that it's an all day trip, one way."

Will's face assumed a pained expression. "That's not good news," he sighed softly.

They heard the back door opening. She retrieved another mug from the cupboard and brought it to the table. Gently placing a hand on her brother's shoulder, she said, "Be patient, honey. Love finds ways."

As Ike removed his coat and hung it on the peg at the back door, Will unfolded the newspaper Ellen had given him and opened it to the chart of the Capitol grounds. He was smoothing the paper with a palm when Ike came to look over his shoulder.

Ike gave the diagram a suspicious eye. "What is that thing?"

Will studied the chart a moment. "It would appear that it's the State's proof that the shot that killed William Goebel was fired from the Secretary of State's office."

Chapter 11

Lines of sight from window and office building steps
to the hackberry tree

Friday, March 9, 1900

"Did you say $100,000?" The loudness of Berry's voice got the attention of everyone in Bradshaw's store, even old Mrs. Cunnad up front at the counter. One of the standing jokes on the Right Fork was that if you could get Mrs. Cunnad's attention from a distance of ten feet, you were a shoo-in for political office. She shot a look of disgust toward the gathering in the back of the store and returned to dictating her order to Bob Bradshaw.

"That's what it said in the paper," Ike replied. "The General Assembly has allocated a fund of $100,000 as a reward for them who can track down the parties responsible for the murder of William Goebel."

"And bribe witnesses and manufacture evidence," Chas Whitt said moving his chair around to turn a fresh side to the fire.

"Hells bells, $100,000 is enough money to convict anybody in the state of any crime you'd care to pick," Berry commented.

"I find it interesting that right after they voted the $100,000 in, they voted down a $15,000 reward for arrest and conviction of the party who did the shooting," Ike said.

"When you've been around it as much as I have, you'll come to understand that there ain't no understandin' the legislature," Berry said. "They're as likely to try to legalize a thirty-six hour day as they are anything else."

"That'd make it a heap easier for a man to get a day's work in," Chas allowed with a grin.

"Thankee, kindly, Mrs. Cunnad," Bradshaw shouted. He moved quickly around the counter to close the door against the blast of cold air her exit admitted to the room.

"Berry, how do you feel about Judge Field gettin' to decide the suit?" Bradshaw asked, moving into place at the stove.

"Lucky."

"How's that?"

"Well, you know that the Democrats filed a suit in the Franklin County court, asking it to uphold the legislature's decision that since Goebel was elected in November, Beckham's the Governor now.

"The fact is, though, that the Republicans had filed suit in the Jefferson County court two hours earlier, askin' the exact opposite. Since the two suits are the same thing, they decided to consolidate 'em. The Republicans filed earlier, so it fell to the Republican-favorable court."

"But, I'd heard that Judge Field voted for Goebel," Ike said.

"So, I heard, too," Berry said. "But anybody would be better for a judge than that damned old James Cantrill."

"The Franklin circuit judge?"

"That he is, as well as a most ardent Goebel supporter and the best friend the Democrats could possibly have."

"You think Field will be handin' down a decision soon?" Bradshaw asked.

"Well, he's had the case for ten days or so now. I'd think he ain't in no particular hurry—things is right peaceful at the present—but, I imagine he'll be havin' somethin' to say pretty soon."

"Either way it goes, somebody will appeal, won't they?" Chas asked.

"Sure will," Berry replied. "All the way to the U. S. Supreme Court."

The door flew open with such force that all eyes turned to the front of the store. As the door flashed through its arc, it yanked Will inside the building. He turned and leaned all his weight into the door to close it against the wind howling through the opening.

"Good day for flyin' a kite, ain't it, son?" Berry laughed.

Will approached the stove, straightening his clothes from the beating the wind had given him. "In like a lion." He managed a smile.

"I was just fixin' to head over to your house, Will," Ike said. "Berry is gonna make your day."

"How's that?" Will wondered, rubbing his hands before the stove.

"Well, you've been making noise about going back to Frankfort ever since you got your hands on that diagram in the paper. Today's the day you get your wish."

"We're going to Frankfort?" Will jumped with excitement.

"Ike and me have business with Governor Taylor," Berry said. "Ike said you'd give your left arm to go. I've got a pass for a free ride on the L & N—they ain't never minded doing favors for judges and legislators and such—so if you want to tag along, it don't matter."

"That chart is driving me crazy. I've just been dying to get a look at the State House grounds."

"Sit a spell, son," Berry said. "The train don't leave Pineville until noon, so we've got plenty of time. What's got you so excited about that chart?"

"Somethin' ain't right about it," Will said. "Rob Franklin hired a civil engineer to draw it up, and it looks pretty good, but there's just something about it that bothers me. I thought if I could get a look at the windows and buildings and all, I might put my finger on whatever it is that don't seem right."

"Why would Franklin hire an engineer?" Whitt asked.

"Well, now, that's a serious question," Berry mused. He leaned his chair back and got comfortable. "That gentleman, as Commonwealth's attorney, is gettin' ready to prosecute. That's why."

"Prosecute who?"

"Don't matter, long's he's a Republican," Berry said thoughtfully.

"That chart points to Caleb Powers, no pun intended," Will said.

Four sets of questioning eyes turned to Will, and four voices chimed in unison, "Huh?"

Will leaned his chair back against the wall, unconsciously emulating Berry Howard. "I'm convinced that they'll use the chart in court to try to prove that the shot was fired from the Secretary of State's office."

"Can they do it?" Ike asked.

"Who knows?" Will answered. "As I said, something bothers me about the diagram. But aside from that, it's a perfect set-up."

"What do you mean by that?" Berry leaned toward Will.

Will was relishing his role in the limelight. For the first time, he felt that he was a full-fledged member of the Bell County men's political organization. Over and beyond that, he was thrilled that Berry Howard was not only interested in his opinion, but hanging on his words. With a glance to ensure that he had Berry's full attention, he went on.

"Well, you know damn well that they're going to try to pin the shooting on the Republicans. They can't get Governor Taylor because his office is on the wrong side of the building, and besides, there was plenty of people in there with him." Will paused.

"But Powers' office was empty," Ike said.

"So, there's nobody to deny that the shot came from there," Will added quickly, shooting a glare at Ike for stealing his line.

"But that don't implicate Caleb," Berry said.

"You ain't thinkin' like an attorney," Will replied, somewhat surprised at his own boldness in speaking to Berry in that tone. "The fact that Powers was gone gives them a perfect excuse to claim that he set it all up and then made his office available to do the deed while providin' himself with an alibi."

"Well, anybody would have to admit that Caleb's office is an ideal place for the shot," Ike said. "But what sense does it make for a man to set up a deal that, to use Will's words, points right back to him?"

"Now you ain't thinkin' like a Democrat," Berry said.

Again the front door flew open and the wind howled through the building. The man who blew in on the gale was a stranger to the group assembled at the stove. He put his shoulder against the door and pushed it closed before he turned to the rear of the store. He was a man of medium height, a little on the chubby side. His well-cut blue pin-stripe broadcloth suit was somewhat disheveled by the wind, but obviously tailor made. His clothing made him as conspicuous in this setting as a plow horse at a thoroughbred race. Bob Bradshaw stood and met the stranger half way between the door and the stove.

"Can I help you, mister?"

"Just came in to get a break from the wind and cold. I'll sit a spell, if you don't mind."

"Don't mind at all." Bob led the way back to the gathering.

"Howdy, men," the stranger said as he moved into the circle, "I'm Tom Cromwell."

"You ain't from around here, are you, Mr. Cromwell?" Ike asked. These Bell County mountain men were suspicious of strangers in general, and doubly wary of one this well dressed.

"No, sir, I'm not," Cromwell replied. "I live down in the bluegrass region, around Lexington."

"You're a long way from home, then." Berry's comment was an obvious request for information.

Although Cromwell was clearly not one of the mountain men, he was also clearly quite at ease among them. His mannerisms and language displayed that he understood these people and knew how to fit in to a situation that would dismay most visitors to the region.

"Yep, sure am," he said. "Just on a little vacation, you might say. I thought I'd get out and see a little of the state I live in."

That comment was not quite satisfactory to the Bell County men. After a awkward lull in the conversation, Cromwell said, "I guess you boys heard about the Goebel killing."

"Anybody that ain't has been in a cave," Berry answered for all.

"Say, this here's Straight Creek, ain't it?" Cromwell said.

"Sure is," Bob answered, "Right Fork."

"Seems to me some of the men that was in Frankfort at the time of the shootin' was from Straight Creek. Any of you boys ever been down in those parts?"

Berry, Ike, and Will exchanged looks of suspicion.

"I've been to Frankfort," Berry said, noncommittally.

Again, an awkward pause settled on the group. At length, Cromwell spoke up again.

"I hear there's a man name of Berry Howard up in these hills some place. I'd sure like to talk to him."

Will opened his mouth to speak, but a warning glance from Berry stopped the words in his throat.

"What about?" Berry asked, ice in his voice.

"Oh, I hear he's one of the political leaders in these parts. I'd just like to hear his views on some of the issues— the shootin', the lawsuits, and all."

"I'll tell him you're lookin' for him, if I see him," Berry said, standing to tower over the visitor. "In the meantime, mister, I'd advise you to keep your mouth shut if you intend to make it through your vacation alive."

The mournful wail of the train whistle floated faintly up the tracks as Ike, Will, and Berry approached the Pineville depot.

"A little different from when we were here last, ain't it?" Ike asked, noting the curious look in Will's eyes.

"A little," Will said. The platform was nearly empty, just a few drummers with their sample cases standing around. Inside, in the waiting room, a few men and women were involved in quiet conversation.

As they moved by the office, Will glanced inside and saw Tom Cromwell talking to the telegraph operator.

"Say, ain't that the fellow who was nosin' around up at the store this morning?" he asked.

Berry peered through the window at Cromwell who was shaking his finger in the operator's face.

"That's him," Berry said. "I'd give my best 'coon dog to know what the hell he's up to."

Conversation was suspended as the train rounded the curve and came hissing and screeching into the station. Will tried to watch Cromwell, but lost sight of him as Berry ushered him and Ike onto a waiting car.

The scenery rushing by the window was all new to Will. He'd been this way before, but that was at night, and in the dead of winter. In broad daylight, with a hint of spring in the air, the trees and grass seemed eager to burst into life. That potential lent a sense of adventure that he had not noticed before.

"Next stop, Richmond," the conductor coming down the aisle shouted above the din. "This train's turning east. Them going to Clay City, Jackson, Hazard, and points east, stay put. The rest of you'll change trains for Lexington, Frankfort, and Louisville."

That announcement brought Will up with a start. "Hazard's in Perry County, isn't it?" he asked Ike.

"It is for a fact," Ike answered. "But we ain't goin' that way. We'll have to wait a little while for the Frankfort train to come through."

The whistle and the screech of brakes told Will that they were at the depot. In the waiting room with Ike and

Berry, his heart sank as he watched the very car in which they'd been riding roll out to the east. East—toward Perry County, and Mary Whittaker.

"You boys heard the news?" The telegraph operator was clearly excited as he moved through the room. His tone wrenched Will's attention back to reality.

"Guess not," Berry said. "What's happened?"

"The Franklin County court has issued arrest warrants for five men in the Goebel killing."

"Who?" Ike, Will, and Berry spoke with one voice.

"Well, let's see here." The man made a show of studying the paper he was carrying, enjoying telling the tale. "Caleb Powers. He's the Secretary of State, you know. His brother, John. I believe he's a militia captain down in Knox County. You know, I recollect the time he come through here. . . ."

Berry jumped to his feet and snatched the paper from the operator's hand. The man started to protest, but seeing Berry Howard at his full height, said nothing. Berry handed the paper to Will. "Who else?" he demanded.

"Caleb Powers, John Powers, John Davis, Charles Finley and William Culton," Will read quickly. He looked on down the page and read aloud, "uh—'committed the crime of being accessory before the fact to the willful murder of William Goebel.'"

"Does it say who provided the information for the affidavit the law requires to issue a warrant?"

Will scanned the report. "Here it is. Thomas Cromwell."

Berry hit the platform at the Frankfort depot before the train had stopped moving.

"Come on, boys," he yelled over his shoulder. "We'd best get over to Captain Davis' boarding house right away." He was off and running down toward the Capitol Square. Will and Ike scampered along in his wake. They caught up just as Berry turned onto Lewis Street on the west side of the office building. In the block just past the Capitol Square, he dashed up the porch steps and into a house.

"Is Captain Davis in?" Berry asked the woman who met them at the parlor entrance.

"Who might you be?" she asked in reply. The look in her eye reminded Will of the look Berry had given that Cromwell man earlier in the day.

"Berry Howard from Bell County," he said without hesitation.

Her face softened. "Captain Davis told me to expect you." Glancing left and right to make sure no one overheard, she went on, "He and Mr. Powers are upstairs in Governor Bradley's room."

"Thank you kindly," Berry said as she walked back into the house. Then to Ike, "You and Will go on up and get settled in our room. I'll go check in with Governor Bradley and meet you in a little while."

Ike and Will were lounging on their beds when Berry came into the room. Although it was late and Will was quite tired, he shook himself awake to hear the news.

"Well, what's going on?" Ike inquired.

"Governor Bradley advised Caleb and John Davis to try to get away," Berry said. "They both protested that they weren't guilty of anything and had no reason to run. The Governor convinced them that they have no chance at all of a fair trial, so they've gone to spend the night at the office building."

A loud pounding at the front door interrupted their talk. The trio moved out into the hall as the housekeeper went to the door.

"Open up in the name of the law." Someone was knocking on the door so hard it was vibrating on its hinges. She opened the door to reveal a group of armed policemen.

"We're here to arrest Caleb Powers and John Davis," the lead man said, pushing past the housekeeper into the house.

"They're not here."

"Culton wasn't at home when we nabbed him at his house a little while ago either," the man said. "We'll have a look around just the same." His head swiveled about as he talked.

Berry motioned Ike and Will back into the room. They managed to be in bed and apparently asleep when the police barged in. Will turned his face to the wall to hide the grin and was asleep before the front door closed behind the disappointed searchers.

"The place is still a powder keg, Will," Berry said. "I just didn't realize that it was going to be this bad. I ain't comfortable with you being here. There's a train leaving here about 8 o'clock tonight, and I think you ought to be on it."

"But I come down here to look at the State house grounds," Will protested.

"And you've got all day to do it. I'll take you over there as soon as we finish our breakfast."

The dining room of the Board of Trade was not nearly as crowded as it had been when they were here before. The pace was leisurely compared to January, and much more to Will's liking.

"Did you find out who that Cromwell fellow is?" he asked over the rim of his coffee cup.

"Sure did," Berry said. "He's the Kentucky correspondent for the *Cincinnati Enquirer*. Betwixt the newspaper management and the Goebel-Campbell-Franklin prosecution team, they appointed him as official fact finder."

"He didn't find no facts until after that $100,000 was voted in though, did he?" Ike mused.

"No, and there weren't no arrests until after that cursed blood money fund come into existence, either," Berry agreed. He wiped his mouth with his napkin and stood. "Come on along, Will. Let's go have a look at the scene of the shooting."

As they moved across the street and into the Capitol grounds, Will compared the actual ground layout with the engineer's chart. Everything seemed to be just as the diagram showed. The chart was a bird's-eye view; it did not show the gentle slope of the ground away from the office building, past the fountain, and across the wide brick walkway to the hackberry tree with a chunk missing from near its base.

"The first thing I want to see is if there's any mark here to show where Goebel was when he was hit," Will said moving up past the fountain. All three searched in vain for some marking.

"Berry, you were here. Where did he fall?" Will asked.

"I didn't see him fall, Will, but his head was on the ground about where you're standing now."

"What difference does it make where he fell?" Ike

asked. "It seems to me that where he was standing when he was shot is what matters."

"It shows on the chart there, don't it?" Berry offered.

"He's got some lines that the paper says are lines of sight from various points, over there and there, and inside the State House," Will said, pointing. "It sure is lucky that each of these people was able to line up where Goebel fell with some fixed object such as a tree or one of the columns."

"Sure is," Ike agreed. "Did the paper happen to say who any of these folks that did this sightin' was?"

"Nope." Will was moving down to the tree.

"What happened to that thing?" Berry asked pointing at the base of the tree.

"They cut out a block containing the bullet," Will explained. Will dropped to his knees to examine the tree trunk. He squinted at the tree and then crawled around to the back side. "Ike, go up there and stand about where Goebel was shot," he directed.

"How the hell am I gonna do that when we don't know where he was?"

"Just somewhere a little past the fountain and over to the right."

As Ike moved into position, Will bent down to get his eye in line with the missing bullet block location on the tree.

"Ike, hold your hand out flat in front of your chest," he yelled.

Ike held his right hand, palm down, parallel to the ground.

Will sighted from the point where the bullet struck the tree, past Ike's body to Caleb Powers' window sill.

"Move your hand up a little," he yelled. "Up a little more . . . just a tad more . . . hold it, freeze right there." He jumped up and ran to where Ike was standing with his hand near the middle of his breast. Will produced a carpenter's rule from his coat pocket and measured from Ike's hand to the ground.

"What in the Sam Hill are you doing, boy?" Berry asked.

"I sighted Ike's hand to line up on the trajectory of a bullet from the window sill to the tree," he said. "It would have been 56 inches above the ground when it passed here, by that method."

"That method don't seem very exact to me," Ike mused.

"It isn't," Will agreed, "but it's just as good as what that engineer Franklin hired did."

"Why? What did he do?" Berry asked.

"He stuck a piece of wire in the bullet hole and just happened to notice that the wire pointed to that window," Will said.

"Why, hell, you could make a piece of wire point to the moon, if you wanted to," Berry observed.

"That sounds like definite proof to me." The sarcasm was obvious in Ike's voice.

"If you're through with this dress dummy here," Berry said, gripping Ike's shoulder, "we need to go over to the depot."

"Just one more thing," Will urged. "Ike, go back over there to where Goebel was and stand for a minute." Will ran back to the tree and squatted down to sight by Ike once again. After a minute, he returned to where Ike and Berry were waiting.

"What now?" Berry asked.

"I verified that there's just as good a line of sight to the office building steps as to the Secretary of State's window. From the steps between the buildings, a bullet could pass between the Capitol building and the columns and get to the tree."

"Do you mean to say that the shot that killed Goebel could have come from the steps over yonder?" Ike asked.

"I mean to say that the bullet they found in that tree could have come from the steps," Will said with a smile of satisfaction.

"Same difference, ain't it?"

"Nope, it ain't. I've read nothing anywhere nor have I seen anything here today that convinces me that the bullet they found in the tree is the one that killed Goebel."

After that thought soaked in, Berry said, "Well, I wish you good luck in your efforts here. Anything you come up with just might prove valuable. Ike and me are goin' over to the depot. You can measure around here to your heart's content. We'll see you at Kagin's at supper time."

⚜

"For your very own," Berry smiled as he handed the paper over to Will.

"This pass allows me to go wherever I want, anytime I want?" It was all he could do to suppress a grin.

"As long as the good old L & N goes there. Now you better get on over to the depot. The train'll be pullin' in any minute now."

Will jumped up without hesitation. He allowed himself a smile as he shook hands with Ike and then Berry. "I'll see you back on Straight Creek," he said as he dashed out toward the station.

Walking along the street in front of the Capitol Square, Will stopped to watch a squad of soldiers march in formation through the gate. He paused to review the scene of the shooting once more in his mind. As he was looking at the Secretary of State's window, he saw the soldiers go in the office building via the door between the buildings. The distances and spatial relationships fixed in mind, he moved along toward the depot.

He paused on the corner to cross the street and heard a racket behind him. He turned to see the squad of soldiers exiting the office building at the door on the end of the hallway opposite where they had entered a few moments before.

Crossing the street, Will's heart was in his throat with thoughts of heading toward Lothair. The soldiers overtook him as he reached the depot door, and he elbowed his way through to the ticket window, arriving just as the train screeched into the depot.

"Does this train go to Lothair in Perry County?" he shouted through the caged window.

"Don't no train go to Lothair," the agent answered. "This 'un goes to Hazard, though. Close enough?"

"Close enough," Will shot over his shoulder, running to the platform.

The train was already starting to move as Will, in the company of the soldiers, scrambled aboard. By the time they had cleared the tunnel, Will found himself sitting in a rearward facing seat, opposite two of the soldiers. He glanced at their faces, and thought he was sure that he had seen one of them before. Will smiled and nodded to the men, who merely stared straight ahead.

A conductor in a dusty, faded blue uniform entered the front of the car calling for tickets. Will fished around in his pocket and produced his pass. When the conductor approached him, he handed up the paper. A pained expression crossed the man's face as he perused the pass.

"Beats me how the company stays in business, givin' these things out to ever'body who has a brother that's as much as a county out-house inspector," he grumbled, handing the pass back.

"How you doin', boys?" he said to the two soldiers, moving on down the aisle.

The men facing Will responded by turning their faces to the window, away from the conductor.

As the train slid along through the humid darkness, Will's mind began to wander to what he'd do when he got to Perry County. He had no idea how far—or what direction—Lothair was from Hazard. Oh, well, as his sister had said, love finds ways. He'd just deal with whatever he found when he got there.

His gaze happened to shift back inside the car into full eye contact with the soldier opposite him, and suddenly he knew where he had seen him. He spoke before he thought.

"You're Caleb Powers, aren't you?" Will's voice was filled with wonder. What was the Secretary of State doing on this train—and in military uniform? The other man looked familiar, too, but Will could not put a name with the face.

The blood drained from Powers' face when Will spoke his name. He drew his neck down into his shoulders, sank lower in his seat and pulled his military cap further over down on his forehead. Will could not imagine what was going on, then he noticed that the other man had a small shaving cut on his chin. He mentally put a long black beard on the man and suddenly realized that he was Captain John Davis, clean-shaven. Then Will was embarrassed for being so slow-witted. These two men were under arrest warrants and were making a run for their freedom. He hastily apologized, keeping his voice low.

"I'm sorry, I didn't mean to call attention to you. Don't worry, you have nothing to fear from me," he whispered.

"You're a Republican, I take it?" Powers said.

"Well, yes, but more than that, I don't think there's any validity to the charge against you," Will answered.

Powers managed a slight smile. "Thank you."

"Do you think this ruse is going to work?" Will asked, leaning toward them to keep his voice down.

John Davis stuck his hand inside his coat and extracted a folded document. "We've got these, just in case it don't," he said. Unfolding the paper, he opened it so that Will could read the beautiful handwriting. Although he could not make it all out, he did see that it was a pardon, signed by Governor William S. Taylor.

The engine whistled for Lexington and began to slow. As they pulled even with the depot, Will noticed that there was a large group of people milling about on the platform. Before the car had come to a full stop, several armed men burst through the doors at both ends of the car.

"Caleb Powers, I know you. Come with me," one of the men shouted. Will noticed that they were all wearing police badges, and most were armed with rifles. The policemen seized Powers and Davis and dragged them off the train.

Aside from the fact that Will did not think they were guilty of anything, he felt sorry for them being dragged through the mob on the platform.

Chapter 12

No Federal Interference
Washington Post, February, 1900.

Saturday, March 10, 1900

Will heaved a sigh of relief when the train finally cleared Lexington. He closed his eyes and turned control of his body over to the clackety-clack rhythm of the wheels on the track. Sleep would not find him, however. At length he gave up the effort and just tried to relax.

"Did you hear about the decision from the Jefferson County court," he heard a voice behind him. Will shifted his position slightly so that he could see the two drummers in the seat to his rear.

"No, did Judge Field hand down a decision on the issue of who's actually governor?"

"Well, in a way," the first man replied. "What he decided was that the judicial system had no authority to pass on what the General Assembly has enacted."

"So, in essence, he's allowed that the Democrats are in, and Beckham's the governor."

"Yeah, but that's just the first round. All agreed that they'd go all the way through the appeal process, you know. So, you can bet that the Republicans will be in the Kentucky Court of Appeals soon."

They were quiet for a few moments, and Will thought maybe they'd fallen asleep. At length, one man said, "Say, Mort, who do you think killed Goebel?"

An answer was slow in coming. "Well, I see four possibilities: there's the Sanford kin—they've got a revenge motive; there's the L & N—Lord knows they're glad to be shed of him; obviously there's the Republicans; and finally, there's the Democrats."

"The Democrats! Why would they kill him?"

"Let's look at who has the most to gain. The Republicans beat him, and are—were, anyway—in office, although they're on the verge of losing the offices. The Democrats, on the other hand, stand to gain the offices because he's dead. Besides, they don't have to worry any more about the son of a bitch ruining their party."

The second man chuckled, and then the conversation fell off. Will tried once again to sleep, but his eyes wouldn't stay closed. After a bit, he sat up and extracted a pencil and paper from his kit. Although he was—as usual—unaware, he spoke his logic aloud as he worked.

"Let's see, the bullet hole was 18 inches above the ground, and according to my figures, the window sill is about 13 feet higher than the bullet hole, but only 8.5 feet above the ground. The place where Goebel was hit is about 100 feet from the window, the tree is about 100 feet further on that line." His voice trailed into a mumble as the figures flowed from the pencil onto the paper. At length, he leaned back and announced to himself that the math said the bullet was about 51 inches above the ground when it flew over where Goebel was struck.

As he put his pencil away, the last thing he remembered thinking was that the math told him about the same thing as he had measured by the rough method of sight.

⚜

He awoke to the mournful sound of the train whistle and the screech of brakes. Sitting up and peering out the coal dust-covered window, Will saw a depot through sleep-filled eyes. The white lettered green board tacked onto the end of the weather-boarded building proclaimed the town to be Hazard. Hazard! He sat bolt upright, suddenly wide awake.

The car ground to a halt exactly in line with the station waiting room. As Will moved down to the platform, the delicious aroma of bacon frying assaulted his nose, making him aware that he was hungry. Giving the first thought since he left Frankfort to money, he dug into his pockets and discovered a total of $1.94. Enough for breakfast, he thought, heading toward the source of the smell, which was a wheeled cart at the end of the platform.

"How much?" he asked the small man behind the cart.

"Bacon, two eggs, toast, and coffee, fifty cents."

"Deal." Will handed over the money. He accepted the tin plate and cup and moved to a wooden bench facing the street to eat. The flavor of the bacon and eggs was better than he'd ever tasted. Must taste better seasoned with anticipation, he thought.

A crew of men slid back the door of a boxcar and began to unload some wooden crates into a stack on the platform. Will worked his way through the eggs and marveled at how quickly the men could empty the car. By the time he'd finished eating, the stack of crates was five feet high, the box car was closed, and the train was getting up steam to pull out.

Will walked back to the cart and handed in his plate and cup. The vendor said something that was lost in the din of the departing train, and then he turned the cart and moved away toward the town beyond. Will suddenly felt terribly alone and deserted on the platform. Before the feeling sunk in, however, he was aware of someone at his elbow. He turned to see the station agent in the standard faded, dusty blue wool uniform.

"Mornin'," the agent said.

"Howdy," Will nodded.

"You ain't from these parts, are ye?"

"No," Will answered, "I'm from Straight Creek in Bell County."

The agent turned to examine Will more closely. "Which Fork?"

"Right," Will smiled. "I take it you know Straight Creek?"

"Good enough to know that the Bell County folks and the Perry County folks smell about the same." He laughed at his own joke.

When the chuckling subsided, Will asked, "How would a man get to Lothair?"

The man pointed southeast, away from town. "He'd go that way."

"Thanks," Will said, starting in the indicated direction.

" 'Bout five miles," the agent called, shaking his head as he went back into the depot office.

Will had walked a mile or so when the dirt road took a sharp, dropping turn to the left. He descended with the grade and found himself facing a steep climb to the top of the next ridge. About halfway up the slope, he sat on a tree stump to catch his breath. Although the day was cool, he'd worked up a sweat and opened his coat to let some of the steam blow off on the spring wind. He'd only rested a few minutes when he heard a wagon start up the hill. He looked to his left and saw a matched pair of Kentucky red mules pulling a coal-laden wagon toward him. He stood and hailed the driver.

"Howdy," Will called.

"Howdy," the driver answered, clucking softly to the mules who clearly understood his command to slow the pace slightly. The incline was so steep, they were happy to obey.

"What in the world are you doin' out here in the middle of nowhere?" the wagon driver called, pulling even with the place where Will stood.

"Just resting a bit from the strain."

"Where you bound?"

"Lothair." Will side-stepped to keep even with the wagon.

"Hop aboard if you want a ride."

Will ran a few steps to catch up and timed his leap so that his right foot hit on the board extending from the wagon bed. In a fluid motion, he bounded from the ground onto the wagon bed and landed next to the driver on the board. He was a small wiry man. A shock of dirty brown hair poked through a hole in his old felt hat. He was badly in need of a shave and was missing two front teeth. He extended his hand to Will.

"Name's Alvie Vaughn."

As Will took his hand, Alvie sent a stream of amber tobacco juice in an arc over their hands into the ditch along the roadway. Will leaned back to clear the path.

"I'm Will Elliott."

"What's your business in Lothair, Will?"

Although he realized that he was in the company of another mountain man, Will's training told him not to be too open.

"I'm lookin' for some folks," he said noncommittally.

"What's the name? I might know 'em."

Guarded or not, he couldn't pass up that offer. "Name's Whittaker. Do you know where they live?"

Alvie let fly another stream of spittle. Will had to admire the art with which he let it form between his widely spaced teeth and then imparted just the right momentum to produce a perfect arc. "Hell, son, half the people in Lothair is named Whittaker. Which bunch you after?"

"The bunch with the good-looking daughter named Mary."

Alvie grinned his toothless grin. "I know just the ones," he said. "That's Silas Whittaker's oldest girl. Matter of fact, we're gonna roll right by their front door here in a bit."

At this news, Will began to beat the dust from his clothing and attempted to smooth the wrinkles. The thought went through his mind that his clothes looked like he'd slept in them. Alvie Vaughn was quite amused at Will's efforts to improve his appearance.

"Friend of mine fixed me up to meet a girl what was a friend of his sister's at a dance one time," he said. "I thought it was a good idee until I got a look at her." He cackled as Will ducked another stream of tobacco juice.

"Ugly, was she?"

"Well, no, she weren't so much ugly, but she was what you might say, hefty. Weighed nigh 'bout 300 pound, in my opinion. Well, sir, she was a friend of a friend, so I'd been warned to be on my best behavior. I'll swan, though, try as I might, I couldn't think of nothin' nice to say."

"What'd you do?" Will asked, beginning to see he was being put on.

"Well, sir, when the fiddlers quit, I said the nicest thing that come to mind."

"Which was?"

"You sure don't sweat much, for a big ol' fat gal." Vaughn rocked back on the wagon seat laughing so hard that the wagon bed shook on the axles.

Vaughn clucked to his mules, and they came to a halt just before the road made a sharp turn to the right. He still had small tears of laughter in his eyes.

"Silas Whittaker's the next house 'round the bend here," he said. "I thought you might want to walk the last little bit."

"Good idea," Will said, climbing down from the wagon. "I surely do thank you kindly for the ride."

"You're welcome, son. Be sure and look me up next time you're up this way."

"I'll do it," Will shouted as the wagon pulled away.

He straightened his clothes as well as he could and started up the road. The day had warmed considerably as the sun approached its overhead position. Rounding the curve, he saw a white house perched high above the road. A narrow, winding path led the way to the porch. He saw right away that the distance was too great to announce his arrival from the road, so he moved up the path to where a gate in the picket fence bounded the yard.

"Hello, in the house," he yelled.

A female figure appeared in the door. Will saw that it

was Mary, dressed in a house dress, before she recognized him. He waved, opened the gate, and moved toward the house.

He had taken only a few steps when she let out a scream, stopping him dead in his tracks. When he looked up to the door again, she had disappeared. Unsure of what was going on, he yelled again and stayed put.

In a moment, a man came to the door. He peered down and then stepped out on the porch.

"Will! I should have known. Come on up here."

Will climbed onto the porch and took George's outstretched hand. "What's all the screaming about?" he asked.

"You've got a lot to learn about women, son. Lesson one is don't go around showing up unexpectedly in the middle of the day. Hang on a minute here, and I'll see if it's safe to invite you in the house yet." He wheeled back through the door and quickly reappeared. "All clear," he announced. "Come on in. We're just about to have dinner."

Will knew it would be impolite to refuse a meal under another man's roof, and besides, he was hungry, so he made no protest. George led him through a sparsely furnished front room into a kitchen where a fire was roaring in the grate. A huge pot of something was simmering over the fire while a woman stirred the mixture with a large cedar ladle. Six children where seated at the table, each one jabbering away and pounding on the table with a knife, fork, or fist.

"Ma, I'd like you to meet Will Elliott," George said. "He's the one Mary told you we met in Frankfort."

Mrs. Whittaker wiped her brow with the back of her hand and then wiped her hand on her spotless white apron. "How dee do?"

"Very sorry to barge in on you," Will apologized. Until George had spoken, it had not occurred to him that he'd receive anything less than the warmest of welcomes.

"Don't matter," she said turning back to her stirring. "We got so many mouths around here, one more or less don't make no difference." The disarming smile on her face reminded him of how he'd been taken with Mary's smile when he first saw her at the Board of Trade. "You boys find yourselves a seat."

Will and George sat. Mrs. Whittaker ladled stew into bowls before each person, and also at two empty seats. Will was about to ask George where Mary was when they heard the front door open. A few moments later, a large man entered the kitchen and hesitated just a moment in the doorway. Finally, he glanced at each of the children and then at the woman. Wordlessly, he hung his hat on a peg and sat at one of the vacant seats. The noise instantly stopped, and each head bowed. When the brief prayer was mumbled, the noise resumed, and the eating began.

"So what in the world are you doin' in Perry County?" George asked.

Will glanced quickly at the parents and then said, "Oh, I was just passin' through on the train, and thought I'd stop and say hello."

"You didn't pass too close to here on no train," Mr. Whittaker observed, much to Will's embarrassment. "Are you sartain my daughter didn't have somethin' to do with it?"

"Oh, Silas, leave the boy be," Mrs. Whittaker said. "You knew the boys'd come sniffin' 'round here sooner or later." Will smiled his relief at her.

"I'd just as lief it be later," Silas said, wiping his mouth.

When they'd finished eating and Mary still had made no appearance, Will finally asked George where she was.

"In the bedroom, primping," he replied. "You'd just as well go to the office with me this afternoon." George ushered him toward the front door.

Will's disappointment was written on his face as they walked down the path and entered the road. "She won't be out of there for hours yet," George said. "Cheer up. She'll be ready for you by the time we get back for supper."

A short walk brought them to a cluster of buildings sitting around an intersection. "Welcome to downtown Lothair."

As George led the way into a doorway, Will noticed a shingle that proclaimed: George P. Whittaker, Attorney at Law.

"I didn't know you were a lawyer," Will remarked.

"Well, you and I didn't have much of a chance to get acquainted in Frankfort, did we?" Moving on into the office, George motioned Will to a chair. "What say we take care of that this afternoon?"

The first topic of conversation that came to mind was, of course, the Goebel shooting. As he began to speak, it crossed

Will's mind that he was getting as involved in politics as Ike and Berry.

"Have you heard about the lawsuits and arrests in the shooting?" Will began.

"I'm one of the lawyers who argued the case before Judge Field," George said flatly. "So, yes, I've heard."

That answered the question Will had had in his mind about why the Whittakers had been in Frankfort in January.

"I'm impressed," Will said sincerely. "Tell me about the position you took before the judge."

George unbuttoned his coat and propped his feet up on the desk. "It's pretty straightforward. I just told him that the court had the power to right a legislative wrong."

"What wrong?"

"Hell, son—declaring Goebel elected. There's not a thing in this world to back the contention that he was legally elected back in November."

"You mean that the contest committees did not examine the vote counts? They just simply declared Goebel was elected, didn't they?"

"Yes. Our position is that, at most, their only legal right was to declare that the November election was void."

"What'd Beckham's Democrat lawyers say?" Will was fascinated.

"Only that the decrees of the General Assembly were final and not subject to review by any other authority." George spat the words.

"Well, ain't that right? Judge Field agreed with 'em, didn't he?"

"No, by God, he didn't agree. He just simply refused to rule on it. If the Legislature's the final authority, this State is in a hell of a fix." George's face was turning red. He jerked his feet to the floor and started pacing the office. Will guessed he was being treated to a replay of what Judge Field had heard in Louisville.

"There's a federal question here, Will. If the constitution of Kentucky gives absolute arbitrary power to either a contest board or the General Assembly to take from the defendants the offices of honor, trust, and emolument to which they were elected by the people of the state, as alleged under false guise of a trial of a contest over offices, the constitution of the state of Kentucky is itself contrary to the constitution of the United States." George collapsed into his chair, drained of emotion.

"That's pretty serious stuff," Will observed.

"You're damn right it is. That's exactly why we filed the appeal in just those strong terms."

"Is that the entire basis of the appeal?" Will asked.

"No, that's not all. The drawings for the contest committees was fraudulently done—seven of the ten democrats on the gubernatorial board had already declared a partiality for Goebel—and perhaps most importantly, the so-called 'legislative meeting' that adopted the contest committee's recommendation was held in the Capital Hotel, not 'the seat of government' as required by the constitution."

"Wow. The Democrats ain't gonna like that appeal much."

"That's why we've asked the federal War Department to send troops to Frankfort."

"Notwithstanding the fact that I'd rather be here anyway, I'm glad I got the hell out of there."

"Never been a better time to head for the hills, so to speak," George smiled.

As the afternoon wore on, George and Will exchanged ideas on a wide variety of topics. By the time the sun was sitting on the edge of the ridge and they started back to the house, they had become fast friends.

Mary met them at the door. She was dressed in the pink and white affair that he'd first seen her in, and Will thought she looked fabulous.

"I'd think you could give a body a little notice afore you show up on the doorstep," was her first comment.

Will observed that she said that with a smile, so he was only momentarily distressed. "If you'd get one of them new-fangled telephones in here, a man could call." He returned her smile.

"As a matter of fact, we've talked about that. George is willing to pay for it, but Pa says that the wires attract lightning, and he won't have 'em attached to his house."

"Well, then, a fellow just has to do what he can, doesn't he?" Will said, moving closer to her.

Mary sneaked a glance toward the back of the house, and seeing that no one was in sight, she kissed him quickly on the cheek. "I'm really glad you're here. How'd you manage it?"

He showed her the pass Berry Howard had given him.

"This thing expires December 31, 1900," she read.

"That leaves me all year to show up here unexpected, doesn't it?" He was beaming.

"We'll work out something."

George stuck his head into the parlor. "Dinner is served," he announced.

Mary rose and Will followed her into the first dining room he had ever seen in anyone's home. He didn't know at first what to expect, but soon came to the realization that the room was designed specifically for eating. That idea required some getting used to.

The children were apparently having their meal in the kitchen; Will could hear but not see them. Only Mr. and Mrs. Whittaker, George, Will and Mary were seated around the table. Will was much more at ease for having spent the afternoon getting acquainted with George. Although he was aching to be alone with Mary, the meal passed pleasantly enough.

When the pie and coffee were finished, Mrs. Whittaker set her husband and son to work clearing the table. "Mary, take Will in the parlor and show him the new stereopticon slides we've got," she said, casting a sidelong glance at her husband.

Will and Mary walked to the front of the house. "It's a beautiful night," she said. "How 'bout we sit in the swing out on the porch?"

"I like that idea a lot."

The air was quite warm for such an early spring night. The usual humidity was not present; the air was so clear that the stars seemed close enough to touch. The swing allowed them to sit close—their bodies not touching, but close enough for Will to feel just slightly uncomfortable.

"I wonder if I should get a sweater," she said.

"You won't need it. I'll keep you warm."

She smiled and gave a slight push with her foot to rock the swing.

He slipped an arm around her shoulders.

"Will, I'm so glad you came by here," she said, dropping her head against his shoulder.

"It took a spot of luck, but I jumped at the chance when

it came along. I just hope we'll have more opportunities."

She sighed as she moved closer beside him. "George will be active in whatever lawsuits come up as a result of all this political foolishness. I always have the option to go with him when he goes off to these court things."

Will tightened his grasp slightly, drawing her still closer. He had in mind to say that it appeared there'd be plenty of work for the lawyers when she turned her face up to him. He kissed her lips softly and held it as long as possible. When she pulled away slightly, she flicked her eyes open momentarily and returned her head to his shoulder.

"I love you," she said softly.

Chapter 13

The Situation at Frankfort
"Republicans have a majority in the house."
Louisville Times, April 4, 1900.

Tuesday, April 17, 1900

Will Elliott was seeing spring of the year come to the mountains for the twentieth time, but it seemed as if this was the first. The forsythia had never shown such a brilliant yellow, and the redbuds had never before displayed such a vivid pink. The pink and white blossoms covering the apple trees scented the air with just the right hint of sweet perfume, and the sunshine had never felt quite so glorious before. He was headed for Bradshaw's, but his feet followed the path along the Right Fork without conscious guidance from his brain. The only thought in his mind was that it was good to be alive.

Entering the store, he was not at all surprised to find the usual crew in their accustomed spots around the stove. Even though there was no fire, the prescribed four-foot circle rule was in effect. He was also not surprised to discover that the Goebel situation was the topic of discussion.

"But McKinley's a Republican, ain't he?" T. J. Ashby was saying. "I'd think he'd be willin' to send the good old U. S. Army to keep a Republican governor in office."

"The President of these United States has got more to tend to than Kentucky," Berry explained. "Besides, he's a politician. He ain't gonna commit himself to nothin' he don't have to."

"So, we'll just have to wait until the U. S. Supreme Court passes on it," Will said as he moved into the circle.

"I think the other half of the court situation is the more interesting, myself," Chas Whitt said.

"I'll agree with that," Bob Bradshaw said from behind the cage. "The criminal side of this thing is gonna heat up real soon."

"It's already hot, ain't it?" T. J. asked. "They done arrested that Youtsey fellow, and you mark my words, they're gonna hang him."

"I'd say you're right, T. J.," Berry muttered slowly. "When I heard that Wharton Golden had been in conference with that Cromwell man and Tom Campbell, I knew that somebody was in for big trouble."

"And that somebody is Caleb Powers, isn't it?" Will asked.

"He's one of 'em," Bob said. "Berry, you was down there for Powers' examinin' trial, wasn't you?"

"I was, and it was a hell of a show."

"Tell us about it."

Everyone shifted their positions to get comfortable for the long tale to come. Bob dropped the mail he was sorting into the basket and came around the counter. Berry tilted his chair back into his tale-telling position, but Will noted that some of the usual enthusiasm appeared to be missing from his manner.

"Just as soon as the judge banged his gavel, a blind man could see that Powers was in trouble," he began.

"The first two witnesses they called were in the State House yard when Goebel was shot. One of 'em, Eph Lillard, was walking with Goebel. He said that he noticed that one of the windows of the Secretary of State's office was up—he insisted that he'd said so all along. Despite he was that observant, he didn't take no particular notice of where Goebel fell, though.

"The next witness was Dee Armstrong, one of the detectives who's lookin' to get his share of that $100,000. He said Caleb refused to tell him where he was or who he'd left in charge of the office."

"Armstrong's one of them high-powered Louisville detectives, ain't he?" Will asked.

Berry snorted. "When the prosecutors got through buildin' him up, you'd believe that he could look at a cow's track here in Bell and tell you the price of butter in New York City."

"Ever'body knows Caleb was on the train on the way to Louisville, don't they?" Chas tried to get the conversation back on track.

"Caleb gave it out to the papers, not to mention that there was a couple of people with him," Berry went on. "Then they called up a few more witnesses who said they didn't know nothin'. That Jones fellow they've got in custody was one of 'em. He said he saw somebody beating on the door to Caleb's office with a hatchet, tryin' to get in 'cause it was locked.

"Then, they brung on the star of the show, Wharton Golden."

"I understood that Golden and Caleb were friends," Ike said.

"They grew up together down in Knox County," Berry said, "but that don't mean much once the prosecution got ahold of him. When the defense got their turn, Governor Brown got Golden to admit that he'd been intimidated."

"You mean ex-Governor John Y. Brown?" Will asked.

"That's him. Caleb hired Brown to defend him," Berry answered.

"What did Golden admit to?" Bob said.

"You boys remember that Cromwell fellow that was in here? Well, he got to Golden and told him that he'd heard a lot of bad tales on him up here in the mountains, but him and Colonel Campbell—being the fine gentlemen that they are—were gonna do what they could to save Golden from being hung."

"That's a joke, ain't it Berry?" Will said. "Nobody would believe that Cromwell learned anything up here."

"Golden did. The boy was scared to death the whole time he was testifying."

"Well, what did he tell?" All present lent rapt attention.

"He said that he and Caleb's brother, John, were hanging around Caleb's office on January 30th, waiting to leave for Louisville, when this black-headed man come in. Golden didn't know the black-headed man, but he says that John Powers give the fellow a key."

Berry let the front legs of his chair drop to the floor with a thud. He leaned forward to continue speaking.

"Now get this. Golden says that the man he didn't know, although he was clearly trying to implicate Youtsey, comes up to him and says, 'You better get out of the way for Goebel is going to be killed this morning.'"

"Hold up here," Ike interrupted. "You mean that this man, who's Youtsey, comes up to Golden, not knowin' him from Adam, and tells him that they're gonna kill Goebel?"

"Yeah," Berry said with a wry smile, "and then Youtsey looks at the key, and says, 'Why, he's give me the wrong key, I'll have to see Caleb.'"

"No one believed any of that, did they?"

"Apparently Judge Moore did. He held Caleb over without bail."

The door opened, admitting a pudgy woman wearing a filthy house dress. Her hands and face were dirty, and her hair had not seen water or brush for some time. While the day was warm, it was not warm enough to justify that neither she, nor any one of the three girls in her wake, wore a coat. Bob Bradshaw went to the front counter. "Howdy, Clorinda. What can I do you for?"

"I jest come in to git some sugar and coffee," she said looking toward the gathering at the rear of the store.

As Bob started to measure the sugar, the woman walked back to the stove. "Cousin Berry, you ain't in here spreadin' lies are ye?" she grinned.

The disgust was evident on Berry's face. "Just because I was related to your late husband don't give you the right to act like you're any kin of mine."

The intended contempt passed right over her head. "I heerd tell you caused a little ruckus down the river."

"Here's your stuff, Clorinda," Bob yelled from the counter.

She turned and walked back toward the front. As she picked up the sacks, Bob said, "Clorinda, you're gonna need to pay a little something on your bill."

"Maybe I'll have some money sooner'n you think," she said, ushering the girls out the door.

"It might be that you'd stand a better chance of collectin' what's due if you was willin' to take it out in trade," Chas suggested. "That middle daughter of hers ain't too bad lookin', you know."

"If it's all the same to you, I'll hold out 'til she comes up with the money."

"Berry, did you say that Governor Brown was defendin' Caleb?" Will asked. "I thought he was a Democrat."

"He is, but he wasn't a Goebel Democrat in the first place, and he sure ain't now. The whole bunch of 'em showed their true colors when the fur started to fly."

"What are you talkin' about?" Ike asked.

"Oh, Judge Denny, another of Caleb's lawyers, got into a shoutin' match with Tom Campbell during the trial. Campbell and Denny both forgot that they were there to try a man for his life. Poor ol' Caleb happened to be betwixt the two of 'em, and at one point, he stood up. When he did, I heard about ten pistol hammers cock. Caleb heard 'em, too, 'cause he sat back down pretty quick. Anyway, that little episode made it pretty clear to all concerned that those men are risking more than professional defeat by defendin' Caleb

Powers."

"Are you sure there's any risk involved?" Will mused. "Sounds to me like defeat for the defense is a pretty sure thing."

"Hell, you boys don't know nothin' about riskin' yore life 'til you've stared into the business end of a Rebel cannon, like I did," T. J. said.

"Aw, T. J.," Bob groaned. "If you're gonna tell us a war story, at least you could tell us one of the entertainin' ones."

"Okay, I will. Did I ever tell you boys about the time over in Virginny, let's see, summer of '63 it was, I ended up camped out in the yard of one of them big plantation houses? Well, sir, the captain had told us to be polite, so I went up to the house to ask 'em 'bout gettin' some water from the well.

"An old gentleman come to the door when I knocked. White suit of clothes, string tie, and gray goatee, you know. I asked him 'bout the water. He allowed it was no problem, and we was just kindly chattin', 'bout the weather and such. Finally, I says, 'You lived here all yore life old man?'

"He straightened up on his cane, looked me right in the eye and says, 'Not yet, I ain't.'"

The old man slapped his knees with glee. The laughter had hardly subsided when the front door flew open and in walked Sheriff Henry Broughton. Looking neither left nor right, he moved straight to the back of the room and into the circle gathered there. "Howdy, boys," he said to no one in particular.

Bob Bradshaw was the only one who spoke to the sheriff. Will followed Ike's example and studied the dirt in the cracks in the plank flooring.

"I guess you boys know that the Franklin County grand jury has been in session for a couple of weeks now," Broughton said.

"I heard about that," Berry replied. "I heard that fate played the same kind of role that it did in the selection of the contest committees."

"How's that?"

"Seems as how it worked out somehow that ten of the twelve jurors are good Goebel Democrats. That's handy, seeing as how it only takes nine votes to bring an indictment."

"I don't know nothin' about that," Broughton said, uneasily shifting his weight to the other foot, "but I do know that Judge Cantrill may be issuing arrest warrants pretty soon."

Although he wasn't looking, Will could see the contempt on Berry Howard's face. Berry slowly rose and faced the sheriff.

"If you got something to say, Henry, spit it out."

Broughton moved slowly to the other side of the stove, obviously enjoying stretching out whatever he was going to say. "Just thought I'd share the news, like any good neighbor would."

The only sound to be heard was the birds frolicking in the sunshine. At length, the sheriff decided to go on.

"I got me a telegram from Frankfort this afternoon. Seems as how the grand jury has returned a few indictments in the murder of Governor Goebel. Yesterday, let's see here." He fished around in his pockets and produced a piece of paper. Unfolding it, he read "'The grand jury in the county of Franklin, in the name and by the authority of the Commonwealth of Kentucky, accuses Henry Youtsey, James Howard, Harlan Whittaker, Richard Combs, and . . .'" he paused in his reading for effect. Clearing his throat, "'. . . and Berry Howard of the crime of willful murder.'" He smiled and went on, "I thought you boys would like to know about it. Today, they brung in a few more. Seems as how Charles Finley, John Powers, Caleb Powers, William Culton, and Wharton Golden are indicted as accessories before the fact." He handed the telegram to Berry. "You might want to read the whole thing for yourself." He turned to leave, but stopped part way to the door.

"Oh, yeah. There is one other spot of news. Rumor is that tomorrow will bring some more indictments, including one W. S. Taylor. I suppose arrest warrants won't be long in coming. Well, I must get on. See you boys." He was laughing heartily as he went out the door.

Again, the chirping of the birds dominated the room. The men simply stared at each other. Will certainly did not have any idea of what to say.

"Well," Berry said at length, "I can't say it comes as a total surprise."

"This thing says you're indicted with these other fellows as 'principal,' Berry. What does that mean?" The concern was etched deeply on Ike's face.

"It means that they're going to try to get one or all of

us for actually pullin' the trigger."

"But, hell, your alibi is rock solid. There are, what, ten or twelve people who can put you upstairs in the Capitol building at the time the shots were fired. How can they indict you for doin' the shooting?" Ike handed the telegram to Will.

A little of the color had returned to Berry Howard's face. "Maybe they think I'm a trick shot artist." He managed a smile.

"If you can do a thing like that, they's a spot for you in Buffalo Bill's Wild West Show," T. J. laughed.

"It says here that Finley, Caleb and John Powers, Culton, and Golden are indicted as 'accessories before the fact.' What's the difference?" Will handed the telegram to Chas.

"Means that they are gonna try to get them on doing something to cause Goebel's killin' afore it actually took place," Ike said.

"Well, they can forget about Finley and John Powers," Berry mused. "Both of them have done fled the state."

"Where's the rest of 'em?" T. J. asked.

"I think Jim Howard is back in Clay County," Berry said. "All the rest of 'em, 'cept me and him, are in the Franklin County jail."

"I still ain't comfortable with this 'accessory' business," Will said. "Ike, you said doing something to cause the killin'. Like what, for instance."

"Like making the arrangements for all of us to go down there on a train, for instance."

"Or hiring somebody to do the shooting," Berry added thoughtfully.

"Who's this Combs named here?" Chas asked.

"Oh, he's a Negro barber from down in Knox County," Berry said.

"What's he done?"

"I guess the same as ever'body else named there," Berry replied. "He's probably guilty of having voted Republican and being somewhere around Frankfort at the time Goebel got hisself shot."

The group sat in silence for a few moments. The telegram eventually made its way to Bob Bradshaw, who studied it closely. At length, he handed the paper back to Berry. "What are you gonna do, Berry? Are you gonna run?"

Berry Howard turned to face Bob Bradshaw, his face

black with rage. "Hell no, I'm not gonna run. I ain't done nothin', and they can't prove that I did. I'll stay right here 'til they come to get me, and when they do, by God, I'll stand trial."

"But, Berry, you just said yourself that there ain't no way of getting a fair trial. Might'n it be better just to clear out?" Ike was deadly serious.

"And leave Caleb Powers holdin' the bag? No sir, not Berry Howard. They'll not intimidate me like they did Wharton Golden."

"Berry," Will spoke calmly and slowly, "you know that when the Goebel press gets into this, they'll portray you as a desperate criminal and a fugitive from justice, just because you aren't in custody like the rest of 'em."

Berry looked straight into Will's eyes. "Are you suggesting that I turn myself in?"

"That would clearly indicate your innocence, wouldn't it?"

"It might do that, but it'd also give them the chance to lock me up and throw away the key, without even so much as a trumped up trial. No, I'll not trip down to Frankfort and give myself up."

"Take the word of an old man, son," T. J. Ashby said kindly. "I wouldn't give myself up either, but it'd be better to make some gesture to show that you're in the clear. Will here's right. The newspapers will have a field day with it."

Berry thought for a minute, then his face brightened. "By hell," he shouted, "it works both ways. If they can use the newspapers, so can I. I'll just run me an advertisement in the paper. I'll state that I'm an innocent man and that I'll be right down there the minute they're prepared to offer me a fair trial."

Chapter 14

A New Kind of Race
In the Bluegrass Country.
Indianapolis Press, March 30, 1900.

Wednesday, May 23, 1900

"I do allow that your wife grows the most beautiful irises in the country," Berry said as he and Ike pulled around in front of the Livingston's house.

Ike clucked softly to the horse, urging her into a gentle trot. "Well, she works pretty hard on 'em," he said. "Seems like a waste to me for the most part, but, at this time of year. . . ." his voice trailed off as both men inhaled the fragrant spring air.

In the yard, Ellen stood up from her weeding chores to wave as they passed. The picture of her in that wide brimmed straw hat with a scarf about her throat was Ike's favorite image of his wife. She smiled a loving smile, and they both waved to her as they passed.

"What is it that Judge Smith wants to see you about?" Ike asked when they had rounded the curve and were out of sight of the house.

"I'm not sure," Berry replied, "but it's probably got something to do with the warrant Henry Broughton's got for me."

"Did he try to arrest you?"

"Not very hard. Somebody said that he came by my house when nobody was home. Knocked on the door, I take it, and then went on back to town."

Ike steered the buggy to the right of the road to dodge a puddle left by the previous night's storm. "Why didn't he try harder than that?"

"Damned if I know. Maybe he's decided that I ain't guilty of anything." Ike noticed that Berry was ill at ease. His eyes were in constant motion, scanning the trees lining the roadway. At length, apparently satisfied, he went on. "Ike, I want you to stop down at Bradshaw's. We'll see who's layin' around there that'd like to ride to town with us."

The buggy moved slowly over the thick mud in the roadway. Ike had been storing up his questions for several days and was glad that he was having a little time alone with Berry. It seemed that one just did not see Berry Howard these days unless he was in a group.

"What did you think of Judge Cantrill granting Caleb Powers' appeal for a change of venue?" Ike began.

"Big deal," Berry said. "He only changed it from Franklin County to Scott County. Holdin' the trials in Georgetown means that it's still in the same circuit, so Cantrill's still the judge, and Rob Franklin is still the Commonwealth's Attorney. Hell, Georgetown is Cantrill's home town—he's probably got the jurors they're gonna use already picked."

"I read all the testimony from the preliminary trial and didn't find anything incriminating. Do you think they're really going to try him?"

"Hell fire, yes they're gonna try him," Berry exploded. "And they're gonna convict him, too. You can bet your bottom dollar that they're going to move heaven and earth to prove that Goebel's death was the result of a Republican conspiracy and that anybody that had any connection with that little January train ride is implicated."

"Caleb admits to helping organize the trip to Frankfort. But, most ever'body that was on the train was done gone home afore Goebel was shot. Where's the conspiracy link?" Ike was puzzled.

"The link's in the minds of Colonel Tom Campbell and Goebel's brothers. The thing is, though, the prosecution controls the most powerful newspapers, and they sure know how to use 'em to influence public opinion."

"But," Ike said, thinking hard, "even at that, they can't get any two people who were there at the shootin' to agree on anything."

"Not much," Berry agreed. "Consensus is that the first shot was clear—probably from a rifle—and the others, which followed quickly, were muffled, like they were inside the building."

"What does that mean?" Ike asked.

"Beats me. I guess we all get to draw our own conclusions."

Ike halted the horse by the bench in front of Bradshaw's. A typical crew of loafers occupied the bench, soaking up the warm sunshine. Will Elliott was seated at one end, giving total attention to Chas Whitt's effort to remove an orange's peel in one continuous strip.

"Howdy, boys," Ike said, dismounting the buggy. Berry remained seated, but nodded to Will and Chas. Ike threw the reins over the hitching rail and sat beside Chas.

"Where are you two started?" Will asked, not taking his eyes from the knife slicing into the orange.

"Judge Smith sent for Berry, and I'm driving him to town. Either of you want to ride along?" Ike asked.

Chas held the orange peel up like a dead snake. It spiraled from his hand to the floor and left a trail of juice on the plank in front of the bench. He flipped the naked orange to Berry and stood, wiping the knife blade on the leg of his bib overalls. "Not me. I got me a date with a big ol' catfish down at the river."

"I'm game," Will said. He and Ike climbed into the buggy.

As Will situated himself in the back seat, Berry turned. "You don't happen to be armed, do you son?"

Will looked shocked. "No," he said simply. "Do I need to be?"

"Oh, I don't reckon so," Berry turned to face forward. "I guess we'll be all right." The motion of Berry's shoulders betrayed the sigh Will could not hear.

Ike clucked the mare into motion, and they began the journey toward Pineville. Will was anxious to keep up with events and assumed he'd have to vie with his brother-in-law for Berry's attention. Attempting to beat Ike to the punch, he asked, "Berry, I've read that the doctors who attended Goebel all agree that the shot that killed him passed through him right to left and slightly downward. What do you know about that?"

"Humph," Berry snorted. "I know that that's just one more little piece of partial evidence designed to help prove that the shot came from Caleb Powers' office."

"What do you mean by partial evidence?" Ike asked, slightly irritated that Will got in a question.

"I mean that Dr. Vance examined Goebel and said that he thought that the wound in the back being the same size as the entrance wound was explained by the fact that the entire bullet did not exit Goebel's body. Now, you didn't read that in no damn Democrat newspaper, did you?"

"Nope. That would kind of blow away the idea of the bullet in the hackberry tree being the same one that hit Goebel, wouldn't it?" Will was interested.

"Sure would," Berry said. "That's why the newspapers don't mention Dr. Vance's statement and why they make so much noise about it being a steel ball that killed Goebel."

"The Goebel press is also making a big deal of the fact that when Powers returned to Frankfort after the shooting, he jumped off the train before it even got to the station. 'Seeking the sanctuary of the State House,' they said," Ike added.

Berry shook his head. "Didn't happen to mention that since he was only a hop and a skip from the Ohio River when he got the news about the shootin', he could have sought the sanctuary of Indiana if he'd wanted to, did they?"

Ike pulled his buggy to a halt in front of the Bell County courthouse. He walked the mare over to the hitching rail and tied her in the shade of a large maple tree while Berry and Will climbed to the ground.

"Do you want Will and me to go in with you, or hang around out here?"

Berry looked up and down the street and inspected all the people on the courthouse lawn. Seeing no danger, he returned his attention to Ike and Will. "Oh, come on in, I guess. I'm not sure what Judge Smith wants, so he may ask you to leave, but if that's all right, come along."

The trio mounted the stone steps and entered the courthouse. Will noticed that Berry shot a quick glance toward the sheriff's office as he moved rapidly across the hall to the stairway. In the upstairs hallway, he was more relaxed by the time they arrived at the county judge's office door.

"Come in, come in. Howdy, boys," Judge A. B. Smith was all smiles as he greeted the three men. "How's ever' little thing out on the Right Fork?" he asked, motioning them to chairs.

"Tolerable, I reckon," Berry smiled. After a slight uncomfortable pause, he went on. "What's goin' on here in town?"

"Berry," Judge Smith began, "you and I have been friends for a long time now, and I know that you're a pretty good fellow. That being the case, I don't aim to let no undue harm come to you." He paused, looked briefly at Will, then Ike, then went on. "On the other hand, I am an officer of the court, and sworn to uphold the laws of this county, state, and nation."

Berry Howard squirmed uncomfortably in his wooden chair. It seemed to Will that Berry looked a little smaller than usual.

"They've got the wrong man, Judge. Ever'body knows I didn't shoot Goebel. There's ten people who'll put me in the other building at the time the shots were fired." Berry spoke evenly and with no display of temper.

"Let me explain the law to you, Berry. I think it will become very important that you understand. Under the indictment and the well-established rules of practice in Kentucky, you could be found guilty of murder if the proof shows that you either fired the shot, or aided and abetted another in doing so." The Judge carefully emphasized the last phrase.

"You're indicted along with several other men, and if any of them are found guilty of firing the shot, then you can be found guilty, also. So, let's say that a jury finds that Henry Youtsey actually fired the shot. Then, obviously, Youtsey is guilty of murder. But if a jury finds you guilty of aiding and abetting Youtsey in the act, then you're guilty of murder, too, even if you were in Egypt, viewing the pyramids at the time."

"But . . . ." Smith cut Berry off with an uplifted palm.

"Just hear me out, Berry. Then you can do whatever you feel you have to do." Judge Smith smiled benevolently and rocked back in his swivel chair. "Now, you are under indictment for a capital crime, and there is an outstanding warrant for your arrest, but the State has made no real effort to apprehend you, and you did run an advertisement in the paper saying that you were willing to surrender.

"In view of all these facts, I'm going to ask you not to wander around town here too much. There's no point in you rubbing Sheriff Broughton's nose in it. On the other hand, I feel that you're entitled to know more about what's going on in these cases than you might learn by reading the newspaper. So, while you're here, I'll bring you up to date on all the progress, if you like."

Berry leaned toward the desk. "And then I go on home?"

Judge Smith leaned forward and put his elbows on his desk. "You go on home whether I talk to you or not," he said kindly.

An obvious wave of relief covered Berry. He leaned back in his chair and smiled broadly. With a jovial glance at Will and Ike, he said, "We're thirsty for news."

"There's a lot," the judge said, fishing some papers out from a pile on the corner of the desk. "For openers, the Governor's race is over. We lost, Beckham's in."

All three mouths dropped open. "What happened?" Ike managed to stammer.

"The United States Supreme Court ruled that they had no jurisdiction and refused to hear the case. Governor Taylor had gone to Louisville for some reason, and when that word came down, he telegraphed Gen. Collier to dismiss the militia and turn the offices over to the Democrats. Then Taylor fled across the river to Indiana."

"Being over there won't make him safe from prosecution, will it?" Will asked.

"Technically, no. But, as a practical matter, yes. Indiana's Republican governor, Mount, won't honor Beckham's requisitions for Taylor or Charles Finley, so they are safe."

"So, that's that?" Berry said.

"Well, the General Assembly did declare a special gubernatorial election for this fall. With Goebel gone, we can let the people actually say who they want for governor." The judge was smiling.

"We'll just win the state offices back, then," Ike smiled, too.

"Perhaps," Smith mused. "Although the publicity stemming from the shooting and trials won't help our cause any. That's the score on the civil side; meanwhile, the criminal process is really heating up."

"We heard about Powers' change of venue," Berry ventured.

"That applies to Davis, Whittaker, Combs, and Youtsey as well. They all pleaded not guilty and got a change of venue to Scott."

"What about Bill Culton?" Will asked, after mentally reviewing the names of the indicted men.

"They've granted him immunity for his testimony," Smith said, matter-of-factly.

"What about the pardons that Governor Taylor issued for Davis and Powers?" Ike asked.

"Cantrill dismissed them out of hand. 'Governor' is the operative word here. The court held that Goebel won the election and was declared to be the governor before the pardons were issued, and, therefore, the pardons were worthless. On

more or less the same basis, he denied them all bail, too."
Smith showed slight anger.

"What kind of evidence have they managed to come
up with?" Berry asked. His voice and manner were much
more concerned now that he truly understood the conspiracy
aspect.

"That's where this thing really starts to get
interesting," the judge said. "Do you know Henry Youtsey?"

"I've seen him around," Berry replied, "but I don't what
you'd say 'know' him."

"Well, he appears to be a pretty weak character," Smith
continued. "I take it that his major concern in the Goebel
affair was that he'd lose his state job. At any rate, soon after
he was arrested, the good Toms—Cromwell and Campbell—
got to him in jail and got him to make a confession."

Ike and Will froze motionless in their chairs. Berry's
face paled. "What'd he confess to?" His voice was barely
audible.

Judge Smith rocked back in his chair and propped his
feet up on the desk. "The boy told an interesting story. He
implicated you, Berry, along with Jim Howard, Combs, Frank
Cecil, and John Powers. He allows that either you, Jim
Howard, Dick Combs, or Frank Cecil fired the fatal shot from
Caleb Powers' office."

"He didn't implicate Caleb Powers?" Will asked.

"Not directly," Smith said. "I suppose that his saying
that the shot was fired from the Secretary of State's office
and that John Powers gave him the key are sufficient to
involve Caleb."

"Hold on, here, Judge," Berry shouted. "This Youtsey
fellow says that I was in Caleb Powers' office when the shot
that killed Goebel was fired from that very room?"

"Well, what he said was that he used the key to let
you, Combs, Cecil, and Jim Howard into the office just before
the shooting."

"I guess I must have hurried on over to the other
building after the shooting, huh?"

"The prosecution ain't puttin' all their eggs in such a
leaky vessel as Youtsey—pardon my mixed metaphors.
They've got plenty of other testimony, too."

"Such as what?" Berry clearly wanted to hear it.

"Our friend Bill Culton had quite a tale to tell also,

once they'd agreed not to prosecute him. He admitted that he'd helped organize the so-called mountain army—I think you boys are familiar with that. He returned Youtsey's kindness by implicating Youtsey, too. Said that Youtsey had showed him some rifle cartridges that contained smokeless powder and steel bullets before the shooting. Then after the shooting, Youtsey told him that he, Youtsey, had ordered the cartridges from Cincinnati, but was not worried about being found out. Finally, he said that Youtsey asked him to say that the two of them were together in the State House when the shots were fired."

"He don't make Youtsey out to be too bright, does he?"

"That ain't nothin' up side what Culton told on Jim Howard," Smith said. "He claimed that Jim Howard more or less told him that he'd done the actual shooting. Culton said that Jim told him how he got out of the office, what direction Goebel and his bodyguards, Chinn and Lilliard, had come from, and on and on. Accepting what Culton said, Jim Howard's the man that pulled the trigger, but Youtsey's guilty too, just as I explained to you."

"Don't none of this involve me, though," Berry said with some relief in his voice.

"While it doesn't involve you directly, Frank Cecil had some interesting comments, too," the judge said. "He also admitted to helping organize the 'army,' and says that he was told to get 'the toughest sons-of-bitches' in Bell County. By the way, he told the judge that 'there was some boys out on Straight Creek that'd answer that description.' He also said that Powers and Taylor both tried to hire him to kill Goebel."

"How's that involve me?" Berry was puzzled.

"Clearly they're trying to establish a connection between the organization of the mountaineer train and the killing. That's the conspiracy angle."

"I ain't no legal mind," Ike said, "but I fail to see the connection. I went down there on that train, I was amongst 'em the whole time, and I didn't hear no conspiracy talk. Besides that, the fact that not a single soul that was on that train has been indicted seems to indicate that there's no connection between the train and the shooting."

Berry stood, laughing. He slapped Ike on the back, "Too bad you ain't gonna be the judge in any of these trials." Turning to Smith, he said, "Judge, I thank you kindly for your warning and the information. If anything new comes up, I wish you'd send for me, so's you can keep me updated."

"I will, Berry," he said, ushering them to the door. "Now you boys try to stay out of trouble out on Straight Creek."

Berry lagged behind and let Ike and Will go first down the stairs. Realizing that Berry was heeding Smith's warning, Will looked toward the sheriff's office as he entered the downstairs hallway. Without speaking, he indicated to Ike, still on the stairs, that the hallway was clear. Ike and Berry came on down and passed quickly outside and to the buggy.

"What say we go have dinner at Mrs. Pat's restaurant?" Berry asked as they climbed into the buggy.

"Sounds fine to me," Ike said, "but ain't you worried about Ellen or Henry Broughton catching us?"

"Tell you what, Ike. You worry about Ellen, I'll worry about the sheriff." Berry was smiling, but shot a glance back toward the courthouse.

"Who's that leave for me to worry about?" Will joked.

"Mrs. Pat." Ike and Berry laughed in unison.

Will wasn't sure just what the joke was, but he laughed along with them, anyway.

Irene Pat was a small woman who obviously worked hard running her restaurant. Her reddish hair was disheveled, and the apron about her tiny waist was stained with a variety of foods. Still, she managed a wry smile as she approached the table where the three men sat. "Berry Howard," she exclaimed. "I ain't seed you in a coon's age. I heerd that you been to Frankfort."

"I have for a fact, Mrs. Pat." Berry was beaming. "I'd like you to meet Will Elliott, and you know Ike Livingston. They both went down the river to see Governor Taylor got his seat, too."

She smiled at Ike and Will. "Well, didn't do a whole lot of good, in the long run, did it?" Moving on to the business at hand, "What'll it be for dinner, boys?"

While they were eating, Leonard Brock and his young son, Wendell, walked into the restaurant. "Leonard," Ike yelled, "come on over and join us. Did you leave anybody at home out on the Right Fork?"

"I left Lize at the house." Like most of the folks on the Right Fork, Leonard was a relative—his wife, Eliza, was another of Will's sisters. "She wanted to get Wendell and me out from under foot for a while, so she sent us on a wild goose chase."

Leonard pulled two more chairs to the table and he and Wendell joined the group. The meal time passed in good-natured conversation.

When the food was finished, the group moved out of the restaurant. On the sidewalk, Will could see through the window that Berry was having a few parting words with Mrs. Pat. Leonard turned to Ike.

"Say, Ike, I got me some things to look after here in town. Would you mind dropping Wendell off at the house as you go by?"

"Don't mind at all. You come along with us, Wendell, and we'll see you get home all right." Berry emerged from the restaurant, and they all loaded into the buggy.

Crossing the river, Berry winked at Will and glanced quickly at the boy sitting beside him. "Did you ever see one of them hoop snakes?" Berry asked.

"You mean those poisonous devils that hold their tail in their mouth to roll after a man?" Will said straight-faced.

"Them's the ones."

"I hear they're deadly poison and fast, too," Ike added.

"Fast? Why, I've seen 'em form themselves into a hoop three feet across and roll down a hill fast enough to catch up with a jack rabbit." Berry sneaked another look at Wendell and suppressed a giggle. The boy's eyes were as big as saucers.

"I was hoein' corn one time when I seen one rolling down the furrow, straight at me," Will said. "He was on me so quick that it was all I could do to jump out of the way, but he did manage to bite the hoe handle as he went by."

"What happened?" Wendell asked, full of wonder.

"Why, that hoe handle swelled up so quick that it just burst itself all to splinters right in my hand." The whole group allowed their laughter to spill out. The look on Wendell's face said that he still wasn't sure about the deadly hoop snake.

The next stop after they dropped Wendell off was Berry Howard's house. "I appreciate you boys going along with me," he said as he dismounted the buggy. "Now, I have a big favor to ask of the both of you." He hesitated for their reaction. Will let Ike take the lead.

"What's that?" Ike was noncommittal.

"They's gonna be trials over this whole mess," Berry

began. "And while I've got to know what's happenin' at them—who swears to what and such—Judge Smith's advised me not to be seen in attendance. So, I wondered, if I pay your expenses, would you two be willin' to spend some time attendin' court in Scott County when the cases are called?"

"I'd not only be glad to do you the favor, I'd certainly enjoy being there," Ike smiled.

Thoughts of Mary Whittaker being in Georgetown ran through Will's mind. "I allow I might be able to go," he managed to say through a beaming smile. "Lord knows somebody will have to keep an eye on Ike."

Chapter 15

Letter written by Caleb Powers from jail to Robert Noakes

Wednesday, June 20, 1900

The L & N Railroad's regular passenger run puffed into the town of Big Stone Gap, Virginia, on time, at 6:45 p.m. The conductor on this run was glad to see the depot come into sight—it meant that he'd get to spend his first night this month at home. After all the passengers were gone, he finished his duties and dismounted the car, heading for home. As he walked into the station office to file his papers, the station agent looked up from his work.

"Hello, Noakes, welcome home."

"Howdy, Jed," Noakes answered, handing in his passenger manifests. "It's good to finally get here. These long runs ain't exactly the best idea the company ever come up with."

"Not from the conductor's view, anyway. Oh, Bob, a fellow name of Maynor telephoned in here looking for you a little while ago. Do you know him?"

At the mention of the name, Noakes's attention was riveted on the agent. "Yeah, he's my lawyer from back in Kentucky. Did he say what he wanted?"

"Said for you to meet him over at the Taylor House Hotel just as soon as you got in. I didn't tell him nothin' other than that I'd tell you if I saw you."

"Thanks, Jed." Noakes tried to ensure that the distress he felt did not show on his face as he hurried out of the station. Thoughts of his wife and a home-cooked meal were suddenly far from his mind as he made his way down the street. A few days earlier, feeling the heat from the attempts of the press to implicate him in the plot and the calls for his arrest, he had conferred with his attorney. J. C. Maynor had said that he'd try to set up a meeting with William Goebel's brother, Justus, to discuss how Noakes might best avoid prosecution.

Entering the lobby of the Taylor House, he saw his attorney in the hotel office.

"Hello, J. C.," he said as he approached the counter.

"Well, hello Bob." Maynor moved out into the room and took Noakes by the elbow, steering him toward a quiet corner.

"Is Mr. Goebel here?" Noakes asked anxiously.

"Keep your voice down, son," Maynor cautioned,

glancing left and right to ensure they were not being overheard. "He's in to supper just now. Let's step up to my room to wait."

They moved down the hall to Maynor's room. In front of the door, Maynor took one more look around before knocking softly and opening the door. At the desk near the window, a rotund man in his shirt sleeves sat, writing on a tablet. Hearing them enter, the man rose and crossed the room. Noakes judged him to be about 5-feet-8 and weighing around 200 pounds. His pate was perfectly bald, but his head was ringed by long shaggy gray locks. In all, he presented a formidable appearance. He extended his hand to Noakes.

"My name's Kleinmeyer," he said, smiling. "Come in, come in."

Noakes entered the room, looking to his attorney for an explanation.

"Sit down here, Bob," Maynor said. "Mr. Kleinmeyer has a proposition I think you'll find interesting." As Noakes turned away, Maynor slipped out the door.

"I imagine he's gone to tell Mr. Goebel that I'm here," Noakes said as much to himself as to the man across from him.

Kleinmeyer fetched a bottle and two tall glasses from the desk. "Now, Bob," he began, pouring a generous portion of whiskey for Noakes, "I'm told that you might be interested in investing some money in the mineral rights in this country. Is that true?"

Noakes picked up his glass and drained it, glad for the release of tension he knew the whiskey would bring. He had hardly returned the glass to the table before Kleinmeyer was refilling it. "Well," he said, "I ain't gettin' rich as a railroad conductor, and I guess I have named the idea to Mr. Maynor before. If there's any money to be made, I might be interested."

Kleinmeyer smiled a knowing smile. "Well, sir, I can assure you that there's coal aplenty in these hills, and who knows, maybe such as copper and iron, too. You can bet that them that owns the mineral rights will do fine in the years to come. Here's to you and me being two of 'em." He hoisted his glass. Both men drained their drinks.

"I allow you're probably right. I know they's coal around here," Noakes said nervously. He glanced at the door, hoping his attorney would reappear.

The next half hour passed in pleasant conversation. Bob Noakes kept looking to the door, but there was no sign of Maynor.

"Yes sir, there's coal and timber aplenty in old Virginny. In fact, the only thing I see wrong with this country is that it's too damned near to Kentucky to ever amount to anything," Kleinmeyer was still smiling.

"Just what do you mean by that?" Noakes asked. The emotion of being offended mixed with the effect of the whiskey caused his speech to slur slightly.

"Why, ever'body knows that there ain't nothing but hillbilly murderers in Kentucky. Civilized people won't even go over there." His smile was now a leer.

"I'll have you know that I grew up in Knox County, Kentucky, and they's as fine a people there as you'll find anywhere else," Noakes said evenly.

"They assassinated their governor, didn't they?" Kleinmeyer's tone was insulting.

"They killed a man who thought he ought to be governor. I'm as sorry as anybody that Goebel got hisself killed, but no man can trample the rights of the people like he did and expect to live." Noakes was almost shouting.

"Sounds to me like you must be a friend of Finley and Caleb Powers." The leer continued.

"That's a fact, and fine men they are."

"Well, I say you've got cowardly assassins for friends."

Noakes rose quickly from his chair and stumbled toward Kleinmeyer. Catching his balance on the table, "We ain't cowards and we ain't assassins," he roared. "I've took up arms along with my friends to fight for what's right, and I, for one, am willin' to do it again if it's necessary." He was obviously drunk now.

Kleinmeyer clapped his hands together and rubbed them gleefully. As he was about to speak, the door opened and J. C. Maynor entered the room.

"How're you gentlemen gettin on?" Maynor asked sheepishly.

Before Noakes could express his anger, Kleinmeyer spoke. "Doin' fine J. C.—I've got everything we need to hang this man."

Noakes's mouth dropped open as he steadied himself with a hand on the table. "Mr. Maynor, what's going on here?"

Maynor put his hand on Noakes's shoulder. "Now calm down here, Bob. We've just been playing a kind of a joke on you. But it's time to come clean. This man you've been speaking with is Colonel Tom Campbell." He gestured toward Kleinmeyer who was smiling widely.

"It's a hell of a funny joke. J. C., I thought you was workin' for me." He was even more angry now, but frightened, also.

"I am, Bob. I'm trying to help you."

"Now, Noakes," Campbell said, "I want you to understand that I've got enough on you to send you to the penitentiary for the rest of your life. Not the least of which is that you've just now admitted that you were involved in the Goebel killing."

"I said no such thing," Noakes thundered. He hoped the volume of his voice hid the uncertainty in his mind about what he'd actually said in the heat of anger.

"Have you seen the articles in the Louisville papers calling for your arrest?" The leer had returned. "They state that there's already sufficient evidence against you, and I expect that Wharton Golden might just make a statement implicating you when I get back. You're in some big trouble, son."

"I ain't got money to fight this thing." Defeat was evident in his voice, and Noakes was near tears.

Campbell winked at Maynor. "Well, I'll tell you what. As a favor to my friend J. C. here, if you'll do just as we say from here on in, I'll get you out of it without no money."

Noakes collapsed into a chair. He smiled weakly and nodded.

"All right then," Campbell said triumphantly. "Caleb Powers' case is due to be called early next month. You be here in Big Stone Gap, oh let's say, Thursday, next week, and we'll arrange to have you arrested and taken to Frankfort. You may have to spend a little time in jail, but we'll keep that to a minimum."

"It'll look funny if we let him out on bond," Maynor commented.

"You're right. Let's see, we'll say that his wife is sick and turn him out with a guard on him. That'll show how humane we can be, too." Campbell was clearly enjoying this play.

"I got no money to pay any guard," Noakes whined.

"Don't worry about that." Campbell was irritated at having his train of thought interrupted. "They's $100,000 to take care of that kind of thing. You just show up in Georgetown prepared to swear to whatever we tell you. That's all you've got to worry about."

Chapter 16

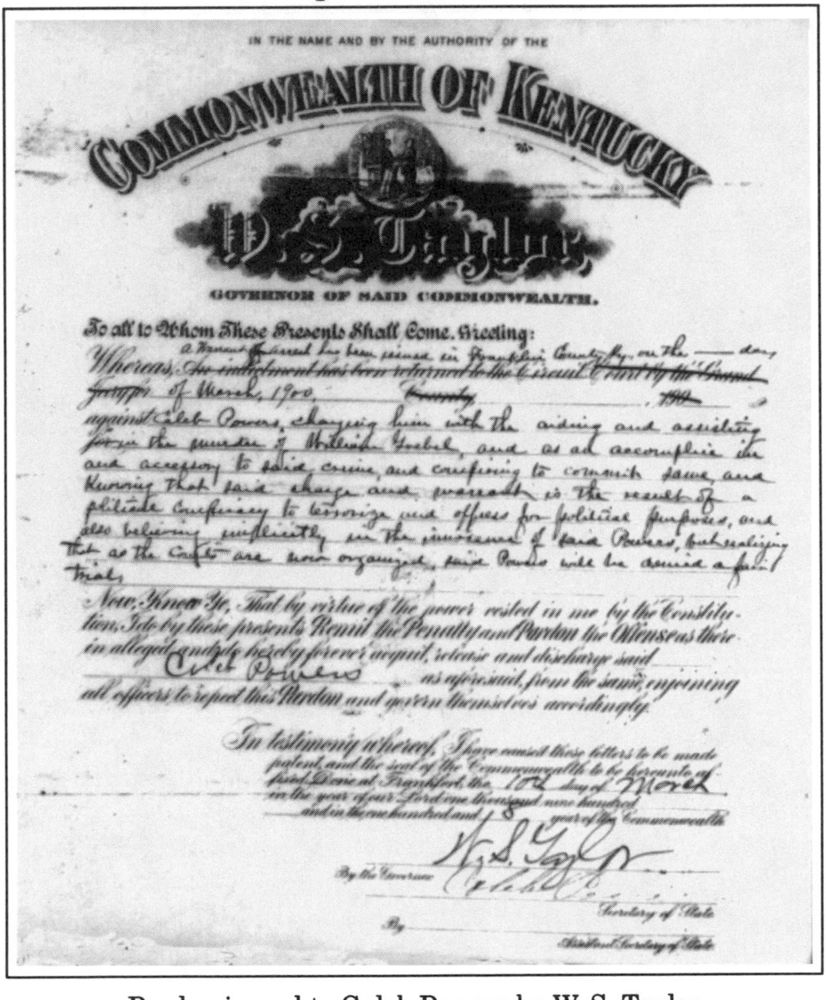

IN THE NAME AND BY THE AUTHORITY OF THE

COMMONWEALTH OF KENTUCKY

W. S. Taylor,

GOVERNOR OF SAID COMMONWEALTH.

To all to Whom These Presents Shall Come, Greeting:

Whereas, ~~An indictment has been returned to the Circuit Court of the~~ A warrant [illegible] has been issued in Franklin County, Ky., on the —— day of March, 1900, ~~County~~, against Caleb Powers, charging him with the aiding and assisting [illegible] in the murder of William Goebel, and as an accomplice in and accessory to said crime, and conspiring to commit same, and knowing that said charge and warrant is the result of a political conspiracy to [illegible] said offices for political purposes, and also believing implicitly in the innocence of said Powers, and realizing that as the courts are now organized, said Powers will be denied a fair trial,

Now, Know Ye, That by virtue of the power vested in me by the Constitution, I do by these presents Remit the Penalty and Pardon the Offense as therein alleged, and do hereby forever acquit, release and discharge said Caleb Powers as aforesaid, from the same, enjoining all officers to respect this Pardon and govern themselves accordingly.

In testimony whereof, I have caused these letters to be made patent, and the seal of the Commonwealth to be hereunto affixed. Done at Frankfort, the 10th day of March in the year of our Lord one thousand nine hundred and in the one hundred and 8 year of the Commonwealth.

W. S. Taylor

By the Governor: [illegible]

Secretary of State

By ——

Assistant Secretary of State

Pardon issued to Caleb Powers by W. S. Taylor

Monday, July 9, 1900

Of all the places to stop in Georgetown, the Wellington Hotel was the classiest. Will was not quite as thrilled as he'd been with the Capital Hotel in Frankfort, but an air of excitement did surround the place. Everybody who was anybody was here for the Caleb Powers trial. Lawyers and journalists abounded, and as they approached the steps, Ike drew Will's attention to a tall, straight man with long white whiskers. "That's Judge Cantrill, standin' there," Ike observed.

"He was one of John Hunt Morgan's company commanders, wasn't he?" Will asked, referring to Kentucky's famous Confederate raider.

"That he was," Ike said. "And, as one of the staunchest Goebel supporters in the state, he's uniquely qualified to hear these trial cases." The sarcasm in his voice was evident.

Will shot ahead of Ike to the desk. "Is George Whittaker registered?" he demanded of the clerk.

The clerk eyed the register. "Whittaker. Uh, sounds familiar . . . oh, yeah, he's here all right."

Ike had joined Will at the counter. "Do you have reservations for Livingston and Elliott?"

"Yep, sure do." He spun the register for Ike to sign. "It's a good thing for you that you made reservations. This is the fullest I've seen it since it was built," he said as Ike signed his name.

Ike and Will turned away from the counter and started up the stairs. "Who's this Whittaker you're asking about?"

Will grinned sheepishly. "I guess I'll have to let you in on it. I met a girl when we were in Frankfort. Her name is Mary Whittaker, and her brother is one of Powers' lawyers. I'm in hopes that she's here with him."

"Why, you sly dog," Ike said with a big smile.

"Now, Ike . . . ."

"I know, I know. You're a big boy now. Well, all right, I won't tease you. But, Berry is paying good money for two sets of eyes and ears here, so I'll not have you swapping spit with some sweet little gal on company time."

Caleb Powers was already in the courtroom when Ike and Will made their way in. He was seated in his position at the defense table in the midst of a dozen or so lawyers headed by ex-governor John Y. Brown. Across the way at the prosecutors' table sat a like number of attorneys. In all, a total of twenty-three of the finest legal minds in Kentucky were ready to do battle. Each was either a Geobelite, an independent Democrat, or a Republican, and so had at least one mortal enemy on the other side. Not to be outdone, Judge James E. Cantrill was as partisan as any and had his grudges with the defense lawyers, too.

Will and Ike found seats behind the defense table. Will twisted in his chair, searching the packed courtroom for Mary. Looking at each face, he noticed that there was not a woman behind him; they were all on the prosecution's side of the aisle. Mary was nowhere to been seen. "Ike," he said turning around, "why are all the ladies on the other side?"

"I heard somebody say that Cantrill ordered them over there," Ike whispered. "I suppose he wants it to appear that Caleb doesn't have any female supporters."

Will looked forward at the cool demeanor of Caleb Powers. "As handsome and composed as he is, I couldn't imagine that he wouldn't have some feminine admirers."

"The judge is just doing his part."

A familiar voice drew Will's attention back to the court. ". . . and, since only five of the 179 witnesses we've summoned are present, we clearly cannot proceed with the trial." George Whittaker was addressing the court.

Judge Cantrill looked sternly over his domain. "The Commonwealth has gone to considerable trouble to assemble us all here at this venue," he said. "Therefore, this court will grant no continuance, but will tender the defendant the compulsory process of this court to secure the attendance of his witnesses."

"Mighty big of 'im, seein' as how the constitution entitles ever' citizen of the state that right," someone behind Will remarked.

The court then took up the examination of prospective jurors, a process that quickly bored Will. "I think I'll get some air," he told Ike.

Outside, he realized how hot it actually was in the courtroom. So many people were jammed inside that all chance of a fresh breeze was eliminated. Will sat on a bench in the shade of a maple tree and closed his eyes.

In a moment, the smell of jasmine filled his nostrils and something brushed against his side. He opened his eyes. "Mary! I was looking for you inside."

Her face was glowing. "Oh, that court stuff is nothing for me to worry my pretty little head about, you know. Besides," she leaned closer and spoke softly, "I only came along in hopes that you'd be here."

"I can't begin to tell you how glad I am," he said, slipping an arm around her waist.

"Behave." She moved quickly and teasingly slapped at his hand. "How about we go back to the hotel and get a glass of lemonade?"

"Best idea I've heard all day," he said, jumping to his feet. "Let me run inside and tell my brother-in-law, and we'll be off." On the way back inside, Ike's remark about company time ran through Will's mind. Racking his brain for a good approach, he slid in beside Ike. Ike turned and as soon as he saw Will's face, he broke into a grin. "Found her, did you?"

"Well, yeah, uh, and I, uh . . . ."

"I understand," Ike said. "Well, go ahead. It's going to take at least the rest of the day to impanel a jury. It's already become clear that unless you're a Goebel Democrat, you ain't fit to sit in the jury box and hear this case. It may take a while to round up twelve of 'em."

"But what you said about Berry's company time . . . ."

"Forget it, son. When the testimony begins, then we'll both have to pay attention. In the meantime, don't do anything I wouldn't do."

Will dashed back outside to where Mary sat. "I got a pass for the rest of the day," he announced.

"As a matter of fact, so have I," she smiled, standing and taking his arm.

The hotel being nearly deserted, they picked the shady side of the porch to have a pitcher of lemonade served. As the waiter poured, Will glanced at the copy of the *Lexington Herald* that someone had left on the table.

"I see that Andrew Robson is appearing in *Richard Carvel* at the Lexington Opera House this evening," he said.

"How about we just catch the train and go see it?"

"A wonderful idea," she replied. "When we finish our drink, I'll run up and change and we'll be on our way.

━◦◦◦◦◦━

Once again, Will found that he had a lot to learn about women. Her "run up and change" turned into the biggest part of two hours before they were actually on the train.

The train ride to Lexington took only about 30 minutes. Will and Mary exited the station and headed west along the street. He had no idea where the Opera House was, but was saved by her suggestion that they have supper in a restaurant they passed.

Although he felt as if he'd had some exposure to women by now, Will had never experienced the kinds of feeling that flowed through him as they ate. His brain was assaulted by the sights and sounds of the lovely lady across the table, and by the time the meal was finished, he was totally under her spell. He had found an opportune moment to ask the waiter for directions, and as he steered her toward the Opera House, he was grasping for words to verbalize his feelings.

"Mary, I know I'm just a dumb old country boy, but... ."

"I'm just a dumb old country girl," she interrupted.

"Look," he feigned anger, "I'm having a difficult enough time with this without your breaking in. I'm attempting to say. . . ."

"Dumb old country boys don't use words like 'difficult' and 'attempting,'" she said gleefully. "If you want to be convincing, try something like, 'This here is hard enough. I'm atryin' to . . .' or something along those lines."

"Well, here's the Opera House, and I still haven't said my piece. I suppose it'll keep until after the play."

"I'm sure that it will." Her smile cut through any frustration that he might have felt.

When the play ended, they walked out into the darkened street. Will realized that he had lost his direction, and had no idea of which way to go for the train station. He was reluctant to let her know that, but by the time they encountered someone to ask, he had no choice but to display his ignorance.

"Pardon me, sir, but could you give me direction to the

train station. We need to get back to Georgetown."

"The station's four squares down that way," the stranger answered, pointing south, "but you ain't going to Georgetown tonight. The last train left at 9:30."

Will was dumb struck. Right at that moment was the first thought he'd had about checking the return schedule. Turning to Mary, he managed to mumble, "We're in trouble. I'm sorry."

The smile had faded from her face. "Well, I didn't think of getting back, either. We'll plead temporary insanity due to love. I do know how to handle lawyers. Let's get to a hotel, and I'll telephone George."

At the Phoenix Hotel, Will registered for rooms on separate floors under the theory that it wouldn't hurt to make the best possible appearance. Meanwhile, Mary placed a telephone call to the Wellington Hotel in Georgetown. Will was waiting in the lobby when she finished.

"Well, he was pretty mad, but I managed to calm him. He's making a lot of noise about being too busy and stuff like that, but it'll be all right. He said he'd tell your brother-in-law what happened." Her smile had returned.

"That part of it is a relief, then. You're in room 14," he said, handing her the key.

The hallway was dark and empty as they came to her door. Without hesitation, she turned and put her arms around his neck. Kissing him lightly, she said, "Will, this has been the most eventful night of my life. I've never known anybody that I'd rather share such adventures with. I love you more than ever."

"Well that's the strangest thing. You know, that's just exactly what I was trying to say when you kept interrupting me," he said as he wrapped her in his arms.

※

"Well, what'd I miss?" Will tried to make the question as light as Ike's glare was hard.

"What'd *I* miss is probably a better question. Just you wait 'til your sister finds out about this." Ike was trying to be serious, but the twinkle in his eye gave him away.

"Some day we ought to have a talk about what you wouldn't do, you know that? Really, what happened in court?"

"Not much. They went through the 24 men called regularly from the jury wheel. Cantrill sent the sheriff's deputies out to drag in talesmen and then interviewed each of them in private afore he'd let the lawyers at 'em. He sent the ones that didn't suit him away. I guess they had to meet his personal standards afore we could see if they met the State's."

"That don't sound right to me," Will mused.

"I asked one of the lawyers about it this morning. He said that Kentucky law allows no review of the jury selection process, so Cantrill's got nothing to worry about from any higher court."

"So we're ready to start the trial?"

"They began late yesterday afternoon. With twelve good, solid Goebel Democrats in the jury box, Governor Brown moved that the court dismiss the case due to the pardon that Governor Taylor had issued to Powers. Cantrill dismissed that out-of-hand, of course."

"So what happens now?"

"Testimony begins. And you better sit up and pay attention."

"I've got no choice. George sent Mary home as soon as we got back here." His voice displayed his unhappiness.

Ike assumed a sympathetic posture. "I'm sure that doesn't make you happy, but perhaps it's best in the long run."

"How's that?"

"For one thing, it'll help you keep your mind clear for the work at hand. For another, it's the most profound thing I could think of to say."

"Thanks for the thought," Will managed a smile.

The opening arguments for the prosecution soon occupied all of his attention. Tom Campbell used his commanding voice to declare that the Commonwealth would show beyond all doubt that William Goebel died as the result of a huge Republican conspiracy, that the bringing of the mountaineers on January 25th was a part of that conspiracy, that Caleb Powers was the primary organizer of the conspiracy, that the fatal shot was fired from Powers' office, and that the state militia was called out to protect the conspirators.

"Does all that sound familiar?" Will whispered.

"It's the same accusations the press came out with right after the shootin', ain't it?"

The state's first witness caught Will's full attention. The prosecution called Meade Woodson, the civil engineer who'd drawn the chart Will had studied. The chart showing the path of a bullet from the Secretary of State's office to the hackberry tree was offered into evidence. Then Rob Franklin asked Mr. Woodson to explain the chart to the jury. As the engineer rattled off heights and distances, Will tried to follow the logic, but was not able to keep up. He turned his attention to the jury and saw confusion on their faces. Leaning closer to Ike, he whispered, "I've spent hours studying that chart and can't understand his testimony. What chance does the jury have?"

Ike did not take his eyes from Woodson as he answered. "He said that the bullet was 4.52 feet above the ground at the point where Goebel fell. How many inches is that?"

"A little more than 54," Will replied after a quick calculation in his head.

"Is that what you got when you worked it?"

"More or less. Listen." Will hushed Ike as Governor Brown asked Woodson how accurate that 4.52 foot figure was.

"I never said it was accurate," Woodson replied. "It is only approximate."

Ike's eyes lit. "Didn't he just say that his testimony ain't worth nothing?"

"Seems like he could have made a stronger case," Will replied.

A procession of doctors came to the witness stand to verify that the shot that struck William Goebel came from his right front, at a slight elevation. The testimony was that the wound in Goebel's chest was 52.25 inches above his heel. When the doctors had finished, Colonel Jack Chinn, who was with Goebel when he fell, testified that he, also, thought the shot came from the right front. As Colonel Chinn stepped down, the expectant faces of the prosecuting attorneys told Will that they hoped the jury believed that the bullet found in the hackberry tree was the exact one that had felled William Goebel, and that it had emanated from Powers' office window.

The days flew by in the sweltering July heat. It seemed that the state was determined to convict Caleb Powers by public opinion. Tom Campbell, who was acting as assistant to the Commonwealth's attorney, took over the trial and made frequent plays to the gallery with little or no interference from

Judge Cantrill. At the dinner break on one particularly humid and breezeless day, Will suggested to Ike that they play hooky that afternoon.

"What'd you have in mind?" Ike asked.

"I hear the blue gill are bitin' down at Elkhorn Creek," Will said enthusiastically.

"You dig some worms, and I'll cut us some poles." Ike's eyes were lit up like a six-year-old at Christmas.

After a few hours on the creek bank, Ike laid his pole aside and flopped on his back in the shade. "Let's take a break."

Will came over and sat beside him.

"What's your best impression of how this trial is going?"

Will leaned back against the trunk of a tree. "Well, I came down here knowing that Caleb Powers was not guilty of doing anything to cause Goebel's death. But, since we've been here, I've become even more convinced of his innocence. That letter to Gen. Collier is the only real evidence they've introduced against him."

"You mean the one in which he asked Collier to order those militia companies to Frankfort?"

"Yeah," Will said, "that comment about 'we must have these men and guns' hurt him, I thought. But, anyway, it looks like to me that they'll have to acquit him."

Ike let out a wry laugh. "You're dreamin' son. Didn't you read that headline that said his conviction was a 'political necessity' in view of the special election this fall?"

"But, it takes proof beyond a reasonable doubt to convict, and the prosecution is a long way from that."

"It don't matter. They ensured conviction when they selected the jury. Then, just to be on the safe side, what witnesses haven't been intimidated into testifying have been bribed. He's convicted, all right, and they'll have to convict at least two others, too."

"How's that?" Will asked.

Ike sat up to look into Will's eyes. "Well, they can't hang pulling the trigger on Caleb, so they'll have to convict somebody of that. Then, to avoid having to establish direct contact betwixt Powers and whoever they put as the shooter, they'll have to have somebody as a middleman. You mark my words, son. There'll be at least three convictions afore this thing is done."

When they returned to the hotel late that evening and handed the mess of fish over to the kitchen staff, Will felt refreshed in body as well as in spirit.

On July 17th, the eighth day of the trial, the prosecution detonated the first of its fireworks. Finley Anderson was called to the stand. Anderson, the telegraph operator at the hotel in Barbourville, testified that Caleb Powers had told him that, "they'd kill off enough Democrats to create a Republican majority in the legislature." He also said that Powers had said, "If we can't get Goebel killed and it is necessary, I'll do it myself."

"It's interesting, Ike, that nobody else was around to overhear either of these damning remarks," Will observed.

"This is happening just like the examining trial. It's what they call 'confession' evidence that can't be contradicted by any other party, because no other party heard it."

"Do you still think they'll convict him on that kind of evidence?"

"Did I ever tell you about the time that wagon wrecked in front of my house?" Will turned his attention to the trial.

On cross-examination, Mr. Anderson admitted that he'd been to Cincinnati looking for a job and ended up in the offices of one Colonel Tom Campbell.

"It's sure interesting that he'd find his way to Campbell's office looking for a job, isn't it?" Will commented.

"That's apparently the story they've decided to use."

"What do you mean?" Will asked.

"'Job' just sounds better than 'bribe,' don't you think?"

Will's interest perked up again that afternoon when the civil engineer was recalled to the stand to furnish some additional information. On cross-examination, Governor Brown really attacked the validity of Woodson's chart.

Governor Brown had requested that Woodson produce the pin he had inserted in the bullet hole in the tree to determine the point of origin. Mr. Woodson had a piece of wire with him, saying that the actual pin he had used was lost, but the one he had "was just like it." Twisting the thin wire in his fingers, Governor Brown asked Mr. Woodson, "Then I understand you to concede that this instrument did not correctly point to the place whence the bullet was fired."

To which Woodson replied, "I would not rely on that. I made no such test as to determine with mathematical accuracy. I never do things with that loose method. If I had wanted to determine with exact accuracy, I would have used my theodlite."

"What's a theodlite?" Ike asked.

"A telescope-type deal they use in surveying," Will answered.

"Then why in the world didn't he get us the exact mathematical answer, if he could have?" Ike's voice was full of wonder.

The next morning brought more of the same kind of testimony from William Culton. He said, in reference to bringing the mountain crowd to Frankfort, that Powers had told him that, "they'd give the legislature 30 minutes to settle the thing or else kill the last damn one of them." After Colonel Campbell refreshed his memory, Culton recalled that Governor Taylor had told him, "Powers is a damned hot-headed fool," and that the ribbon badges were handed out so that "in case of trouble or killing, we would not kill our own men."

At a break in the testimony, Ike asked Will if he'd noticed the sheaf of papers Colonel Campbell held in his hands.

"I have," Will said. "What do you suppose that is?"

"I don't know, but he uses it to refresh a witness's memory when they don't remember what they're supposed to say."

On cross-examination, Culton admitted that prior to the trial, he'd said that he "did not know a single word or act that would incriminate Powers," and that he'd "never heard a word about harming anybody." In addition, the defense forced Mr. Culton to admit that he'd been indicted for forgery and embezzlement, thereby impeaching his character.

In the afternoon session on July 20, Robert Noakes calmly walked to the witness stand and took a seat. As an excited stir went through the ranks of the prosecuting attorneys, he glanced toward the defense table, looked directly at Caleb Powers, and nodded slightly. Noakes then proceeded to testify that Caleb and John Powers had both asked him to procure smokeless powder steel bullets prior to January 25, 1900. In response to a question about a private conversation he'd had with Caleb, Noakes said that Powers had said, "Bob, I understand that you have two men in your company who, if you would tell them you wanted a certain man to be killed, you would find him a corpse the next morning."

When the prosecution finished, Will leaned over to Ike. "Whose turn is it to cross-examine?"

"Judge Simms, I think. They've got so damned many lawyers up there, it's hard to keep 'em straight."

"I hope it is Simms," Will mused. "He'll break up that pack of lies pretty good."

"We'll see," Ike said as Judge Simms began his cross-examination.

"Mr. Noakes," Simms said, "when was the last conference you had with the prosecuting attorneys?"

"Last night at the Wellington Hotel," Noakes answered.

"Who was present?"

"Colonel Campbell and my personal attorney, J. C. Maynor."

"In the presence of Colonel Campbell, you wrote out your statement?" Judge Simms seemed puzzled.

"No, sir." The confidence that Noakes had first displayed seemed to be ebbing away.

"Who wrote it out?"

Noakes squirmed in the witness chair. "I had a talk with Colonel Campbell, and after we had talked, he called in a stenographer and dictated what the stenographer was to write. After he did so, I read over what he had dictated."

"How much more clearly could he say that Tom Campbell scripted his testimony?" Ike asked.

A little later in the examination, Judge Simms came to the heart of the matter.

"You've been arrested in this case, have you not?"

"Yes sir."

"How long did you spend in jail?"

"Two nights."

Judge Simms frowned. "After two nights, you were allowed out on bond?"

"No, sir. I was released with a guard."

"You've been arrested and spent two nights in jail." Simms paused for a moment, thinking. "Have you been indicted?"

"No, sir."

Judge Simms then went for the throat. "Did you ever conspire with anyone to kill Goebel?" he asked.

Noakes glanced toward Colonel Campbell, then said, "No, sir. My evidence before the jury is sufficient to show how far I went."

"Did you have any conference with Caleb Powers or anybody else for the purpose of killing Goebel?"

"Not any further than my evidence shows."

"Well, Judge Simms got the best of that exchange, I thought," Will said as they walked out of the courthouse.

"What you think don't matter," Ike said. "It's what the jury thinks that counts. We'd best get to the restaurant before it fills up with the suppertime crowd."

The interior of the Wellington Hotel was bedlam. The little town of Georgetown just was not equipped to deal with the volume of people who had descended on it for this trial. In line at the entrance to the restaurant, Ike heard the manager say that they only had a table for four open.

"We're a party of four," a man behind Ike shouted. Moving between Ike and Will, he took each by an elbow and forged into the restaurant. The manager gave them a harried look and showed them to the vacant table.

"I'm Irvin Cobb," the stranger said, shaking hands. "This here is my friend and partner in crime, Charley Michaelson." Will knew right away from Cobb's ready smile that they'd get along.

"You're here for the trial, I guess?" Will asked Cobb.

"Who isn't?" Cobb laughed. "I'm a reporter for the Louisville *Post*, and Charley here is with the Hearst papers in New York."

"Wow," Ike said, "I'm impressed."

"You can be impressed with Charley if you like," Cobb laughed. "I'm just a Kentucky country boy, and besides, this is the first big trial I've ever covered."

"Be that as it may, I'd be interested in the opinions of you professional observers," Ike said.

Charley Michaelson spoke first. "Aside from the obvious rehearsed testimony, I thought Mr. Fetter's testimony was most interesting."

"He's the man that printed the Taylor badges, isn't he?" Will asked.

"Yes," Michaelson said. "He was coming up the walk behind Goebel when the shot sounded."

"I remember him," Ike said. "He said that they had the spot where Goebel fell marked wrong, didn't he?"

"That's right. He allowed it to be about six feet farther

away from the Capitol steps than Woodson's chart shows."

Will was quick to respond to that. "If Mr. Fetter's right, that chart isn't worth much, is it?"

"I think that's why they've tried to sweep his testimony under the carpet," Cobb said.

"What did you gentlemen think of that Steffy boy's story?" Ike asked as he poured iced tea for all hands from the pitcher.

"He's the telegraph runner that saw a rifle sticking out of the window?"

"That's right," Ike said. "If he saw a rifle barrel out the window, I don't understand why they haven't made more of that."

Cobb threw back his head and roared with laughter. "Because, he identified the wrong window. To do any good for Campbell, the rifle barrel has to be in Caleb Powers' office window. Nowhere else will do. I'll bet he wishes he had a witness who saw a rifle barrel in the Secretary of State's office window."

※※◎◎※

The next morning, Colonel Campbell got his wish. The prosecution called George F. Weaver to the stand. From the waiting room, a short stocky man with a sandy mustache emerged. Will noticed that the prosecuting attorneys glanced at each other expectantly as Weaver sat in the witness chair. He said that he was a barber from Denver, Colorado, who was currently working as a traveling organizer for the Woodsmen of the World, and just happened to be in front of the State House in Frankfort when Goebel was shot.

"What's Woodsmen of the World?" Will asked.

"It's a fraternal organization. Hush up," Ike whispered.

Weaver, turned loose by Colonel Campbell to tell his story, declared that he was on the pavement west of the fountain next to the hackberry tree when the shot was fired. He heard the bullet impact the tree and then glanced toward the office building, just in time to see "what he took to be a man's hand on a gun barrel, taking it back into a window." He was quite sure that the gun was in one of the windows of the Secretary of State's office. Weaver thought it was the one in the southwest corner of the building.

The lawyers at the prosecutor's table were all smiles. Here, at last, was their definitive proof of the shooter in Powers' office.

Behind him, Will heard Charley Michaelson whisper to Cobb, "In every big murder trial at least one volunteer perjurer turns up. This fellow here is a candidate for the job."

"What makes you think so?" Cobb asked.

"After a few of these trials, you'll be able to tell. I'll make a little bet I'm right."

As Judge Simms stood to begin his cross-examination, Will could see that Simms didn't believe a word Weaver had said. After some preliminary questions, Simms went after Weaver.

"How long had you been in the Capitol Square before the shot was fired?" he asked.

"I would say between one-half to three-quarters of an hour."

"What were you doing all that time?"

"Just strolling around."

Judge Simms scratched his chin. "You were from a half to three-quarters of an hour strolling along the walk until you heard the shot?"

"Possibly so." Weaver was quite unperturbed.

"What kind of weather was it that day? A pleasant day?"

"I really don't remember just what kind of day it was."

"It was a nice day for strolling?" Judge Simms' frustration was evident.

"I don't remember anything very remarkable about it."

"What is your best recollection about the weather that day?"

"I really have no recollection about it."

"Did it rain?"

"I don't remember if it did."

Judge Simms circled the witness stand to face the jury. "Did it snow?" he shouted.

"I think not. If it did, I don't remember."

"As I recall, it was colder'n hell and blowing snow that morning," Ike commented. "You'd think anybody that was there would remember the weather that day."

"Yep," Will agreed. "I saw a Frankfort lawyer with his hands in his own pockets."

When they came downstairs for breakfast early the next morning, Will and Ike found Cobb and Michaelson already seated at a table. As they pulled up chairs and poured coffee, Cobb smiled and pitched a newspaper to Ike. "Charley wins his bet," he grinned.

"About Weaver?" Ike asked, unfolding the paper.

Neither Cobb nor Michaelson bothered to answer. The headline said it all: "The Strolling Barber Strolls to Jail."

The story went on to detail how it had been discovered that at the time of the Goebel shooting, Mr. Weaver had, in fact, been more than 150 miles away, organizing a lodge at the other end of the state. "Well," Ike said, "so much for that witness. What does the prosecution do now?"

"Colonel Campbell's still got Wharton Golden up his sleeve," Cobb said.

"Yep, and I allow that Campbell was up half the night writing out what Golden will say, too," Will quipped.

Wharton Golden walked to the stand with a confident look in his eye. As he sat, Colonel Campbell shuffled through his sheaf of papers until he had placed the one he wanted on top. Thus prepared, he turned to question the witness.

Campbell had to refresh Golden's memory several times, but the witness did remember that he'd heard Charles Finley say, " . . .and if the legislature doesn't listen, we'll kill the last damned one of them," and Caleb Powers reply, "By God, that's just what we'll do."

"He's slipped up here," Will said. "He's allowed a third party to hear one of these damning conversations."

"Not quite," Ike mused. "That third party has fled the state and ain't about to show up here to confirm or deny the conversation."

On the cross-examination, Judge Simms got Mr. Golden to admit that he knew nothing about any conspiracy, and had, in fact, supposed that any killing would happen in the legislative halls. Then Judge Simms went through a now familiar routine about just how it had happened that Arthur Goebel had found a job for Golden.

While Golden was explaining that, Ike leaned over to Will. "Does it strike you as a little strange that the Goebel boys keep finding jobs for these fellows that helped kill their brother?"

"You said it. 'Job' is a better word than 'bribe.'"

After Golden's testimony, the state rested its case. On Monday, July 30th, the defense made its opening argument and called Caleb Powers to the stand as its first witness.

Powers readily admitted to helping organize the crowd of people that came from the mountains to Frankfort on January 25th. He said that he had done so at the request of Governor Taylor, and that Taylor had "also suggested that if the men came armed, they had a constitutional right to do it." He denied all the private conversations that Finley Anderson, Robert Noakes, William Culton, and Wharton Golden had claimed to have had with him, and accounted for his whereabouts at the times the alleged conversations took place. Powers testified that the only meeting at which he had heard talk of any kind of violence was when Sheriff Burton of Breckenridge County had exhibited some rifle cartridges and said, "a few of these exploded in the right places would settle this thing." Powers explained that he understood that Burton had died in the interim and hence could not testify.

As they left the courthouse, Will heard a shout from behind.

"Will, Ike, wait up."

They turned to see Irvin Cobb running down the steps. He caught up with them but did not stop where they were waiting. "We'd best get over to the restaurant before it fills up," he threw over his shoulder.

Ike and Will quickened their pace to keep up with Cobb as they headed for the hotel. Once seated in the restaurant, Cobb had time to converse. "Well, what did you boys think of Powers' testimony?"

"There were no surprises," Ike said. "He said about what I expected—denied everything."

"I was impressed with his sincerity," Will added. "He certainly made me believe that he was telling the truth."

"The real fun will begin in the morning when Campbell cross-examines him." Cobb was displaying his usual good-natured smile.

Ike took a break from the steak he'd been sawing with a knife. "If Campbell tries his usual tactics of putting words in the witness's mouth and confusing the issue, Caleb Powers might just prove to be his match."

"Powers is nobody's fool, he's made that clear," Cobb agreed.

"Irv," Will said while slowly swirling the ice in his glass, "I heard a story I'd like to ask you about, if you don't mind."

Cobb placed his fork on the plate, giving Will his attention. "What's that?"

"I heard that right after Goebel died, you made an effort to discover what his last words actually were. Is that true?"

"That's a fact," Cobb burst into laughter. "We reporters didn't much believe that 'fearless and brave' stuff, so I decided to see if I could discover the facts—not for publication, you see, but just because I wanted to know.

"It seems that Goebel was fond of oysters. On the day he died, he was begging the doctor to let him have his favorite meal. They knew that he couldn't last long anyway, so they ordered him up an oyster.

"The fact is, that just before he slipped into a coma, he spit it out and said, 'Doc, that was a damned poor oyster.'" All three men laughed heartily.

"That'll look fine carved in the base of the statue," Ike giggled.

"What statue?" Will asked, wiping the tears from his eyes.

"The statue memorializing William Goebel that you know damn well the Democrats are going to put up."

The courtroom was packed to overflowing as the sheriff escorted Caleb Powers in. Word had spread that today's activity would be spiced by a battle of wits between Powers and Campbell. Farmers had left tobacco standing and merchants had locked their stores to attend today. They didn't have long to wait before the battle was joined. As soon as Powers was seated, Colonel Campbell attacked.

"The only time you heard anything about bringing about the death of Senator Goebel or threatening him in any way was at the meeting you have told us about?"

The expression on Powers's face did not change. "I said that is the only meeting in which I had ever heard threats of any character," he replied evenly.

"And the only man you ever heard say anything of that nature is dead. Is that right?" Campbell was referring to Sheriff Burton and directed that remark at the jury.

"I said that I don't know whether he is dead or not." Powers looked straight into Campbell's eyes.

Campbell looked away. "It is your information that he is dead?"

"Yes, sir."

"And that man was sheriff of Breckenridge County, I understand."

"Yes, sir."

"Could you give us the names of all those who were present at the meeting where Mr. Burton proposed the assassination of Governor Goebel?" Campbell was looking at Judge Cantrill.

At the defense table, Governor Brown had heard enough. Leaping to his feet, he addressed the court. "We object to this mode of interrogation. The Colonel has just asked about the assassination of Mr. Goebel being suggested at the meeting. My recollection is that Mr. Goebel's name was not used; that a cartridge was displayed and that Sheriff Burton suggested that it would be a remedy."

Campbell glanced at the judge. "Perhaps I am wrong, and on reflection, I think the Governor is right." He appeared somewhat deflated.

"The first round goes to the defense," Will whispered.

"And without any help from the judge, either," Ike replied.

The remainder of Powers' cross-examination went off in much the same fashion. Campbell exhibited how he had earned his reputation for intimidation and insinuation. He employed every weapon in his arsenal in an attempt to put words in Powers' mouth or trap him into some admission of guilt. He failed. Powers maintained his composure throughout the long examination, and bested Campbell at every test of wits. Despite Campbell's tactics, Powers made no disrespectful replies and fell into none of Campbell's well-laid traps.

Following Powers to the stand was a line of well over 100 witnesses for the defense. Powers' attorneys left no point of the prosecution's case unquestioned as the dog days of August crawled by in the cramped courtroom. At last, the defense rested its case and the closing arguments began.

The courtroom drama surrounding this trial was the focal point of the news in Kentucky, if not the nation. Each attorney intended to take full advantage of his time in the limelight. Many of the words that fell from the speakers mouths' were directed at neither judge nor jury, but rather were pointed political barbs aimed at the heart of one of the opposing attorneys. In all, the summaries occupied a solid week as a cap to the five weeks of testimony. After Judge Cantrill had issued his instructions, the jury filed out of the courtroom—Caleb Powers' fate, at last, in their hands.

Ike and Will wandered outside to enjoy some fresh air in the shade. Seated on a bench under a huge old elm, Will said, "Ike, how do you suppose those jurors can keep straight all the testimony and arguments they've heard?"

"You heard Cantrill's instructions. They don't have to worry about testimony or arguments, or truth or justice for that matter."

"What do you mean by that?"

"Why, hell, son, after those instructions, if they failed to convict Powers, they'd be in contempt of court." Ike's voice was edged with sarcasm.

"I didn't understand that part the judge tacked on to the seventh instruction." Will looked to Ike for an explanation.

Ike pulled the printed instruction sheet from his vest pocket. "The part Cantrill added defines the phrase 'unlawful act'. So now, here's the whole thing, as amended." Ike's eyes fell to the paper.

> "The Court instructs the jury that if it believes from the evidence, beyond a reasonable doubt, that the defendant, Caleb Powers, conspired with W. H. Culton, F. W. Golden, Green Golden, John Powers, John Davis, Charles Finley, W. S. Taylor, Henry Youtsey, James Howard, Berry Howard, Holland Whittaker, Richard Combs, or any one or more of them, or with some other person or persons unknown to the jury acting with them or either of them, to do some unlawful act, and that in pursuance of such conspiracy or in furtherance thereof, the said Henry Youtsey, James Howard,

Berry Howard, Holland Whittaker, Richard
Combs, or some one of them or some other
person unknown to the jury acting with them
or with those who conspired with the defendant,
if any such conspiracy there was to do the
unlawful act, did shoot and kill William Goebel,
the defendant is guilty, although the jury may
believe from the evidence that the original
purpose was not to procure or bring about the
death of William Goebel, but was for some other
unlawful and criminal purpose.

"The words, 'some unlawful act,' as used
in this instruction, means some act to alarm,
to excite terror or the infliction of bodily harm."

Ike wadded the sheet in his fist and flung it with
disgust.

"In other words, Cantrill says that if Powers organized
the train ride, as he openly admits he did, then he's guilty of
murder."

"But, surely, after the defense they put on, you don't
still think they're going to convict him, do you?"

Before Ike had a chance to reply, a shout came from
the courthouse steps. "Jury's comin' back in!" Ike pulled his
watch from it's pocket in his trousers.

"After six weeks of argument and testimony, it took
'em less than 40 minutes to reach a verdict. Does that answer
your question?" Ike snapped his watch shut as he stood.

Caleb Powers was being led back into the room as Ike
and Will found their seats. As he passed near the rail, a young
lady handed Powers a rose bud. He did not speak, but smiled
his thanks as he sniffed the flower and faced the court.

"Have you made your verdict, gentlemen?" Cantrill
asked.

The chairman of the jury slowly rose. "We have," he
said as he unfolded a slip of crumpled paper. His eyes slowly
fell from the judge to the paper and he read: "We, the jury in
the case of the Commonwealth of Kentucky versus Caleb
Powers, find the defendant guilty as charged and fix his
punishment at imprisonment for life in the state penitentiary."

Chapter 17

Letter submitted as evidence, purported to be
from Gov. Taylor to Jim Howard

Tuesday, November 6, 1900
Election Day

Ike closed Bradshaw's door as quickly as possible, not only to conserve the heat being generated by the stove, but also to avoid the wrath of the gathering should he let in too much cold air.

"Why, hello, Ike. Welcome to the second annual Gubernatorial Election meeting," Will said as Ike moved toward the stove. Will and Chas Whitt scooted their chairs aside to make room for Ike in the circle around the stove.

"Howdy, boys," Ike said, glancing around the circle at Chas, T. J. Ashby, Berry Howard, Leonard Brock, and finally back to Will. "You plannin' on electin' a governor ever' year, are you?"

"It were a year ago tomorrow we was sittin' right here talkin' over Taylor's chances again' Goebel, you'll recollect," T. J. said.

"That's right," Berry said, "but the picture's a little different this time. With Goebel and his election law both dead and in hell, we've got a real chance to get our man, Yerkes, elected."

"Well, I ain't one to tell no good after the Democrats, but I'll have to say that Beckham did right by repealin' that damned Goebel election law. That makes the picture some brighter," Bob Bradshaw allowed from behind the post office grill.

"Some," Berry agreed, "but the adverse feeling from all these trials ain't helping our party's cause any."

"The Democrats have tried Powers, Jim Howard, and Youtsey and convicted 'em all. Three out of three, ain't they?" Chas asked.

"Yeah, they are, but their witnesses keep proving to be liars, and I allow the appeals court will overrule the Powers and Howard verdicts," Berry said.

"Who's a liar?" T. J. asked.

"That Finley Anderson from down at Barbourville filed an affidavit last week stating that Campbell and the Goebel brothers had bribed and intimidated him into lying on Caleb," Berry said.

"His conscience must've started bothering him," Ike laughed. "I allow we'll see more of that kind of thing afore it's done."

"Ike, you and Will was at all of the trials, fill us in on what happened at Jim Howard's trial," Bob urged. Whitt and Ashby nodded in agreement and leaned forward expectantly.

Ike walked the legs of his chair around so that he could lean back against the wall. Pulling his feet up to a rung of the chair, he clearly relished being the focus of attention.

"Well," he began slowly, "Jim didn't ask for a change of venue, so Judge Cantrill heard the case in Frankfort. That didn't make much difference—the jury selection and Cantrill's rulings went about the same as for Powers in Georgetown. Worked out about the same, too. After hearing a mass of testimony, it took the jury about 30 minutes to find him guilty and sentence him to hang."

"I heered that any judge other than Cantrill woulda throwed it out of court in the first place," T. J. commented.

"Cantrill let Campbell do pretty much as he pleased," Ike agreed. "In his opening argument, Campbell stated that Jim Howard had killed those two men down in Clay County— said it as a fact. Since he ain't been convicted of either one, that, as I understand it, should have caused a mistrial."

"Not with Judge Cantrill on the bench, though," Will commented.

"What kind of evidence did they have on Howard?" Chas asked.

"As far as physical evidence goes, it was a laugh. They produced a letter hand written on Western Union letterhead addressed to Jim Howard at Manchester. Someone had scratched out the Western Union heading and written in 'Executive Offices, W. S. Taylor, Governor.'"

"What'd it say?" Bob asked.

Ike smiled. "It said that if Jim was interested in 'the performance of a certain act,' he should come to Frankfort right away and report to one Henry Youtsey at the Executive building."

"Who signed it?" Chas inquired.

Ike smiled again. "It was unsigned. Can you imagine that they had nerve enough to ask anybody to believe that was a real document? What a joke."

"What kind of testimony did they hear?" T. J. asked.

"Same kind they had on Powers," Ike replied. "And from the same sources, too. Culton and Wharton Golden supplied the most damaging testimony."

"Now you want to talk about a liar," Leonard laughed. "Some of them that knows him told me that come feedin' time, Wharton Golden has to get his neighbor to call the hogs for him." That brought a laugh from everyone.

"What'd they say?" Bob had put the mail away and nudged into the circle.

"Golden told more or less the same story he'd told before about John Powers giving Youtsey a key to Caleb Powers' office. He also said that Jim had told him that Goebel's bodyguard, Chinn, had run like a rabbit after the shooting.

"Now, Culton really came up with some good stuff. He told as how Jim had bragged to him about having done the shooting. Said that Jim showed him some smokeless cartridges and even explained how he managed to get out of the building and grounds afterwards."

"I liked the part about the lining up on a tree, though," Will said. Ike shot him a glare as the others' attention shifted to Will.

"Your hackberry tree?" Chas asked.

"Culton said that Jim Howard had told him, 'If you want to make a dead shot on a moving object, take a sight on a tree, and when the object passes the tree, you will make a dead shot every time.'"

The whole group snorted in unison. "My Pa taught me that you'd best lead a moving target if you plan to hit it," Chas said.

"You'll not hit no Johnny Rebs by aimin' at trees," T. J. said.

"It does lend credence to the idea of the bullet that hit Goebel ending up in the hackberry tree, though," Ike commented.

"And that's just exactly why they had him say it," Berry added.

"If the shot that hit Goebel came from the second or third floor, like some said, that'd explain the steeper angle, wouldn't it?" Leonard asked.

"I've thought about that, and yeah, it would explain the angle, but then the bullet would never have made it to that tree," Will said. "It would have gone into the ground well short of the tree."

"Will, did you ever make heads or tails out of that engineer's chart?" Chas asked.

"I think I finally decided what was bothering me about it. According to Woodson's figures—and mine, too—a bullet would fall about eight-tenths of an inch per foot between the window sill and that tree. But the doctors said that the bullet came out of Goebel's back almost two inches lower than it entered his chest."

"So what?"

"So," Will went on, "either Goebel's chest was over two feet thick, or the bullet had to come from a steeper angle."

"Or the bullet deviated in its trajectory." Berry's eyes were closed in deep concentration.

"The doctors ruled that out, Berry," Will explained. "They were all quite sure that the bullet went straight through him."

"So what are you sayin'?" Bob asked.

"I'm saying that, in my opinion, that bullet in the hackberry tree was a plant." Will glanced at Ike, hoping for confirmation of such a bold opinion.

"If it was a plant, how and when did it get in the tree?" Chas was clearly puzzled.

"That's a hell of a good question," Will admitted. "I have to confess that I can't figure it out."

"But you still think it's not the bullet that hit Goebel?" Bob asked.

"I've never seen a man's chest that was over two foot thick. So, I've got to think that the bullet that went through Goebel was falling at a steeper rate. If that's the case, it would have hit the ground before it got to the hackberry tree."

"I'm a mite confused, son," T. J. said. "Are you sayin' that you don't think the bullet they found in the tree came from Powers' office window?"

"No, I'm satisfied that the bullet found in the tree was fired from Powers' window. But, I don't see how a bullet fired from that window could have gone through Goebel's body at the angle a bullet did and still end up in that tree."

"So the bullet in the tree ain't the same bullet that killed him?" Berry spoke with his eyes still closed.

"I just can't figure how it could be," Will sighed. After a pause, he added, "although I'll have to admit that if it's a plant, it's a damned clever one."

"Well," Ike said, attempting to draw the group's attention back, "I've heard all the testimony, and I'm confused about a lot of things."

"According to what I read in the paper, it's cut and dry," Chas said. "When I read a Democrat paper, Powers, Jim Howard, and Youtsey are as guilty as sin, and when I read a Republican paper, they're as innocent as newborn lambs."

"In both cases, they're ignoring whatever part of the evidence doesn't fit the chosen theory," Will said.

"You know," Ike said seriously, "I'd come to that exact same conclusion."

The whole group was interested. "What, for example, are you boys talking about?" Bob Bradshaw asked.

"Well, like Will was just saying, if you want to believe that the bullet in the tree was the identical bullet that hit Goebel, you'll have to ignore the angle through Goebel's body. Conversely, if you want to think that it ain't the same bullet, you have explain how it got in the tree."

"In the same way," Will added, "if you want to believe that Jim Howard did the shooting, you have to ignore the witnesses who say he was at the Board of Trade Hotel at the time the shots were fired."

"There's lots of questions, either way," Ike said. "They brung in a lot of testimony to show what a dead-eye shot Jim Howard is. I was sitting there wondering: if he's so good, why didn't he just shoot Goebel in the head and be done with it."

"Too far?" T. J. suggested.

"About 100 feet. I ain't the best shot in the hills, but I think I could lay a rifle up on a window sill and hit somebody in the head—no further than that—myself," Ike remarked.

"The conspiracy aspect is what confuses me," Chas said. "To hear the prosecution tell it, the train that went from here was a big part of the conspiracy. That'd involve, what, 1,000 people?"

"And that's only the start," Berry added. "You've got to add in everybody that wore one of them badges, including 42 Republican members of the House and 18 senators. Also, according to the prosecution, the state militia is in on it, so throw in another three to four hundred of them."

Will leaned forward in his chair. "You know, boys, on

the conspiracy angle, the fact that there wasn't nobody in the State House yard the morning Goebel was shot is mighty curious to me."

"And you ain't the only one, either," Ike added. "The prosecution in all the trials made a great show of pointing out that all the 'mountain army' seemed to be elsewhere that morning."

"So what?" T. J. asked.

"So they were clearly trying to show that somebody—who was in on the conspiracy—ordered 'em out of there just in time."

All eyes turned to Berry Howard for an answer. Will was remembering that Berry had insisted that he and Ike get out of town that morning.

Berry seemed content to cradle his chin in his hand and study the red-hot sides of the stove.

"It is confusin', ain't it," T. J. commented to break the silence.

"It is for a fact," Ike agreed. "Sometimes I think it's better to believe whatever you want and go on."

"That's fine for us," Will said earnestly, "but for the judges and juries of the courts to do that. . . . Well, it's disgusting."

The group again fell silent as Will's voice trailed off.

"What about Youtsey's trial?" Chas asked, breaking the spell.

Ike and Will both started to speak at once. Their eyes met; Will deferred to his elder and motioned Ike to go on.

"Strangest damned thing you ever saw," Ike began. "Right off, the prosecution called Arthur Goebel to the stand. He started to tell about an interview he'd had with Youtsey the day of the arrest. Then Youtsey threw a fit."

"Threw a fit?" T. J. said.

"Youtsey jumped to his feet, pointed at Goebel and shouted, 'It is untrue; there's not a word of truth in it. I never said a word to that man in my life, nor he to me. Never.'

"Well, sir, let me tell you about the scramble in that courtroom. Deputies were trying to get control of Youtsey, and spectators were clawing for the door. Youtsey was fighting off those trying to hold him and screaming, 'I hope God may kill me dead if I ever said a word to that man or him to me. I never heard his voice and he never heard mine.'

"His pretty wife was there, and she said, 'You have run him crazy—I hope you are satisfied,' to Tom Campbell. Youtsey was still trembling and screaming. He said, 'Let me go, let me go. I tell you Goebel is not dead. All the demons in hell couldn't kill him.' Finally, the policemen overpowered him."

"What the hell was the judge doing all this time?" Chas asked.

"He'd been pretty content. At that point, Cantrill said, 'If the defendant don't behave himself, Mr. Sheriff, you put a pair of handcuffs on him.' Then, cool as you please, the judge says, 'Proceed with the trial.'"

"You're pullin' my leg, ain't you?" Bob said.

"I'm tellin' it exactly like it happened, ain't I Will?"

"That's just the way it happened," Will said. "By this time, Youtsey was stretched out on the floor like he was in a coma, and the lawyer started to ask Mr. Goebel another question."

"One of Youtsey's lawyers jumped up," Ike took the lead back. "He says that he thinks the court ought to recess. Cantrill considered on that and said, 'Yes, I think it is due to you, counsel.' Youtsey's lawyer, Crawford his name was, didn't bat an eye; he says right back, 'I think it is due the defendant, sir.'

"I'm not sure Cantrill caught the sarcasm of that, but anyway, he simply allowed that he was willin' to overlook some of these outbursts, seein' as how Youtsey'd been in jail and all.

"Finally, Rob Franklin, God bless him, said that he had no objection to postponing the trial until nine the next morning. So that's what they did."

"What happened then?" Ike had the whole group under his spell.

"Court met and adjourned each morning for the next four days. Youtsey's doctors said that he was in no shape to stand trial. On the fifth day, Cantrill said he'd postpone no more. He ordered Youtsey brought in and the trial to proceed. They carried Youtsey in on a bed, set him down and went right on with the testimony."

"With him in a fit?"

"If you couldn't have seen his chest move when he breathed," Ike said, "you'd have thought he was dead."

"Was he really in a conniption fit?" Bob asked incredulously.

"Tom Campbell didn't think so," Ike replied. "He pointed out that Youtsey ate whatever they put afore him and answered the call of nature by himself. Campbell allowed that Youtsey was shamming."

"So they just went on with the trial?"

Will nodded agreement. "And, that ain't even the worst of it. When the right time come, they called him to the witness stand."

"Nah. They didn't?" Bob shook his head in disbelief.

"Sure did," Will said. "They put question after question to him, him all the while as much dead as alive, but he said nothing—if he heard the questions. If his lawyers had any chance of gettin' him off, it went out the window when he threw his fit."

Ike cut off Will's explanation. "The prosecution made a pretty strong case agin' him, anyway," he said.

Will shot a sidelong glance at Ike. "If you was to go to a funeral, you'd want to be the corpse, wouldn't you?" Ike took the hint and fell silent.

"I thought the State proved pretty conclusively that Youtsey did order smokeless powder, steel bullet cartridges from Cincinnati, and that he'd discussed various schemes for killing Goebel with several different people." Seeing that he'd hurt his brother-in-law's feelings, he added, "You agree, Ike?"

Ike looked up from the floor. "Yeah. Also, they showed that Youtsey ran down the stairs to the basement of the office building yelling that Goebel was shot just about the same time that the shots were heard outside."

"How long did it take the jury to decide on that one?" T. J. asked.

"Just a few minutes," Ike replied. "They sentenced him to life."

Berry Howard let the legs of his chair drop to the floor. "But, they didn't establish no conspiracy, did they?" he growled.

"Not directly; but—as Ike predicted down in Georgetown—they've got a shooter in Howard, an organizer in Powers, and a go-between in Youtsey," Will said.

Ike looked pleased that Will had remembered his thought. "Berry, do you think that those three convictions will be enough to make Tom Campbell and the Goebel boys happy?"

"It probably would be if they all stand up. But, I expect that we're going to elect a Republican judge to the appeals court today; and if so, that'll give us a majority on that bench. It figures then, that they'll overturn both Jim Howard's and Powers' verdicts.

"What about Youtsey?" Bob asked.

"He didn't appeal," Berry said. "The Democrats take that as evidence that he's guilty. Anyway, if the convictions don't stand up, they'll have to try Jim and Caleb again. They've lost the testimony of Finley Anderson and the strolling barber, so they'll need some new witnesses."

"After all this time and so many trials, where are they gonna find new witnesses?" T. J. was puzzled.

"Just indict a few." Berry spat the words.

"What do you mean by that?" Chas asked.

Berry heaved a sigh and made an obvious attempt to calm himself before he spoke. Leaning back in his chair, he shifted to a comfortable position. "Well, most prosecutors use a grand jury inquest to develop evidence, but that ain't good enough for our friend, Colonel T. C. Campbell. Nosiree, the good Colonel gets the grand jury to bring an indictment agin' somebody and then uses that as a lever to elicit testimony."

Will leaned back to get out of the line of Berry's sight. He turned to his left and whispered in Ike's ear, "Sounds like he knows what he's talking about, doesn't it?"

Ike did not take his eyes from Berry's face, only nodded his head slightly to acknowledge Will's observation.

"But, it's been almost a year now," Chas said. "A man would think that they'd have all the indictments in by now."

"A man would think that," Berry allowed, "but, it ain't necessarily so when it comes to Colonel Campbell and his tactics."

"That's another thing that's been bothering me," Ike said. "Berry, do I understand correctly that the testimony of one alleged conspirator can't be used to convict another alleged conspirator?"

"The way Judge Smith explained it to me," Berry replied, "is that any story told by an accused conspirator has to be corroborated by somebody who's not accused before the jury can believe it." A strained look crossed Berry's face.

"Then that means that the testimony offered up by

Golden and Culton ain't worth bothering with, don't it?"

"Right. They're both indicted as accessories, and the conversations they say they had with Jim Howard and Caleb are not verified by anyone else. That's one of the reasons I'm pretty sure the appeals court will reverse the decisions."

"So, you think there'll be more trials?" Chas asked.

"I'm sure they'll try Caleb and Jim again," Berry said. "They've let Whittaker, Combs, and John Davis go, so I doubt they'll bring any of them to trial. By allowing them bond, they've as good as said that they've got nothing on them."

A sharp pain shot through Will at the mention of the Whittaker name. It'd been more than four months since their night at the opera house, but Mary had not been far from his mind in that time. He had looked expectantly for her at the Howard and Youtsey trials, but her brother had simply said that it had been decided that she'd best stay at home. The sudden realization that conversation had stopped brought him out of his thoughts.

"Will, I said what was that question you were wanting to ask about the keys to Powers' office," Ike repeated.

"Oh, uh," Will brought himself back to the present. "I was just wondering how many years the same locks had been on those doors, and so how many people there might be that'd have had access to a key."

"That's another good question," Bob said.

"There's still lots of good questions," Ike added. "They brought in a couple of men from Howard's home in Clay County to testify that he was down there bragging about having done the shooting."

"And the defense brought in a bunch of witnesses to testify to the bad character of those men," Will added.

"In his summary argument, Campbell pointed out that those of bad character are just the ones Howard would have associated with and bragged to. If men's lives weren't involved, it'd be right comical," Ike said.

"It ain't funny to us under indictment," Berry muttered, causing everyone's smile to fade.

"Well," T. J. Ashby said, broaching the subject that everyone had been avoiding, "thar's still you up the prosecution's sleeve, ain't they?" All eyes turned to Berry.

Berry Howard slowly got to his feet. Not even the slightest flicker of his usual good nature was evident in his face as he towered above the small frame of the old man. Will observed that Berry's hands were tightly clenched as he rose, but quickly relaxed into a more normal position. "I'll say this," he said in a husky voice, "they'll have to put me on trial or just forget me. By God, they'll not intimidate Mrs. Howard's baby boy into testifying agin' anybody." He cleared his throat and settled back into his chair. "They've got nothing on me, so I've nothing to fear," he added as he sat.

Will wondered whether Berry felt as confident as his words indicated. He understood that Berry probably felt no guilt, but in his heart, he knew that innocence hadn't shielded Caleb Powers.

Picture of
Will Elliott's
sisters–
Sallie Elliott,
front right;
Ellen
Livingston,
front center

Sallie Elliott
Howard

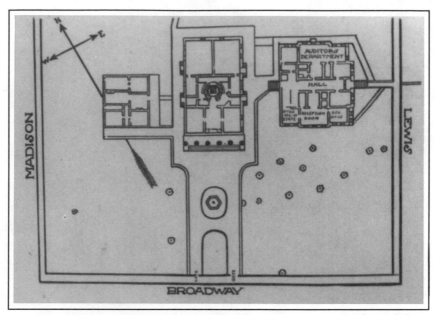

A Plan of the
Capitol Grounds

View from the
hackberry tree
Photograph by John Snell.

Holland Whittaker
  Robert Noakes
Henry E. Youtsey
  Captain John Davis
Berry Howard
  James B. Howard
Some of the Others
Indicted for the
Murder of William
Goebel.

Judge James E. Cantrill

Statue of William
Goebel erected in
1904. Old Capitol
in background
Photograph by
John Snell

Brass plate in the
sidewalk right
behind the statue of
William Goebel
at the
Old State Capitol
Photograph by
John Snell.

Chapter 18

Seal of Kentucky—Revised
Minneapolis Journal, February 1, 1900.

Wednesday, December 10, 1901

"Berry Howard, halt in the name of the law."
Berry turned to find himself staring into the business end of Henry Broughton's Colt revolver. "What's the problem, Henry?" He tried to sound casual.

"I've got a warrant here for your arrest. You're wanted in Franklin County for the willful murder of William Goebel." The sheriff motioned to his deputy without taking his eyes off Howard. "Newt, check him for weapons."

The deputy ran his hands quickly over Berry's body and nodded to the sheriff. "Let's get on down to the jail," Broughton said. "A man from Frankfort will be along soon to escort you down the river."

"Henry," Berry said as they entered the courthouse, "would you mind if I stop by the clerk's office for a minute?"

The sheriff looked puzzled. "I reckon not, but what do you want in there?"

"Well, you know," Berry said with a smile, "that when a man goes to the pen he loses his vote."

"Yeah, what of it?"

"I'm gonna change my registration from Republican to Democrat. If one party is gonna lose a voter, I'd rather it be them than us."

Chapter 19

Telegram sent by Caleb Powers arranging train trip

Wednesday, April 16, 1902

Berry Howard was seated at the defense table when Ike and Will first entered the courtroom at the Franklin County Courthouse. He was engaged in earnest conversation with his team of lawyers, headed by Colonel D. G. Colson and Judge A. B. Smith. Colson's face was turning red as he spoke to Berry. Although their seats were only two rows behind the rail, they could not overhear the conversation.

"There isn't the same fever of excitement here as there was at the other trials, is there?" Will observed.

"Well, it's been two years since Goebel was shot, and Berry Howard is a small fry, anyway," Ike said glancing around at the crowd. Although the courtroom was full, spectators were not hanging from the rafters as they had been at the previous trials.

"The prosecution sent the first team, though," Will pointed out, spotting Campbell, Rob Franklin, and Franklin County attorney James Buford across the aisle.

"Yeah, they did," Ike agreed. "And there's the standard twelve solid Goebel Democrats in the jury box."

Judge Cantrill rapped his gavel and called for order. The prosecution called the civil engineer, Meade Woodson, as its first witness. "As many times as they've been through this, you'd think the jury would already know what he's gonna say," Will said.

"It's interesting that they start off Berry's trial by still trying to prove that the shot was fired from Caleb Powers' office."

Adhering to the established pattern, the next witnesses were the doctors who had attended Goebel, and then Eph Lillard who was on the walk just ahead of Goebel when the shots were fired. All of their testimony was just as at previous trials. Will's attention started to wander.

Then the court called William Lyons to the stand. "Who's he?" Will wondered, not having heard that name before.

"Shut up and we'll find out."

Lyons testified that he was the doorkeeper of the House of Representatives during the 1900 session. He stated that on January 25th, Berry Howard and Bill Culton had approached the door and demanded admittance. Lyons said that Berry had told him that he had a right to enter because he was an ex-member. When he refused to admit Culton, an ugly scene ensued in which Culton threatened to kill him and pulled a pistol. According to Lyons, Charles Finley appeared at that time and took Howard and Culton away, saying, "Lyons, don't get in trouble with these people, for they will hurt you. They are desperate men."

The morning dragged by for Will, with little interesting testimony. Just when he was starting to think that he'd heard all the witnesses before, another new name was called—Frank Burch. Will remembered him from the train.

Colonel Campbell stood and silently eyed Burch for a long moment before he spoke. When he did begin, his voice was soft.

"Where do you live?"

"Knox County," Burch replied.

"You were in Frankfort on January 25, 1900?"

"Yes, sir."

"How did you get here?" Campbell's voice was just slightly louder.

"I came on a special train from Barbourville at the request of Captain John Powers," Burch recited emotionlessly.

"You stayed on after most of the mountain army went home?"

D. G. Colson shouted, "Your Honor, we object to the use of the term 'mountain army' with reference to the men who came to Frankfort on the train."

Colonel Campbell turned and smiled at Colonel Colson. "I apologize if that term offends you, sir. I considered it as common usage to describe that group. Would you have any objection to 'mountain crowd' as a description?"

"Do you suppose Campbell will allow the judge to make any of the rulings this time around?" Will whispered to Ike.

"Yes, sir. I stayed until after Goebel was shot," Frank Burch continued without further prompting.

"Where were you when the shots were fired?"

"I was in the red brick building to the left of the State House."

Campbell turned to look past the witness at the jury. "In the building that's commonly called the Agricultural Building?"

"I believe that's what they call it, yes."

"Did you see the defendant, Berry Howard, in there?"

"Yes, sir, I did."

Campbell walked around the witness chair, positioning himself so that Berry was in his line of sight as he faced Burch. "What was he doing?" The volume of his voice increased another few decibels.

"When the shots were fired, Berry Howard was holding the door of the building shut. Me and some of the boys ran over there to see what was happening. We'd been expecting trouble all week and figured that it was starting, but Berry wouldn't let us out."

Campbell smiled across the witness at Berry. "Did he say anything?"

Frank Burch frowned in deep concentration. "I don't remember that he did."

Campbell moved a few steps so he now faced Judge Cantrill. "To refresh your memory, did the defendant not say, 'Son, you can't go out until we get further orders'?"

Burch's face brightened. "Yes, sir, that's just what he said."

"Tell the jury what happened after that. Take your time and tell it in your own way." Campbell smiled benevolently.

Burch adjusted his position in the chair. "Well, after that, somebody said that they ought to have a captain over us—that somebody ought to be in charge. Somebody nominated Berry Howard, and he was elected captain over us. He sent some of the boys upstairs to get the guns and then posted us at the windows of the building."

"There were guns stored in there, were there?"

"Yes, sir. Like I said, we'd been expectin' trouble all week, and we had the guns in there, at the ready. After the shooting, Berry Howard posted different ones of us at the windows with guns."

"When did you leave Frankfort?" Campbell adjusted his position once again so that he was facing the defense table.

"I went home on the train on Friday after the shooting."

"That'd be the second of February?"

"I guess so." Burch seemed bored at that question.

"Who was on that train with you?"

"A bunch of the boys that come down the week afore.

Fifty or sixty of us, I guess." Burch paused a moment, then added, "Berry Howard was in charge of the car."

Colonel Campbell glared at the witness. "No more questions," he said as he took his seat.

D. G. Colson rose slowly from his chair at the defense table. He moved toward the witness stand until he was within a few feet of Frank Burch. "Who all did you say was in the Agricultural Office with you?" he began.

Burch shifted uncomfortably in his chair. "The best I can remember, Tom McDonald and Bob . . . ."

"Bob who?"

"McDonald. And Zack Steele and Mr. Howard." He spoke quickly.

Colson moved to the other side of the stand so that he now faced Judge Cantrill. "Which Mr. Howard?"

Burch twisted his body in response to Colson's new position. "Berry Howard. And it seems like Frank Cecil was in there, too. I won't say for certain that's all I knew. There might have been some others."

Colson moved a step back from the witness stand. "Are you positive however, that this defendant was there?" His voice was a little louder than it had been on previous questions.

"Yes," Burch answered.

"I thought everybody knew that Berry was upstairs in the State House when the shots were fired," Will whispered to Ike.

"They do," Ike said. "Colson's just making the point."

The prosecution called John Alford to the stand. On direct examination, he testified that Berry Howard was in charge of the train car in which they went home. When Mr. Franklin finished, Judge Smith stood.

"What do you mean when you say that Berry Howard was in charge of the car?" he asked.

"I mean that he was the man that satisfied the conductor," Alford said evenly. "We didn't pay any fare."

"Mr. Howard was not the conductor on the train?"

"No, sir."

"Or brakeman or engineer?"

"No, sir."

"Captain of a company or colonel of a regiment?"

"No, sir."

Judge Smith turned as if to return to his seat at the

table, then turned back to the witness. "Did Mr. Howard conduct himself civilly?"

"Yes, sir."

"You did not see him do anything unusual?"

"No, sir."

Taking note of the puzzled look on Will's face, Ike leaned close to him. "They're still trying to tie the train ride into a conspiracy," he said. "Judge Smith's just makin' sure that the jury hears that Berry was not an official on the train."

Will and Ike exchanged looks of surprise at Colonel Campbell's next move. He stood and faced the gallery. "The Commonwealth calls Clorinda Howard," he boomed.

"Clorinda? What does she know about anything?" Will wondered aloud as she took the stand and identified herself in response to Campbell's questions.

"Be quiet, and we'll find out," Ike said without moving his eyes.

"Did you at any time have any conversation with Berry Howard shortly after Senator Goebel was shot?" Campbell asked.

Clorinda's face clouded in concentration. "Well, yes, of course I . . . we had a conversation together at Sim Bailey's house."

"Could you tell these gentlemen what that conversation was?" Colonel Campbell smiled as he gestured toward the jury.

"Yes, sir," Clorinda began hesitantly. "Mr. Bailey, he come in and said to me one evening that the news had come into Pineville that Berry Howard was the man that killed Goebel. It appeared like I kept studying about it, and it bore on my mind. You see, they had all come down here, a whole lot of them—three or four train boxes full—and they all come back and he did not come at that time. It passed on—well it was three or four days, anyway—and then he returned and come in there. Of course, I always liked Berry and love him yet. I said to him, says I, 'Berry Howard, I have heard bad news on you,' and he said, 'You have?' and sort of laughed. I said, 'Yes, and I may as well tell you as anybody else.' Says I, 'They tell me you are the very man who killed Goebel.' He said, 'I didn't do it, I didn't kill him,' but he put his hand in his pocket and pulled out three cartridges and said, 'This is the very sort of cartridges that killed Goebel. When they fire, they don't make any smoke.'

"I never axed him any more questions about that then. I just quit." Clorinda paused, a confused look on her face. Then, she went on. "He said then that what kept him so much longer that he was back down here fixing up to pay the board bills. That is all I know." She sank back in the chair and heaved a sigh.

"You got all that?" Will whispered.

"It sounded rather rehearsed to me," Ike said. "She just ran it off—who said what and all—just a little too smoothly."

"Smoothly?" Will said. "I was just sitting here wondering what the hell she said."

"Well, I mean it was like she knew what she was supposed to say, but she just couldn't get it in the right order."

By the time they finished discussing her examination, Colonel Colson was questioning Clorinda. "How did your husband happen to die?" he was saying.

"We object to that question," Mr. Franklin shouted.

Judge Cantrill glanced at Rob Franklin, then turned his attention to Colonel Colson. "I don't think that is material here."

Colson took one step toward the bench. "That is not the case; it is material. I will make it competent."

"Very well. I will indulge you, on that assurance." Judge Cantrill stroked his whiskers as he settled back.

Colson walked over to the table and studied some papers for a few moments. At length, he let the papers fall to the table and turned back to the witness. "When was it that you first saw Berry Howard after Senator Goebel was killed?"

Ike and Will turned to each other. "Why did he just let that go about her husband's death?" Ike asked. Will simply turned his palms upward.

"To whom did you first tell this conversation which you say you had with Berry Howard?" Colonel Colson was saying.

"I told it to my husband and when I told it to him, he said 'Now, you will be a witness agin' Berry Howard in Frankfort.' I said, says I, 'Daniel, if that is so, I'll never tell it again.'"

"To whom did you next tell it?"

"I never would tell it no more. He told it. He'd get to drinkin' and he'd tell it the best he recollected and then he'd say, 'Clorinda, now tell it.' And I would say, 'No, I said I would not tell it, and I ain't going to.'"

It appeared that Colson was working hard to contain his laughter. "When was the next time you heard him tell it to anybody?"

"Ever' time he got to drinkin', he would tell it." She paused, then added, "And he got to drinkin' pretty often, too."

"Of course you can name some of those he told it to?" Colson was clearly enjoying this scene.

Clorinda folded her arms across her chest and stuck out her chin. "Now, I ain't gonna tell any more," she said defiantly.

From the prosecution table, Campbell said, "Tell everything. The court will tell you when not to tell. That is all right."

Colson spun around to address the judge. "I think they turned the witness over to the defense," he roared.

Judge Cantrill leaned forward and nodded at Colson. "Yes, and I think you are entitled to interrogate her without interruption."

Still seated at the table, Campbell lowered his head and made a show of shuffling through some papers.

Judge Cantrill waited a few moments and then consulted the clock at the back of the court room. "It's pert nigh supper time," he announced with a rap of the gavel. "Court adjourned 'til tomorrow morning."

At the restaurant that evening, Ike and Will were seated with a drummer named Melvin Ballenger from Chicago. After some introductory remarks, the conversation turned, as usual, to politics and the trials.

"Well, up in Chicago," Ballenger said, "all we hear out of Kentucky is about the conspirators being convicted. The way I got it, Powers and that Jim Howard fellow have both been convicted twice now. Ain't once good enough for you Kentuckians?"

Ike laughed. "You see, Mr. Ballenger, the appeals court has a Republican majority. So, the Democratic-packed juries convict 'em, and the appeals court reverses the decision. It might go on like that for some time yet."

"I guess I understand that," Ballenger said, "but in view of the recent convictions of Powers and Howard, and with Youtsey in the state penitentiary all this time, why are they still bringing new indictments and trying people?"

"We have our ideas," Will said. "They indicted Frank Cecil and Zack Steele just to force them to testify. In the case of that Ripley fellow—and Berry, too—I'd say that they both refused to offer any testimony agin' anybody. So, it's either try 'em or let 'em go. The State ain't about to just let 'em go, so they have to bring 'em to trial."

"They tried that Captain Ripley, but I never did get straight on who he is, or what they had on him," Ballenger said.

"He was captain of the militia company that guarded the Governor's mansion right after the shooting," Ike answered. "As for what they had on him, he was supposed to have known a lot of damning things on Governor Taylor. But, if he did, he wouldn't tell it to the prosecutors, so they brought him to trial."

"And he got acquitted? That doesn't make sense," Ballenger said.

"The evidence was so thin, not even a packed Goebel Democrat jury would go along with 'em."

"The Goebel press found a way to make the best of it, though," Ike remarked. "They made much of the fact that the innocent get acquitted while only the guilty get convicted."

<hr />

"Your husband mentioned this in the presence of Rankin Slusher?" Colson was smiling broadly as he continued with Clorinda to begin the day's session. The same shabby dress she had worn yesterday looked as if she'd slept in it.

"You must not ask me too many questions. I ain't going to tell any more. I know you want to get me . . . I ain't going to tell it no further." Clorinda sat back with an air of satisfaction. Will thought that her resolve had stiffened overnight.

After a few minutes of questioning in the same vein, Colson tired of the game and changed directions. "Mrs. Howard, have you talked with any of the attorneys in this case since you came to Frankfort?" he asked.

"No, sir."

"None of the attorneys in this case had any talk with you about this case this morning?" Colson's voice was tinged with anger.

"No, sir," Clorinda said emotionlessly.

Colson walked to the defense table and turned slowly back to face the witness. "Did Colonel Campbell talk to you about this case this morning? Colonel Campbell is one of the attorneys."

A look of surprise came over her face. "Is he? He never said nothing to me—only just he said to testify the truth—to answer the truth."

"When did he talk to you?" Colson was animated again.

"It ain't been just a few minutes ago."

"Didn't you say a while ago that none of the attorneys had talked to you?" Colson's smile had returned.

"I don't know the attorneys." Clorinda was getting a little ruffled.

"Do you know that gentleman?" Colson asked, pointing to Campbell.

Clorinda squinted and leaned forward. "I don't know him, only they told me," she said.

"All right then, have you met him?"

"Yes, sir. They told me he is Mr. Campbell. That's all I know about it."

"Did he talk to you about this case?" Colson's voice rose.

"He just told me to testify the truth." She glanced at Campbell as she wrung her hands in her lap.

"Tell the jury what he said to you."

She glanced quickly at Campbell. "I told him that it was just what I aimed to do—tell nothing but the truth."

"Have you told all you know about this case?" Colson appeared satisfied that he'd made his point.

"Yes, sir, I have."

"The Commonwealth calls Judge A. B. Smith to the stand."

Ike and Will looked at each other, amazed. "Why in the world are they calling Berry's own lawyer to testify against him?" Ike said.

"They sit around the courthouse and talk," Will said. "I guess they want some of the gossip repeated here."

"You have said previously that Berry Howard tried to get you to come to Frankfort on January 25, 1900?" Rob

Franklin asked.

"Yes, sir."

"What did you say to Mr. Howard about it?"

Judge Smith twisted uncomfortably in his chair. Glancing at Berry Howard, he said, "I think that when I told him that my business was such that I could not come, he said that it would not cost me anything to come down here. But I declined to come."

"Did you see Berry Howard after he came back?"

"Yes, sir." Smith turned toward the defense table. "He was in my office one day along with C. W. Short, W. D. Rollins, and Judge Bingham."

Franklin consulted his notes and then returned his attention to Smith. "Will you relate the conversation?"

"Mr. Howard came in my office. He and Judge Bingham commenced talking something about the murder of Senator Goebel or the contest. Mr. Howard said, in the line of conversation, that the man Whittaker who was arrested—I think the words he said were, 'If we had seed him, we might have got some more of them' or words to that effect."

Franklin let his notes drop to the table and smiled at the witness. "What else was said at that time?"

Judge Cantrill leaned forward. "About what?" he boomed.

Franklin looked quickly at the judge, then back to Smith. "To refresh your memory, didn't you hear Berry Howard, there at that time and in that presence, say that he was there at the time Goebel was shot with 'Nancy'—or 'Betsy'—across his knee and he saw Goebel, how he squirmed after he fell, and that he knew exactly who shot him?"

Smith's face turned red. He scooted to the edge of his chair and shouted. "No, sir. If I heard any such statement, I don't remember it."

Franklin recoiled a step as if the force of the reply had pushed him back. "Are you saying that you didn't hear it or that he didn't say it?" he managed to ask.

Smith took a deep breath. "I never heard it. I could not say whether he made such a statement or not," he said with attempted calm.

"Didn't you see Mr. W. D. Rollins a short time after Mr. Goebel was shot and did you not talk the matter over with him and repeat to him that you had heard Berry Howard make that statement, and say that the Commonwealth would give $1,000 to know what Berry Howard had to say?" Franklin regained the step toward the witness.

"I think so, about that substance." Smith looked slightly deflated.

"After being before the grand jury, you were noted of record as one of the counsel for Mr. Howard?"

"Yes, sir."

Franklin smiled broadly at Judge Cantrill. "No more questions," he said abruptly and sat down. Colson slowly rose to his feet.

"Where was it that this conversation occurred?" he asked softly.

"At my office in Pineville." Smith's voice matched Colson's.

"Who was present?"

"I remember Judge Bingham, Judge Short, and W. D. Rollins."

Colson retreated to the table and sat down. "What was the conversation that occurred there?"

"As I remember it, Judge Bingham was standing over from the table where Howard was sitting, and they commenced talking about the assassination. Berry said that if they had seed the parties who arrested Whittaker, they would have got some of them."

Colson whirled. "Did he say 'we' or 'they'?"

Smith frowned. "I'm not sure."

"Did Judge Rollins say anything?" Colson asked, leaning back.

"He may have, I don't know."

"What did Judge Bingham say? Anything?"

"I don't remember a word he said. The conversation was between Mr. Howard and Judge Bingham."

"Where was this remark you made to Judge Rollins about $1,000?"

"I remember that it was in front of the courthouse."

Colson's face brightened. "No one else was present?"

"No, sir."

"Thank you, Judge Smith," Colson said as he smiled at Campbell.

The remainder of the day was consumed with the parade of familiar witnesses for the Commonwealth. The only point of interest Will could find in the mass of testimony was the effort the prosecutors were putting forth to convict Caleb Powers. At supper that evening, he said as much to Ike and Melvin Ballenger.

"It seems to me," Ballenger said, "it's the same thing we were talking about before—as if they're afraid that the previous convictions of Powers and Howard won't stand up, and they have to keep piling up new evidence."

"I agree with that, and I allow that the most recent convictions won't stand," Ike said.

"What makes you so sure?" Ballenger asked.

"There's a Republican majority on the appeals court," Will reminded him.

"Yes, and the Democratic judges didn't help their own cause much with the dissenting opinion they published the last time, either." There was fire in Ike's voice.

"How's that? I didn't see it. What did they say?" Ballenger was interested.

"Once you wade through all the legal mumbo-jumbo," Ike said, "what they said was that since Powers was guilty anyway, justice was served and so any errors of law made no difference. The general public, even many Democrats, didn't care much for the minority appeals judges taking that kind of stance."

"It seems odd for the appeals court to pass on the facts of the case as well as the applicable law," Will said.

"Let it never be said that the Commonwealth of Kentucky spared any effort to bring the guilty to justice," Ike said, his voice laced with sarcasm.

Just as they were leaving the table, Clorinda Howard entered the room in the company of a man Will and Ike did not know. The familiar faces evoked a broad smile from Clorinda. "Howdy, boys," she grinned.

Ike did not return her smile. "Clorinda," he spat, "I've been wantin' to ask you something about your dealing in this business. Do you know what collusion is?"

"Yes sir," she replied pertly. "I seed one on the railroad up at Pineville one time. It was a terrible mess."

Clorinda's face went blank as all within hearing exploded with laughter. It was evident that she had no idea of what they found humorous. Even as angry as he was, Ike Livingston threw back his head and roared with mirth.

As they approached the courthouse the next morning, Will thought that half the men from Bell County were hanging around outside. When the prosecution started calling its witnesses, he learned why they were all in attendance. Grant Mason testified that Berry Howard had arranged for him to come to Frankfort on the train on January 25th and paid the bills for the entire group. Will Ingram told a similar tale and related some of the stories circulating around Pineville. Ike and Will took great interest when Isaac Hopkins, one of Henry Broughton's deputy's, took the stand. After the preliminary questioning, Colonel Campbell asked Hopkins where he was when the shot was fired.

"I was sitting in a chair in the private office of the Secretary of State," he said calmly. An excited murmur went through the crowd.

"In what building?" Campbell asked, looking around the gallery.

"In the Executive Office building." Hopkins, too, cast a puzzled look around the room.

Campbell appeared puzzled, then the cause of the excitement apparently dawned on him. He soon had Hopkins clarify his whereabouts to indicate that he was in the waiting room located between the offices of the Governor and the Secretary of State. Upon that disclosure, the gallery quieted.

In response to Campbell's questions, Hopkins told of conversations with Berry Howard, Wharton Golden, and Frank Cecil. The bulk of the testimony indicated that all these men knew of the shooting in advance and were involved. He even stated that Berry Howard had told him, "not to worry, Taylor will pardon us out" of any trouble. A hush fell over the room as Colonel Colson rose to cross-examine.

"Are you sure that at the time Senator Goebel was shot, you were in the room between the office of the Governor and the office of the Secretary of State?" he asked quietly.

"I am." Hopkins appeared to be prepared to be challenged.

"You were not in the Agricultural Building?"

"I was not."

"Thank you," Colson said as he took his seat.

"That was short and sweet," Will said. "What do you think he's trying to do?" He searched Ike's face.

"Looks like he's emphasizing the fact that Ike Hopkins ain't too sure about where he was," Ike commented.

The next Bell County man called was Steele Redding.

"You were in Frankfort on January 25, 1900?" Franklin asked.

"I was."

"Did you see Berry Howard that day?" Franklin smiled.

"Yes, sir. I saw him upstairs of the State House."

"Tell these gentlemen what he was doing," Franklin said as he returned to his seat.

"There was a bunch of men lined up on the stairs. As each one come up, Berry was showin' him—pointin' through the window." Redding was nervously twisting his hat in his hands.

"Tell us what he was pointing at," Franklin said.

"At Mr. Goebel," Redding said.

Standing to cross-examine, "How do you know he was pointing at Mr. Goebel?" Mr. Smith asked.

Redding looked as if he did not understand the question. "He was in there," he said.

"There were other men in the Senate chamber also?"

"Yes."

"Could Berry have been pointing to someone other than Goebel?"

Redding shot a quick glance at Campbell. "I suppose so."

"Did you hear anything that was said?" Smith walked away.

"No, I was too far from them to hear."

After the dinner break, the prosecution called William Culton to the stand. The story he told was as familiar to Ike and Will as the bends of Straight Creek. Culton recited his tale as well as if he were an actor in a play, replete with all the details to implicate Powers, Jim Howard and Henry Youtsey. The only difference between this and previous versions was that Culton denied the testimony of both William Lyons and Frank Burch, insisting that the encounter described by Lyons did not take place. With regard to Burch, Culton maintained that both he and Berry Howard were upstairs in the State House at the time of the shooting, and arrived at the Agricultural Building only sometime after the shots were fired.

"Did all that serve any good purpose?" Ike asked.

"I suppose they like to keep Culton in practice," Will said.

Late in the day, the prosecution called the State House policeman, Wingate Thompson, to the witness chair. Campbell asked Thompson some questions about the Whittaker arrest, and finally got around to Berry Howard. "Did you see this defendant that night?" he asked.

"I saw him at Kagin's restaurant that night," Thompson replied.

"State what transpired."

"I was in the restaurant with some friends. I said, 'There is Berry Howard, and I think he knows as much. . . .'"

A. B. Smith fairly leapt into the air. "We object to this," he shouted.

Judge Cantrill waited a moment for Smith to descend. With a sidelong glance at the prosecution, he said, "Objection sustained."

Campbell drew a deep breath. "Who was with Berry Howard at that time and place?" he asked.

"Jim Howard," Thompson said without hesitation.

"That's right," Will declared to Ike. "You remember that we met 'old bad Jim' at Kagin's that evening?"

Judge Cantrill rocked forward in his chair. "It being Saturday, that'll be enough for today. Court adjourned until 9 o'clock Monday morning." A rap from the gavel cleared the courtroom.

As they started to exit, Berry shouted to Ike and motioned to him. "Go ahead," Ike said to Will, "I'll catch up with you outside."

Will lounged on the courthouse steps, enjoying the beautiful spring weather. He inhaled deeply, tasting the delicious fragrance of the flowering crab apple trees lining the street. Just as the weight of the trial was beginning to slip away, Ike came down the stone steps wearing a concerned expression.

"What's up?" Will asked.

"Not much. Berry asked me to go visit his nephew over at the penitentiary. Want to go along?" Ike spoke slowly.

"No, thanks," Will replied, "I don't care much for that place."

"I don't blame you. I don't like it much either. Do you think you can stay out of trouble if I leave you to your own devices?"

Will laughed. "Yeah, I expect so. There's a chore I've been meaning to attend to, anyway. I'll see you at supper time."

As Ike moved away, Will started walking through town headed for the State House Square. Crossing the railroad tracks, he moved through the same gate that William Goebel entered a moment before the shot felled him. Just past the fountain, he saw the marble marker embedded in the brick pavement to denote the spot where Goebel fell. He paused a moment and found himself wondering just what the marble square marked. Was it the spot where Goebel was standing, where his head hit the ground, or what? Will stood on the marker and observed that he was in the direct line from the Secretary of State's window to the hackberry tree across the walk. I guess that's why the marker is where it is, he thought as he mounted the steps to the office building.

Inside, he moved down the hall, glancing to his right at the door Youtsey said had admitted Jim Howard to the office. On the left, Will found the auditor's office. The pretty young lady seated at the reception desk looked up as he entered the room. "May I help you?" she smiled.

Will found himself looking into a deep pool of baby blue eyes. "Well, uh," he stammered, trying to remember why he'd come into this office, "is this the auditor's office?"

"Yes, it is," she said in a soft voice. "What can we do for you?"

Recovering his composure somewhat, Will said, "The auditor's annual report is a matter of public record, isn't it?"

"Why, yes," the lady replied. "As a matter of fact, we're rather proud of our reports to the public."

"Could I see the reports for the last two or three years, please?"

"Certainly," she said laying two volumes on the counter. "These are for 1900 and 1901. This fiscal year isn't finished yet."

Will took the two books and sat at a table along the wall. After two hours of scanning the tiny print, the only reference he could find to the $100,000 Goebel reward fund stated simply that as of December 31, 1900, $7,000 had been spent. There was no mention of to whom the rewards had been paid.

"The Commonwealth calls Anthony Broughton to the stand," Colonel Campbell announced.

"Your brother, Henry, is the sheriff of Bell County?" Campbell asked to begin his examination.

"That's right." Broughton grinned at Berry.

"You and your brother escorted some prisoners to Frankfort on the train along with the mountain arm—excuse me—the mountain crowd on January 25, 1900?" Campbell turned to smile at Colson.

"Yes, sir, I was here when the shootin' took place."

"State whether or not you were present at a conversation between Caleb Powers and your brother." Campbell paced the room.

"Yes, sir; I heard that." Anthony Broughton's face was a study in concentration.

"Your Honor, we object," Judge Smith said from the defense table. "What conversation are they talking about?"

"Overruled," Judge Cantrill said, nodding to Campbell to proceed.

"Powers asked my brother who would be a good man to get to do the shooting."

Campbell moved around the witness stand. "Do what shooting?"

"To kill Goebel, I reckon. He just said 'to do the shooting.' He didn't say no more."

"What did your brother say?" Campbell turned so that his back was to the witness as he faced the jury.

Broughton squirmed slightly in his chair. "He told Powers that he didn't know or something that way—that he didn't know who would be the best man, or something that way."

"What's this got to do with Berry?" Will whispered.

Before Ike could reply, Campbell spun on his heel. "Do

you know Frank Cecil?" he said in a loud voice.

"Does that answer your question?" Ike said.

"Do you know Zack Steele?" Campbell pressed on.

"Yes, sir," Broughton looked puzzled.

"Have you told all you recall of this conversation with Powers and your brother?" Campbell seemed slightly irritated.

Broughton screwed up his face in concentration. "That is the best I remember," he said.

Campbell sighed. "To refresh your memory, I will ask you if the name of Frank Cecil was mentioned in the conversation."

Broughton's face brightened. "I believe that my brother did tell Powers that Frank Cecil or Zack Steele would be a good man." He assumed the look of a puppy due a treat.

"A good man to do what?"

"A good man to kill Goebel, as I understood it."

"They're still doing their best to convict Caleb Powers, aren't they?" Ike whispered.

"Yeah," Will replied, "and they're implicating Frank Cecil and Zack Steele for future use, too."

"Did you talk with Berry Howard after he returned to Pineville—after the shooting?" Campbell was asking.

"My brother, Henry, and I happened to be at the depot when they come back on the train. We discussed the thing some."

"What was said between you at that time and place?"

Broughton shifted uncomfortably in the chair. "He said that he went down there to help give Taylor his seat and he stayed until he helped to do it," he said without hesitation.

Campbell consulted his notes. "Had Berry anything in this hands at the time he was talking with you?"

"He had a gun in his hands."

Campbell paused as if waiting for the witness to continue. At length, he asked, "What did he say about the gun?"

"I asked him what he was doing with the gun. He held it up and said, 'That was the gun that killed the Gobbler.' That's all I can recollect that he said." Boughton relaxed.

Will leaned close to Ike. "As I recall, what he said was that he was gonna shoot a turkey."

"Maybe that's what Broughton meant by 'gobbler,'" Ike whispered.

"To refresh your memory, I will ask you whether you made any statement to Howard about getting into trouble," Campbell pressed on.

"Yes, sir. I asked him if he was not afeared he was in trouble and he said that if he was, Taylor would pardon the boys out."

On cross-examination, Mr. Forrester, the most junior of Berry's defense attorneys, attempted to break down Broughton's testimony, but met with no success and finally gave up.

Late in the day, the prosecution called Mrs. Irene Davis to the stand. "Who's that?" Will asked.

Ike pointed across the room. Mrs. Pat was making her way to the witness chair. She was dressed in a low-cut red dress that clung to every curve of her body. "I guess she got married again," he said, his eyes, like all others, glued to her every movement.

"Yes, sir. I ran a restaurant in Pineville at that time," she was saying.

"Did Berry Howard come in there?" Mr. Franklin asked.

"Quite often."

"Tell us some of the talk you had with Berry in your restaurant."

She leaned comfortably back in the chair and crossed her shapely legs as she smiled at Rob Franklin. "Back in January 1900, he come in and he said, 'Mrs. Pat, I am going away and will be gone for a while. There is getting up too much trouble down in Frankfort, and I am going down to see if I cannot help settle the disturbance between Governor Taylor and William Goebel.' He said, 'I am gone, and you won't see me anymore for a while.'

"Sometime after that, he come back in there and he said, 'Well, Mrs. Pat, I am back with you again. I have been down to Frankfort to help settle the trouble between Governor Taylor and William Goebel.' He said, 'After us mountain men got there, I will tell you that William Goebel didn't last but a damned short time.' That is all. He didn't say that he killed him nor nothing about that."

Mr. Franklin smiled contentedly. "Thank you."

Mr. Forrester slowly rose to his feet. "Where were you first married?"

Mrs. Pat's smile faded. "Breathitt County, Kentucky."

"How old were you at that time?"

"I don't remember." She squirmed uncomfortably.

"How many times have you been married?" Forrester smiled in a friendly manner.

"Three times," Mrs. Pat said emotionlessly.

"Who did you marry first?"

She hesitated just a moment before answering. "A man named Long."

"How long did you live with him?"

"I don't remember," she said, twisting in the chair.

Mr. Forrester moved around to face the jury. "Do you know a man by the name of Warren Wilson?"

"Your Honor, I object," Campbell and Rob Franklin shouted in unison.

"Who's Warren Wilson?" Will asked.

"You know him. He's the man she lived with between marriages."

"I don't understand what's going on here," Will whispered to Ike.

"Hell, son," Ike smiled, "don't you know that you can't believe a single word uttered by a woman of loose morals?"

"The Commonwealth rests," Campbell announced.

Judge Cantrill glanced up at the clock. "In that case," he said, "court's adjourned until 9 o'clock tomorrow morning."

⚜

"How's your friend's trial going?" Melvin Ballenger asked as the waiter poured coffee into his cup.

"I'm not sure," Ike answered, shifting slightly aside to let the waiter fill his cup. "I really don't think the prosecution presented much of a case."

"You think he'll be acquitted then?"

"I can't say as I do," Will said.

Ballenger tilted his head to look at Will in confusion. "If they didn't make a good case, why don't you think he'll get off?"

"For the same reason Caleb Powers and Jim Howard didn't get off," Will said bitterly.

"Have they presented any damaging evidence?" Ballenger asked.

"Not really," Will said around the hunk of roast he'd

just stuffed in his mouth.

"Didn't your mother teach you not to talk with your mouth full?" Ike teased. Then to Ballenger, "It appears to me that their main concern has been to build up evidence for future trials. It looks like they're trying harder to convict Powers than Berry."

"That lends credence to the idea that they only brought the indictment to elicit testimony, doesn't it?" Ballenger said.

"Not in this instance," Will said, swallowing his food. "Berry's been under indictment for two years. I'm sure that at the time, they never thought it'd come to this."

"What do you mean by that?" Ike was as puzzled as Ballenger.

"Well, they indicted Berry on the strength of Youtsey's original statement. Then they as much as admitted that it was worthless when they let Combs go. What do they do, then, with Berry? If he wouldn't turn State's evidence—which he evidently refused to do—then the only options they had were to let him go, too, or bring him to trial."

Even Ike Livingston was impressed with Will's observations. "You keep thinkin' like that, son, and you might end up presenting arguments in court yourself some day," he smiled.

Will stuffed another chunk of roast into his mouth. "By the time we finish this Goebel business, I think I'll have logged enough courtroom time to do me forever."

⚜

Most of the next day in court was consumed by Berry Howard, testifying on his own behalf. He stated his whereabouts at the time the shots were fired and explained his involvement with the train trip. He told the court that he had left Pineville on January 22, 1900 and traveled to Louisville to meet with ex-Governor John Y. Brown, seeking Brown's help to secure a pardon for his nephew in the penitentiary. Berry said that Governor Brown had provided him with a letter to Governor Taylor. He arrived in Frankfort, he said, early on the morning of January 25th, intending to speak with Governor Taylor that day. Ike and Will knew that story to be largely true and admired how Berry flatly denied any knowledge of, or involvement with, a conspiracy to murder

William Goebel. In reply to a question, he reluctantly agreed that there was ill will between he and the Broughton brothers as well as between himself and Clorinda Howard.

Before court adjourned for the day, the defense called several witnesses who all verified Berry's statement that he was upstairs in the State House when the shots were fired.

⁂

"We'll see some fireworks now," Ike said the next morning when Mr. Forrester called Henry Broughton to the stand.

"How do you suppose they caught him sober enough to testify?" Will giggled.

"What's the relationship between you and Berry Howard?"

Henry looked confused. "I don't understand you," he said.

"Do you like Berry? Are you friends?" Forrester smiled.

"Yeah, I guess you could say that," Broughton answered.

"Did you and he not fall out after your election campaign for Bell County sheriff?"

"Well," Henry glanced at Campbell, "I suppose it'd be fair to say that I wasn't as fond of him afterwards."

"Do you know Ike Hopkins who's testified here?" Forrester was still smiling at the witness.

"Yes, sir. He's from Pineville, too."

"Did you not meet Ike Hopkins at the Bell County courthouse three weeks ago and tell him that he'd have to help you 'make proof' against Berry Howard?" The smile was gone.

"No sir, I did not," Broughton said adamantly.

⁂

"The defense calls Ike Hopkins," Colonel Colson said.

"Did you meet with Henry Broughton in front of the Bell County court house three weeks ago?" Colson asked.

"Yes, sir."

"What did you and he discuss?"

"I don't remember." Hopkins' face betrayed no emotion.

Colson then asked a series of questions that became quite familiar over the remainder of the trial: "Are you acquainted with Irene Davis, formerly Mrs. Pat?"

"I am."

"Are you acquainted with the general reputation of Mrs. Pat among the people of the community for truth and veracity?"

"I am."

Colson moved to face the jury. "What is her reputation?"

"Well," the witness said slowly, "it is bad."

"Do you know Clorinda Howard?"

"I do."

"Are you acquainted with her general reputation in the community for morality?" Colson was smiling broadly now.

"It is bad," Hopkins did not return the smile.

Tom Campbell charged forward to cross-examine. "Do you know what 'veracity' means?" he roared.

"Tellin' the truth, I reckon," Hopkins said.

Campbell's face was beet red as collected his thoughts. "Looks a tad deflated, don't he?" Will giggled.

"What kind of morals is Mrs. Clorinda Howard deficient in?" Campbell said at length.

"Well," Hopkins drew the word out as he eyed Berry, "it is claimed by some that she keeps a bad house . . ." He hesitated as if finished speaking, then added, ". . . her and her daughters."

A parade of witnesses moved across the witness stand, each answering the same sequence of questions designed to impeach the testimony of Clorinda Howard and Irene Pat Davis. After some twenty such episodes, just before 6 p.m., the defense rested.

"In the matter of the Commonwealth of Kentucky versus Berry Howard, we, the jury, agree and find the defendant not guilty," the foreman said laconically, as the courtroom virtually exploded with shouting.

Ike turned to Will, the corners of his mouth showing strain from the wideness of his grin. "How about that?" he yelled above the din.

"Who would have thought they'd do that?" Will shouted.

"Evidently Berry did," Ike said pointing across the room to where Berry Howard was in front of the jury box shaking hands with each juror in turn. Ike and Will made their way through the crowd to congratulate Berry. As Will moved close behind, he heard Berry say to one of the jurors, "I knew you'd do right by me."

Chapter 20

er slipped and started down my left pants leg.
hand upon it and thus running in a limping
to the rumor that I had been wounded.
the west steps I ran up them and then into
m of the Executive office to learn the situ-
greatly excited in that office, and it was
re we could learn who was hurt.
ively no information or knowledge as to the
the shot was fired, who fired it, from what
was fired, and I have never been present at
had any conversation with any one in relation
connected with the shooting of Senator Goebel
m or to any one else, nor did I ever hear the
assassination of the shooting of him discussed
to the time that he was actually shot, and I
eeting, conference or conversation being had
not have I ever heard of such conversation
such as has been published in the papers
g of Senator Goebel.

H. E. Youtsey.

until that time did he have any communication, either

indirect, with the said James Howard.

Henry Youtsey.

My commission expires Jan/16th 1904

Two affidavits submitted at trial reported to be signed by
Henry Youtsey. Shows differences in signatures of documents

Tuesday, September 1, 1903

Ellen Livingston hurried across the room in response to a yell from the gate. She peered through the screen door to see the large bulk of Berry Howard on the path below.

"Hello, Berry. Come on up," she shouted.

Berry was puffing from the exertion of the climb when he reached the porch. Ellen held the screen door open, inviting him inside. Once in the front room, he paused momentarily to catch his breath. "Howdy, Ellen," he said. "Is the old man about?"

"He's down to the store right now, but I expect him back directly." Motioning him to a chair, she said, "You remember my sister, Sallie, don't you, Berry?"

"I certainly do," he smiled, bowing slightly. "How are you, Miss Sallie?" Berry sat in Ike's favorite chair, facing the two women.

"Tolerable," Sallie said, smiling.

After a slight uncomfortable pause, Ellen said, "I was just about to pour us some lemonade. Would you like a glass?"

"Sounds mighty good," he replied. "It sure is hot today."

Just as Berry was trying to think of something to say, he heard the back door slam and Ike's voice in the kitchen. In a moment, Ike came into the front room, Will Elliott in tow.

"Hello, Sallie," Ike said. "Berry Howard, where in the world have you been? I ain't seen you in a coon's age."

"I just come back from Georgetown the other day," Berry answered with a sidelong glance at Sallie.

Ellen came in from the kitchen bearing a tray of full glasses. After serving everyone, she took a seat on the bench between Sallie and Will.

"You've been down there for that Powers man's trial?" Ellen asked.

"Yes, that's right," Berry replied. "It was his third."

"I'm surprised that he appealed from the last conviction," Sallie said. She lowered her eyes as Berry turned his gaze to her.

"It took some courage," Berry said. "Tom Campbell had let it be known that if they tried Powers again, he'd ask for the death penalty."

"Why was he willing to risk it?" Ellen asked. "He had to know that they'd convict him yet again."

"Yeah," Will said, "and there's a Democratic majority on the appeals court now. A death sentence means he'll probably hang."

"He said that he'd rather die trying to prove his innocence than sit in jail, branded as a murderer. I personally took that as strong evidence that he's as innocent as he says he is," Berry said.

Ellen started to ask another question, but her husband cut her off. "Is there any more of this lemonade out there?"

"I'll see," Ellen took the hint. "Come along, Sallie," she said, getting to her feet, "I might need your help."

"Well, let's hear it on the trial," Ike demanded as soon as the women cleared the room.

"We're all ears," Will said, edging forward on the bench.

"Caleb hired all new lawyers," Berry began. "I don't suppose that there was anything wrong with the ones he had, but apparently he figured that a new crew wouldn't hurt anything. Then, too, he managed to get Judge Cantrill thrown off the case."

"How'd he manage that?" Ike asked.

"Caleb's lawyers filed an affidavit which detailed some of the stuff Cantrill had pulled at the last trial, and the appeals court ordered Cantrill to vacate the bench."

"What kind of stuff?" Ike asked, leaning forward.

"Oh, they alleged that Cantrill had adjourned court while one of Powers' lawyers, W. C. Owens, was right in the middle of his closing argument, for one thing. Also, they accused that while Rob Franklin was making his argument, Cantrill passed a note reminding Franklin of some fact he'd failed to mention."

"Did they mention that Cantrill saw fit to adjourn for the day any time one of the prosecution's witnesses began to flounder under cross-examination?" Will added.

"And Judge Cantrill vacated the bench?" Ike asked, amazed.

"Not right away. They gave him the choice of vacating or being ruled in contempt," Berry said. "He chose to vacate. Then, Governor Beckham appointed Judge James Robbins to hear the case."

"Robbins?" Ike asked. "Ain't he the man that

introduced William Goebel at his first campaign meeting?"

"The same," Berry said, "and presided over the convention that nominated Beckham, too."

"And Powers was better off?" Will shook his head.

"What about the testimony?" Ike asked.

"Most of it was the same as before," Berry replied, "but a few interesting things did happen. Frank Cecil testified, and he did tell quite a tale."

"Frank Cecil?" Will said. "I heard that he'd skipped the country."

"He did," Berry said, "but Campbell got him back from California."

"What did he tell?" Ike urged.

"He talked about some meetings he'd been in where he heard a lot of wild talk, but the most interesting part of it was that he claimed that Powers had said that there was a man across the hall who wanted to kill Goebel from Powers' window."

"That'd be Youtsey," Will spoke as much to himself as anyone.

Berry did not acknowledge Will's comment but went right on. "He said he asked Caleb what was the problem with that, and Powers said that he didn't trust whoever it was. Then, according to Cecil, Powers—out of the clear blue   says, 'We are looking for a man in the morning, and if he comes, he will do it.'"

"Jim Howard?"

"That all sounds a little too neat," Ike said thoughtfully. "What did the defense lawyers do with Cecil?"

"Burned him pretty good, I thought," Berry laughed. "The first thing they hit him on was why he'd suddenly decided to come back from California."

"What'd he say?" Ike asked.

"Said that he got tired of being on the run—he's under indictment, you know. They really got after him about something he'd supposedly told Mrs. Pat, though.

"Sam Wilson asked him if he hadn't told Mrs. Pat that he was the identical man that killed Goebel, but that the prosecution wouldn't let her tell that at my trial because they were trying to convict me, not him. He denied it, of course, but it got a big laugh."

"Was he a believable witness?" Will asked.

"Well, the defense destroyed him," Berry said. "In the end, he admitted that he didn't know anything at all about any conspiracy to kill Goebel. Mr. Wilson asked him specifically if he had any agreement with Culton, Wharton Golden, Taylor, Powers, Dick Combs, Harlan Whittaker, Jim Howard, Youtsey, Zack Steele, or me to shoot anybody, and, in each instance, he said he did not."

"Did they bring out the criminal record he's managed to run up around here?" Ike asked.

"Sure did," Berry grinned, "rape and all."

"Then, his testimony didn't amount to much, did it?" Ike was shaking his head.

"Say, Ike, is there any more of this lemonade? My throat is getting pretty dry."

Ike opened his mouth to yell into the kitchen, but before he could get out a word, Sallie tiptoed in and handed Berry a full glass. With a slight blush, she wordlessly turned and left the room.

"Will," Ike said, "I want you to have a talk with that sister of yours."

"Women should be seen and not heard," Will laughed.

"Looks more like they hear but are not seen," Berry observed.

"Anyway," Ike said, peeking into the kitchen, "wet your whistle and tell on about the trial."

"The prosecution brung on Youtsey as the star witness," Berry said, after taking a long pull at the lemonade.

"He testified at Jim Howard's third trial a little while ago, didn't he?" Will asked.

"Yeah, he did," Berry said. "They'd had a couple of years to dream up what they wanted him to swear to, and he'd learned his lessons pretty good, too."

"Hold up, here," Ike said. "Youtsey's been in the penitentiary ever since his conviction. What did they have to hold over him?"

"Better treatment. It come out that he'd been stoking the furnace in July and locked up on bread and water on Sundays until he saw fit to write out a statement and show up in court. And I'll tell you something else, too—he looked to be in much better health than he was during Jim's last trial."

"What did he have to say about it all?" Ike asked, getting to his feet and starting to pace the floor.

"It was a caution," Berry said, smiling broadly. "I can't remember all the details as good as Youtsey did, but one of the first things he had to say was that there was somebody named Dr. Johnson who was willin' to do the shootin' for $300, but that fell through because Culton said not to do it; that the Legislature was going to decide in Taylor's favor.

"The next scheme he told about started out with somebody introducing Dick Combs to Youtsey. Only he was told that the man's name was Hockersmith. That's why there's been confusion on those two all the time. Youtsey allowed that it was all fixed up for Combs—or Hockersmith—to shoot Goebel from Powers' window on January 29th. Youtsey said he went into the office that morning and told John Powers what was afoot and that John gave him a key to the office, which Youtsey then transferred to Hockersmith/Combs and went on his merry way. That didn't work because, according to Youtsey, it was the wrong key.

"He allowed that he told Caleb Powers about it, and that—get this now—Caleb agreed to leave his office unlocked."

Ike stopped abruptly. "Golden testified at the previous trials that Powers locked both doors when they left on the 30th."

"The defense lawyer asked Youtsey about that. He simply said he didn't know anything about what Golden had said."

"So, Cecil testified that Powers didn't trust Youtsey to do the shooting while Youtsey says Powers trusted him enough to leave the door open. Kind of contradictory, don't you think?" Will said.

"That took care of the Powers connection?" Ike asked.

"Yep, and then, he moved right along to Jim Howard. He said that he told Governor Taylor about all this, and Taylor dictated a letter to Jim Howard saying that Howard was to report to Youtsey in Frankfort right away.

"Like the trusting soul that he evidently is, Jim showed up in Youtsey's office, letter in hand, on January 30th. Youtsey took Jim across the hall and posted him at Powers' office door—which according to what he'd just said—was unlocked. Youtsey goes around through the reception room, into Powers' office through that door, locked it, and let Jim in the other door."

"Nobody saw any of this, I don't guess?"

Berry's smile broadened. "Not a living soul, accordin' to Mr. Youtsey. But, there was witnesses in the reception room who saw Youtsey go through there and others who swore that nobody went into that room.

"Anyway, Youtsey fixes Jim up with the rifle loaded with the steel bullets and smokeless powder cartridges Youtsey'd ordered the week before. He said that Jim told him he wanted a pardon for killin' George Baker, and Youtsey allowed that was not a problem."

"Who's George Baker?" Ike asked.

"A man Jim supposedly killed in one of them Clay County feuds."

"I think I'd have said something about wanting a pardon for the shooting I was about to do, if it'd been me," Will remarked.

"If it'd been me, I'd have worked that out long afore," Berry said. "At any rate, Youtsey said he looked away for a minute and when he looked back, Jim had laid two pistols up on a stack of books. Jim told Youtsey that he was going to use them to make people think there were a dozen men in there."

"Strange that he'd want to draw attention to the room, ain't it?" Ike observed.

"You know," Will said, "I've wondered about those pistol shots. If they were fired inside the building, as ever'body seems to think they were, why hasn't anybody ever found any bullets holes?"

"Give Campbell time, son." Berry laughed. "If these trials go on long enough, them bullet holes will show up in Powers' office floor in the outline of a footprint that's Jim Howard's exact size."

"Did Youtsey say he saw Jim fire the shot?" Ike asked.

"He did at Jim's last trial, but this time, he said that he left the room and ran outside before the shooting."

Ike stopped pacing to stare at Berry. "What did the lawyers do with that inconsistency?"

"Not much," Berry replied. "Youtsey just reverted back into the testimony he clearly had memorized. He declared that he was on his way down the stairs inside the building when the shot was fired. He said he ran out the back door and then back in through the east side steps, and back into the reception area, when he helped break into Powers' office."

"Nobody in there, I don't guess," Will said.

"Nope, but Youtsey said that he did grab the Marlin rifle which was still there. He said that he ejected the empty shell and kept it."

"Where's the rifle and shell now?" Ike asked, sitting once again.

"Youtsey destroyed the shell, and doesn't know about the rifle."

"It all fits together pretty neatly, doesn't it?" Will said.

"Just about as neatly as those nimble legal minds could make it all mesh," Berry said thoughtfully.

Ike sat up straight in his chair as if he had just been jolted from deep sleep. "Didn't one Henry Youtsey—while he and Caleb Powers were in the Louisville jail—sign an affidavit to the effect that he knew nothing whatsoever incriminating on Powers?"

A laugh of contempt fell from Berry's mouth. "They had that covered, too. Youtsey said that he did sign that paper, but only with Caleb Powers' promise that the affidavit would never see the light of day."

"Huh," Ike snorted. "What did Youtsey think he was going to do with it, use it in the outhouse?"

Before Berry could answer, Ellen entered carrying a fresh jam cake on a platter. Sallie followed with a pitcher of milk in one hand and a pitcher of lemonade in the other. "Take a break," Ellen said. "It's time for some refreshment."

When everyone was served, to make conversation, Berry asked, "Miss Sallie, are you teaching this year?"

"Why, yes, I am." She blushed slightly. After a brief pause, she said, "Something rather amusing happened at school yesterday. I asked little Jill Atkins to spell the word 'straight'."

"Jill's old man Atkins'—the moonshiner's—youngest gal, ain't she?" Will asked.

"That's her," Sallie said. "Anyway, after she spelled it, I asked her what the word 'straight' meant. Quicker than a wink, she said, 'It means not mixed with nothing.'"

When the snack was finished, Ellen and Sallie gathered the plates and glasses and headed for the kitchen.

"Youtsey signed an affidavit for Jim Howard too, didn't he?" Will asked as soon as the women had cleared the room.

"Sure did," Berry answered, "and it was introduced into evidence at this trial, too. I managed to sneak a look at the two pieces of paper, and I'm tellin' you, a blind man without a cane could see that the signatures were not the same."

"Didn't the lawyers ask about that?" Ike asked.

"Youtsey swore that he'd signed both of 'em. It appeared to me that ever'body in the place knew that his testimony was just a pack of prearranged lies anyway, so they just let it go." Bitterness was evident in Berry's voice.

All three men were silent for a moment while the significance of that idea hung in the air. At length, Will said, "Youtsey is the man that implicated you in the first place, wasn't he?"

"Yeah," Berry said emotionlessly, "back when this mess all started up, he told Campbell that he let Dick Combs, Jim Howard and me into Powers' office."

"Well, what did he have to say about that now?"

Berry smiled broadly and leaned back in his chair. He stretched his legs in front of him and folded his hands across his ample chest before he began speaking. "Well, sir, it was interesting," he began. "Youtsey allowed that Arthur Goebel came to visit him at the jail soon after his arrest. . . ."

"Hold up here," Ike interrupted. "He went into a conniption fit denying that very point at his trial."

Berry's smile became even wider. "That's right. This time, though, he readily admitted that he'd talked with Arthur Goebel—and Campbell, too."

"Didn't they ask him about the fit?" Will asked, wide-eyed.

"He admitted that it was faked," Berry said. "He said that it 'seemed like the best thing he could do at the time.'" Berry's laughter caused the glasses to dance on the table.

"Anyway," Berry said when his laughter subsided, "he allowed that Arthur Goebel was the one who said that Combs, Jim Howard, and me were responsible for the killing. He said that Goebel insisted that the three of us had to be in Powers' office."

"Youtsey didn't have the guts to stand up to him?" Ike asked.

"Well, let me tell you that when you're locked up in a cell, it's pretty damned hard to argue with them what's in power," Berry said.

"You know, this whole thing is getting ridiculous," Ike said. Will nodded his hearty agreement.

"Before you make that conclusion final, consider this," Berry said. "Youtsey said that the reason he allowed Arthur Goebel to use him to implicate Jim and Combs and me was that, since it wasn't true, any one of us could disprove it, and that'd discredit Arthur's testimony."

"Then why the hell didn't he do that rather than throw a fit?" Will wondered.

Berry simply turned his hands palms up.

"What else happened?" Ike asked.

"Noakes testified," Berry said. "When the defense got ahold of him, they demonstrated that Campbell had intimidated him into swearing to whatever the script called for." His smile was gone.

"How'd they do that?" Will asked.

"Noakes had filed an affidavit telling about how they'd caught up with him over in Virginia and threatened to indict and try him if he didn't cooperate."

"I read in the paper that Powers addressed the jury himself," Will said expectantly.

"I hope to tell you that he did," Berry said, smiling once again. "He began speaking at the night session and spoke for two hours before court was recessed for the day. The next morning, he started at nine and spoke until noon. After dinner, he spoke for another two hours—about seven hours in all."

"In that amount of time, he must have touched a lot of points."

"He mentioned every aspect of the case, including the packed juries, the specially chosen judge, the law concerning conspiracy, and the mistakes that the prosecution has made. It was such a good argument, that you had trouble rememberin' that he was the defendant. And he made some tellin' points, too."

"Like what?"

"Like that if he was the kind of person to assassinate somebody, he'd have knocked off Poyntz when the other two election commissioners resigned. He pointed out that if somebody had done that, Taylor would have had the power to appoint three new members, and they'd have sent Bill Goebel home, choking on his own election law.

"He finished up by talking about his aged mother in Knox County, sitting in her rocker, awaiting his exoneration. I'm tellin' you, boys, when he got through, there wasn't a dry eye in the house."

"And they convicted him anyway?" Ike and Will said, nearly in unison.

"They sure as hell did." Berry let the legs of his chair fall forward. "Sentenced him to hang, too."

Chapter 21

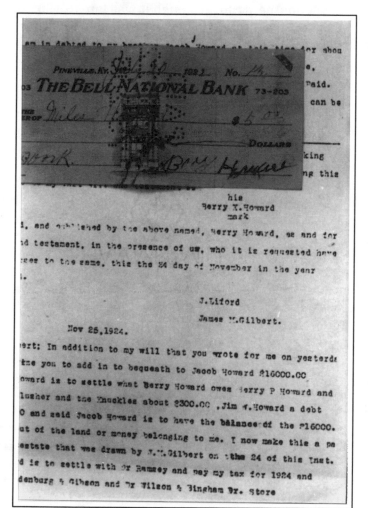

Berry Howard's Will bearing his mark
and check bearing his signature

November, 1994

Caleb Powers did not hang. He appealed that third conviction and—in a move that surprised most observers—the appeals court, despite its Democratic majority, reversed the verdict. Powers was, therefore, forced to endure yet another trial, although it was late in 1907 before it was called. Due—in part, at least—to the fact that Tom Campbell had died in the interim, most observers agreed that Powers came as close as was possible to a fair trial this last time.

The Commonwealth presented basically the same evidence as at previous trials (less Frank Cecil, who had disappeared), while the defense made a mighty effort to impeach Youtsey's testimony. One witness swore that he had overheard a 1900 jail house conversation in which Dick Combs had told Youtsey, "You didn't aim high enough to kill him," and Youtsey's reply, "It seems to me he is pretty dead. I had him in line to make a dead shot." After hearing a mass of testimony, the jury eventually declared that it was "hung," the last vote being 10-2 for acquittal.

Caleb Powers' case was scheduled to be heard for a fifth time, but before the case was called, Republican Governor Augustus Willson, elected in November 1907, granted a pardon. Powers had always said that he would not apply for a pardon, that only being acquitted by a jury would be satisfactory. In the end, he did apply and a petition bearing some 500,000 signatures did not hurt his cause. By announcing his decision on June 13, 1908, Governor Willson brought Caleb Powers' prison stint to an end at a little over eight years.

Powers was subsequently elected to the United States House of Representatives where he served eight undistinguished years. He liked to tell listeners that he served as many years in the United States Congress as he did in prison. Caleb Powers died in 1932, proclaiming his innocence to the end.

On the same date as Powers' pardon, Governor Willson also granted liberty to James B. Howard. Mr. Howard returned to his Clay County home and lived the remainder of his long life in obscurity, resisting many attempts at interviews. One remark that does survive provides some insight into his feelings. Mr. Howard chanced to be in Georgetown on the day of Judge James Cantrill's funeral. Asked if he planned to attend, he answered, "No, but I don't mind letting it be known that I'm heartily in favor of these proceedings."

Governor Willson's pardons covered every person who needed one, with the notable exception of Henry Youtsey. Others who had been indicted but not tried—Dick Combs, Harlan Whittaker, John Davis, Zack Steele, W. S. Taylor, Charles Finley and John Powers—were all pardoned in 1909.

Henry Youtsey was granted his liberty via parole seven years later, in 1916. It fell to Democratic Governor James Black to pardon Mr. Youtsey in 1919. When Mr. Youtsey walked out of prison after having served almost 20 years, the judicial processes of the Goebel killing, at long last, came to an end. Mr. Youtsey died in his native Campbell County in 1942.

In that same year of 1919, Ike and Ellen Livingston left Bell County and took up permanent residence in Lincoln County. Somewhat of a real estate dealer, Ike owned various parcels of property before he finally decided he was a farmer and bought some acreage in the Green River section. Ike died of natural causes in 1944; Ellen died a natural death in 1955.

Will Elliott and Mary Whittaker were married in 1909 and went right to work on becoming my grandparents. In 1921, they followed the Livingstons to the Green River section of Lincoln County, purchasing the farm adjacent to Ike and Ellen. Will died of typhoid fever in 1934; Mary died of old age in 1975.

In 1918, Berry Howard married Sallie Elliott, making him my great uncle. Berry purchased, with cash, a 165-acre farm near Crab Orchard in Lincoln County in 1904. He apparently lived there for some period of time before returning to Bell County. (I once asked my Dad where his Uncle Berry got that money. He responded by asking me if I'd ever heard about the time that wagon wrecked out in front of Uncle Ike's house.)

On November 24, 1924, Berry Howard filed his last will and testament, leaving all his worldly goods to Sallie. The next day, November 25, he added a codicil, specifying that the sum of $16,000 should go to his brother, Jacob. Berry died one week later, December 1, 1924. It is interesting to note that although Berry Howard could sign his name, only "his mark" appears on the will.

Early in 1925, Sallie appealed to the Bell County circuit court. Despite the fact that her signature appears as witness on Berry's will, she stated that her husband had died intestate, and that there were many more claims on the estate than she could possibly pay with the worth of his property. The court appointed an adjuster, who directed which of the many debts were to be paid. Sallie died in Harlan County in 1962.

One interesting aspect of the Goebel affair seems to have escaped the notice of all observers. William S. Taylor's lieutenant-governor, John Marshall, is totally absent from all accounts of this period in our history. That he was a native of Louisville is the only fact I could find. The fact that he somehow managed to elude indictment and even public suspicion leads one to wonder if he was in on some plan or had money or political influence enough to keep clear.

As for the $100,000 fund, I could find very little information. The State Auditor's report for 1901 states that $7,000 had been spent at that time (as Will found out). In his closing argument at Caleb Powers' third trial, Colonel Tom Campbell asserted that only $14,000 had been expended from the fund. Finally, in his remarks accompanying the pardons, Governor Willson stated that $15,000 of it had been dispersed. None of these mentions gave any details of to whom the money was paid. What became of the remainder is an open question.

So, that still leaves the question of who shot William Goebel. The answer is that we don't know. Since William Goebel fell, nearly a hundred years have passed; everyone who was involved has gone to the grave and took any knowledge they possessed along. In all that time, no letter, no diary, and no deathbed confession has ever come to light. We don't know now who killed Goebel; we probably never will.

But, we can speculate. Of the characters we know, Henry Youtsey seems the most likely candidate to be guilty, although it certainly does appear that Uncle Berry knew something on somebody. One school of thought says that if the Commonwealth of Kentucky, with virtually unlimited financial and judicial resources, couldn't prove any of these men guilty, they probably weren't. Another school contends that the guilt of Caleb Powers was proved well beyond any reasonable doubt. My personal opinion is that Caleb Powers was totally innocent and James Howard could not possibly have been stupid enough to have behaved as the prosecution accused. I'm not convinced that Henry Youtsey had the courage—he was apparently a rather weak personality—to have actually fired the shot. Perhaps an unknown assassin—possibly a paid hit man—did the deed and simply walked away. Given the circumstances of the day, that would not have been difficult.

As you approach the old State House in Frankfort today, look to your right as you step onto the brick walk where William Goebel entered the grounds a century ago, and you'll see a statue of "our martyred Governor." The granite base of the statue is engraved with quotes and platitudes that the 1904 Legislature felt were necessary to describe the deeds and acts of William Goebel for future generations. Walk about fifty yards to just past the fountain, and you'll see a one-foot square brass plate that proclaims: William Goebel fell here Jan. 30, 1900.

The hackberry tree was felled by lightning in 1980; on an extended line from what was Powers' window to the brass plate, you'll find a depression in the ground that marks the spot where it stood. As I stood on that brass plate and observed how it is placed to align with the window and the tree, how I wished that the stones and trees and bricks could tell what they've seen and heard.

Book"marks"

Please feel free to initial or make a special "mark" in the square to keep track of books you've read.
